"It was beginning again. Elizabeth looked around the room from face to face. She saw rage, fear, tears. She saw the monster; his face covered with hair and his nostrils flaring. His feet were heavy and thick, but he looked weak. She needed to run, get to her safe place. She moved back toward the closet and quickly disappeared."

PRAISE FOR *A PARTING GLASS*

"This is a page turner. I hated to put it down! So descriptive, insightful and charged! The language is colorful and it brings the picture directly to my mind's eye. This is my favorite phrase from the book: "Hurt sometimes came when she least expected it, based on some unknown feeling, and popped up like a jack-in-the-box. Hurt and fear, tied together."

~ Connie Shidler

****

"I read A Parting Glass *all day yesterday. I did not pass GO, I did not collect $200. I only ate once, I did not pee because I was slightly dehydrated from non-stop reading. I could not put it down because I wanted to know more about the lives of this family, these kiddos. I wanted to know how their story ended.*

It was light and happy while at the same time heavy and dark. The characters were distinct, easily recognizable and consistent. I felt I knew them immediately. Their behavior and thoughts were insightful, delightful and sometimes heartbreaking. I laughed at out loud (here...alone in my house) several times or thought "that's a good one"—I love the main character, Elizabeth, for being her perky, spacey and special little self."

~ Joyce Cussimanio

****

"Each character was fully realized, which is no small accomplishment when you are writing about a family with many children. I do believe the author hit this one out of the park as we used to say at our old softball games."

~ Kathy Sutton

"The relatable and comforting (at times painful and deeply penetrating) description of Midwest Catholic family life was truly charming and lovely to read, like the feeling of being in a space you remember but have never been. I loved the subtle and witty humor. An enthralling journey about how a family deals with pain and seeks happiness together."

~ Liz Calloni

****

"I am blown away by this touching, strong, beautifully-written story. I want to wrap my arms around this family (not Junior) who I feel I have known but yet not really known. I honestly did not want to put the book down once I got started reading. As I read, I experienced a sense of concern and sadness that was quickly replaced with anticipation, excitement hope and finally joy. It's a book I will long remember! Well done!"

~ Debbie Wilson

****

"Surrounded by monsters, in her home and at her school, imaginary and real, unwitting heroine Elizabeth O'Sullivan finds a unique way to deal with a not-so-happy childhood and a path to happiness. The reader is allowed a glimpse into Elizabeth's world of make believe where Gary Cooper becomes her friend, a special nun floats and protects, and a paper saint dances and winks and makes her feel special. A compelling read from beginning to end."

~ Maureen Carroll

A Parting Glass

A PARTING GLASS

a novel

Tess Banion

Anamcara Press LLC

Oh, Sweetie, monsters are real, and they look like people.
~ Anonymous

Published in 2018 by Anamcara Press LLC

Book design by Maureen Carroll, https://maureencarroll.com/.
Palatino Linotype and Tahoma.

Printed in the United States of America.

Elizabeth O'Sullivan is an eleven-year-old girl with uneven bangs and a rich imagination. She fights monsters, real and imagined, in a small Kansas town in the 1950's. A tale of resilience and hope.

ANAMCARA PRESS LLC
P.O. Box 442072, Lawrence, KS 66044
https://anamcara-press.com/

Ordering Information:
Quantity sales. Special discounts are available on quantity purchases by corporations, associations, and others. For details, contact the publisher at the address above.
Orders by U.S. trade bookstores and wholesalers. Please contact Ingram Distribution.

Publisher's Cataloging-in-Publication data
Banion, Tess, Author
A Parting Glass / Tess Banion

ISBN-13: A Parting Glass, 978-1-941237-13-7 (Paperback edition)

ISBN-13: A Parting Glass, 978-1-941237-19-9 (Hardcover edition)

[1. FIC045000 FICTION / Family Life / General. 2. FIC002000 FICTION / Action & Adventure. 3. FIC066000 FICTION / Small Town & Rural.]
"The Parting Glass"is an Irish folk song that can be traced back to the 17th century.

Dedication

First, to the person who has lived this story day in and out, who I love to the moon and back, my dear husband, George Wanke. Thank you for the years, laughter and tears. This book would never have happened without you.

To my mother who loved me unconditionally and my father who never got a chance to change. To my siblings, the Banions, Mike, Tom, Pat and Doug who are the threads that make up the cloth of my life, thank you for always loving me.

Special to Tom Banion whose support enabled this project. He believed it was a good story, long before most, based on truth, partial truth and flat out lies. My brother Mike Banion who sailed away too early leaving sweet memories of kindness. My younger brother Doug Banion whose very voice makes me giggle when I hear it and who is glad to make my acquaintance. And, my beloved sister, Pat Banion Russell, whose absence is a daily reminder of what she brought to my life.

To my beautiful children and their exceptional offspring, and for all the laughter, love and inspiration they bring to my life: Hilary Banion Wanke and Colin Banion Wanke and their spouses Josh Campbell and Lindsey Wanke and their growing families; Flynn, Isla, Darwin, Agrippa, and baby girl yet to arrive.

Chapter One

A passenger train sails up and down the soft rolling hills of Central Kansas that are populated with only a scattering of houses, lonesome steers, and church steeples.

Elizabeth, the fourth child in the traveling family, clutched a small paper cup filled to the brim with ice cold water. With a steady gaze she mysteriously transforms the paper cup into a water glass. Elizabeth owned the ability to see the world as she wanted it to be and to make something out of nothing. A handy skill to have in a family cursed with hard realities.

She slowly walked down the aisle, her gait wobbly but determined. The train heaved from right to left and back again, clank, clank, as it passed over the rails. Elizabeth steadied herself. She must evade the centurions just feet away and win the release of her fellow compatriots. She was Joan, Joan of Arc, saint, martyr, and divinely guided military leader of France.

The train heaves and the contents of the glass spill out onto the floor and Elizabeth must right herself. Now she had to return to the water cooler, what an inconvenience. A thin man with sunken eyes smiled. He is one of the King's men, she imagines. She must keep her eye on him, never let him know that she knows. As she replenishes the imaginary glass, she watches the soldier with her eye cocked. Slurp, slurp, she pretends to drink.

The passenger train was filled to capacity. Old and young, families, single women in hats, men in their tired suits, they all traveled by train. The clanking melody of the lumbering locomotive sets heads in motion, weaving back and forth. The sweet smell of bananas, bologna and peanut butter move through the car like a creeping fog, slowly settling on all those awake and asleep.

For railroad families, it was a tradition, a benefit, a club, a way to travel from Topeka to Clovis, or La Junta to Marceline, or any other place on the line of the Atchison, Topeka and the Santa Fe that stretched from Chicago to Los Angeles.

The Super Chief, the monster train, red-orange and yellow, commanded all that it passed. At places so small the Super Chief would only whizz by, folks climbed fences and waved. The whistle bellowed, and memories were made.

Families moved when they worked on the railroad, leaving friends and places of comfort for the next stop on the line. Grandfathers, dads, uncles, and even mothers worked for the railroad—a long and proud history. There were other railroads, but for the O'Sullivan family, there was only one.

In the back of the passenger car, two seats were turned to form an enclave of four seats; linoleum covered the floors. This special feature kept families together. The seats were scratchy and worn with tiny balls of fabric on the surface. On the head rest, white napkins were secured, making it impossible for Brylcreem, a "little dab will do it," to soil the top of the seat. At the end of the line, in Chicago or Los Angeles, the napkins would be changed and floors swept.

In one four-seat area, James, a sturdy, muscular, bigger than expected thirteen-year-old boy with cropped auburn hair and deep green eyes wrestles with his brother Patrick, a slightly built twelve-year-old with quick reactions and deep blue eyes and blondish hair. Their haircuts matched, but nothing else. The boys, brothers to Elizabeth, served as her foes. They threw each other from seat to seat, intense in their struggle. Giggles interrupted the contest as one conquered the other. It should not be a match at all. James, the bigger, the older, and the stronger should always win, but he didn't. Patrick had the fight of the Irish in him.

As Elizabeth approached her brothers, she looked up at her mother, Susanne. Her complexion was the color of cream with an occasional freckle, and her strawberry blond hair was straight from Scotland courtesy of her mother. Her vibrant blue eyes came from her beloved Swedish father; they were the signature of an immigrant, wide and innocent. Elizabeth had her mother's eyes, but not her hair. Her hair was dark like her father's, almost black. She was a combination child in looks, but not for one minute like either her mother or her father in personality.

Next to Susanne sat Katherine, pencil thin, the twin to Patrick but with the height of an older sister. The strawberry refractions that glistened in Susanne's hair, given as a gift at birth from her mother to her first daughter, caused people to stop and stare. Katherine read to John, a chubby three old with a laugh that would fill any void, especially his mother's.

Katherine looked up at the boys, pensive, wondering when the conductor would come and what he would say. She couldn't stop them from wrestling so she continued reading. Katherine's regal demeanor made her seem older than her years. Elizabeth knew that her sister was more often right than wrong, and fully understood that Katherine was the anchor of the family, much like a mother should be—the one who kept chaos at bay. However, all of that did not stop Elizabeth from occasionally challenging the "surrogate mother's" wishes. It was as if she needed to challenge someone. She couldn't challenge Susanne because she was too soft and fragile, or her older brothers who would just ignore her, and certainly not her father who was too dangerous.

In a flash, John freed himself from Katherine and leapt onto Susanne's lap. Brought back into the present,

Susanne welcomed John with a kiss. *This* boy was never without kisses. Just feet away, James' face contorts; he's sweating and holding Patrick in a headlock.

James looked up as Elizabeth dumped water on his head. "Now melt, you evil dogs," she said as the water cascaded on the boys at play. She had seen the Wizard of OZ and she knew what water could do.

James shook off the drops of water. "Elizabeth," he said with a sense of annoyance. He loved his sister, her spark. He could never truly be mad at her, and she idolized him. He was in so many ways such a mystery to her. He was strong but not too strong, smart but not in a way that made anyone feel uncomfortable. There was no show. He was bigger than life for Elizabeth and she trusted him completely.

In a flash, James caught Elizabeth's eyes and smiled just as Patrick lunged forward and flipped him. The match would be a long one, however; that was not Elizabeth's problem. Who won or lost was of no concern to Elizabeth. The brothers would get enough water poured on them to fill a swimming pool.

The train jerked suddenly with a force that tossed Elizabeth into the aisle. She landed and looked up into the glare of Katherine. She ignored the piercing eyes, gathered herself up and danced down the aisle to the water cooler, much to the chagrin of a tight-lipped, hat wearing woman who stared first at Elizabeth and then at Susanne.

Elizabeth would continue to water the boys until they grew tired of the wrestling match or the conductor told her to stop. The real threat was the conductor. He sported a badge, wore a rigid hat, rarely smiled and probably had a gun. Although Elizabeth had never seen a conductor pull out a gun, she knew deep down that he could. He was powerful. No one messed with the conductor because he could throw you off the train if he wanted, and he had done that very thing once to her father who seemed drunk at the time. Junior had tried to explain, "too much insulin and not enough sugar," but the conductor knew a drunk when he saw one, and he would not tolerate a drunk on his train. Elizabeth admired the conductor's power, but knew it couldn't be hers. In her world, women had babies, a husband and stayed at home.

"Well, I never!" said the tight-lipped woman to Susanne and anyone else listening.

Katherine, all too familiar to the sounds of exasperation, and always aware of glaring eyes, looked up from her reading at her mother. Susanne, glued to her view, looked straight into the setting sun, never acknowledging the stares, or the wrestling boys. She was lost in remembering the sweet days of her youth: church recitals, school performances and friends—the friends who had moved away or stayed away. She remembers the excitement of listening to music on the radio from far away places like New York City. How different her life had turned out.

Elizabeth walked slowly down the aisle, carefully holding onto the sides of the seats as the train heaved left and right. She sat down in an open seat and peered out the window as tiny towns with small houses flashed by. Cars waited on dusty roads for the train to pass. The familiar clang of the crossing guard suddenly filled Elizabeth's senses. Small children sat on wooden fences and waved as the mammoth train bellowed "hello." Elizabeth smiled and put her hand up to the window.

The moment was broken with the cough of the conductor. He was a giant of a man with a stone face, heroic in his uniform and hat. He motioned for Elizabeth to return to her seat.

Elizabeth jumped up and scurried down the aisle. She stopped for just a moment to take in an image of a mother feeding her baby while a father and daughter peered out the window. The father looked up at Elizabeth with kindness. She felt strange but not afraid. She didn't know very many men. Priests didn't count. Most men, even her grandfather, didn't pay much attention to her. For just a moment she wanted to stay and join that family, but the pull of her own family was just feet away.

Elizabeth liked being part of a big family. She loved having brothers to bother and a sister to look after her when she needed it. Her family was small potatoes compared to the O'Brien family, who had less money than Elizabeth's family because they had ten children. In Elizabeth's mind that was a family that could definitely provide ample entertainment.

Elizabeth knew most of the O'Brien children by name except for the older ones. She rarely ran into them so there wasn't much need to know their names. If it was lunch time and there happened to be a neighborhood kid roaming the yard, Mrs. O'Brien just added another plate to the table. For all the chaos in the O'Brien family, they never seemed to fight. Maybe, Elizabeth thought, it was because they were like a giant arcade game with steel balls bouncing off each other, never really stopping.

Yes, the O'Brien mother looked angry, but many of the mothers in her neighborhood had that look. Elizabeth hoped when she grew up, she wouldn't look angry. Her mother didn't look angry; she just looked sad. Elizabeth thought that anger and sadness were like her cousins. There was some resemblance, something that connected them but they didn't see each other very often, and when they did, there was little reason to think they even knew each other—just like anger and sadness.

Elizabeth was next to last in the family. Patrick could have been lost in the middle but he was a twin and that was special, and he was very smart. Katherine was the first girl and a twin. The only thing that beat being a twin was to be the oldest and a boy, first son of a first son. That was James. He was his mother's protector.

Elizabeth often stared at James' model airplanes, carefully displayed in the room occupied by the children. It was a known fact that no one was ever allowed to touch the model airplanes, Elizabeth knew the consequences.

These airplanes were James' most treasured possessions and made each of the children proud just by being related.

The favorite child was the baby John; they all truly loved him, flesh and blood treasure. First, he made his father laugh with his antics and tantrums which was no small feat. He had a fat, round face and body, the epitome of health among a family constricted by a diet of past grievances. He had unconsciously convinced his siblings that he was, in some exotic way, anointed. He had escaped it all. They knew there would not be any more babies. How could another baby come into this family and take his place? It would be impossible.

From day one, his position was established. He was big for his age. Elizabeth knew that mothers liked big babies. She heard them talk about it anywhere there was a gathering of married women. "He has such a great appetite." Of course he does, Elizabeth thought, he eats what he likes and always throws what he doesn't on the floor. She remembered the day they brought John home from the hospital. She immediately knew that her place as the last child had been usurped by this very large lump of screaming cuteness.

Susanne's fingers glided along her knees, a makeshift piano. She gazed out the window oblivious to the antics of the boys just feet away. Elizabeth slid in next to Susanne and moved as close as she could. She kissed her mother's arm and looked up at her battered neck. Susanne smiles, happy to see Elizabeth. The daughter with the great imagination that was sometimes a challenge. She lightly touches Elizabeth's head. Her eyes linger on Elizabeth's face as if looking for someone.

"It will be dark when we get home," Elizabeth offers, knowing there will be no response. Susanne looks out into the sunset. The piano ritual began again. Elizabeth watched her mother's fingers and imitated the moves. Susanne hums a tune with fragments of words flowing over her battered vocal cords arriving as a whisper: *To memory now I can't recall, so fill to me . . .*

Chapter Two

Cigarette smoke danced out of a car window and lifted into the air. A dark-haired man with brooding eyes smoked and slouched in the front seat of an old Hudson, a car known to have the biggest back seat on record, one that could hold five children. Junior waited with hope and longing. He resolved to do better; he always tried. The train's whistle startled him, and he quickly sat up, flipped his cigarette out the window and reached over to touch a small box on the seat next to him. He smiled, "They're home."

The train station, a brick building with dark awnings, stretched along the tracks. Ancient lights hung from poles filtered by an early morning fog. Large wooden baggage carts were parked along the worn brick platform. The imposing train idled, waiting for the next travelers to start their journeys and the conductor to sing out, "All aboard." Sleepy passengers emerged through the fog while Junior searched for his family. Susanne appeared first with John in her arms, followed by James and Patrick each carrying a large suitcase. Katherine, with a book, guided a yawning Elizabeth.

The drive home was quiet, almost too quiet for Junior. Susanne must have some news of his mom and dad, his brothers and sisters, especially his little sister

Marilyn. Susanne's stay with his family after the accident was surely long enough to evoke extended conversations. But the car was silent.

Susanne had little to say; her thoughts were her own and he could not pry them out—not with sweet talk or jokes, or even the gift box that he slid across the seat, or the hand that gently touched hers. Besides, her voice was barely back. There were few weapons at her disposal and silence was one of them.

Susanne cuddled John who was nestled in her lap and peered out into the darkness. She glanced over her shoulder at the sleeping children in the back seat. All breathed deeply. Except for Katherine, sleep was only an opportunity to pretend. She was ever vigilant, ever watchful, and her sleep was never her own. Her eyes closed, but her thoughts raced.

Once home, the quiet of their small house didn't stop Junior from finding Susanne in the dark of night. She wondered how something so intimate could be so available when there were so few feelings. Unlike Susanne, Junior didn't mind the emotional distance, but normally he would never wake her up in the middle of the night, "like some men at the railroad," he often said. But they were both awake and she had been gone for a week and that was a long time.

"A married man should never have to be without." That's what he told her soon after they were married in 1943. He never intended to eat a meal out, or go without from that day forward. The honeymoon was over and Junior had changed. During the war before they were married, they ate out plenty and there was no sex—not real sex anyway, just heavy petting.

Junior didn't go to war. There wasn't room for a diabetic. He resented his disease the most when it limited him. He would have loved to kill a few Japs and Krauts. He stayed put and met Susanne who came to replace a man who did get called up. Although she and Junior lived in railroad towns just a stone's throw away from each other, they had never before met.

Susanne was as pretty as spring, soft and lovely. That's what Junior thought when he saw her for the first time, but it was the color of her hair that gave him the opportunity to flirt. "Hey, copper penny," Junior said.

She glanced up from her work on the telegraph machine; her blue eyes pulled him in. Susanne took his breath away, but she thought him bold. Who was this man and why did he think he could be so familiar? She didn't know him and she thought she probably didn't want to.

Although attractive, Susanne didn't have a boyfriend. There was a sweet guy who followed her with his eyes, but he had never made a move. He was far too shy. He left for the war and she was sure he would be killed. How could he not? He was too kind to last in the war. But, he did. He came home, and found that Susanne was already taken.

Even though Susanne fought her feelings, Junior was the handsomest man she had ever seen with his brooding black eyes, thick hair, and mischievous smile. It took only a few months and Junior had worked his magic. He got a "yes" when he proposed. After two failed attempts to find a best man— perhaps that was an omen— Susanne and Junior were married.

Men were tough to find in those days. On the railroad, you were called in and sent out because the nation was at war, and goods and services needed to get through; railroads ran on time. In the end, they found a guy in a bar who seemed to be sober, and he stood up with them at their wedding. Her engagement ring was small and the wedding band smaller yet, but it bound them together. Years later she pawned the ring to pay a bill; it was not a very big bill.

In the small double bed, Junior and Susanne again went through the motions as the moon poured into the sparsely furnished room. Junior panted, groaned and reached climax. Susanne stared at the ceiling while a small tear ran down her cheek. She lay still and then gently pushed Junior off. Almost asleep, he didn't object. She slipped out of the bed and slowly crossed the room. Against an open window, the moon's light shone through her sheer gown outlining her body as a gentle breeze lifted her hair. She looked good for a woman with five living children.

Their first child, a beautiful little girl with dark hair like Junior's, died at birth. The labor had been hard but the baby, when presented to the grieving parents, looked perfect. They named her Bonnie Sue, a pretty name but not a good Catholic name. That was before they converted.

It was said that Junior's great affection for his riding-the-rails buddy, Gerald, a good Catholic who never missed mass, prompted Junior to announce to Susanne, "I am going to become a Catholic. You can be anything you want."

The conversion came soon after the death of their first child and left many to wonder if the two events were tied together but they were not. Gerald saw in Junior pieces and remnants of a young boy with so much personality, so much charm, and who liked people and knew that people liked him. Junior loved his friend Gerald for seeing that part of him and, in his own way, loved his son Patrick Gerald, the most.

Susanne wiped away a tear and reached over to pick up the gift wrapped in blue tissue paper with white ribbon and a small bow on top. She gingerly removed the ribbon and bow, setting them on the windowsill. Reaching in, she pulled out a music box adorned with a ballerina figurine straight out of Swan Lake. She wound the music box slowly, convinced Junior would never wake from his sleep. He didn't. The tiny ballerina was dressed in a stiff white tutu, her feet wrapped in slippers, and her hair pulled up into a knot. She moved in a circle, swirling in sync to the music. Susanne's fingers lightly touched the surface as she studied the object, remembering the story of a princess turned into a swan by an evil sorcerer. The irony of her own situation caused her to reflect.

Susanne's father was as different from the man she chose to marry as the sun was to the moon. He was quiet and unassuming, much like his ancestors who had come from Sweden. Her mother's family immigrated from Scotland. They boarded ships along the North Sea and English Isles coasts, leaving tundra and hard lives behind. Both of Susanne's parents were the youngest in their large families of twelve and thirteen. The Swedes produced one more child than the Scots, or maybe one more that lived than died. Their descendants, her parents Henry and Isabella, were the only ones born in their adopted homeland.

Isabella Leishman made clothes for farm families while Henry Peterson was a farm hand. Both were considered ancient when they married—Isabella in her late 30s and Henry already in his fourth decade. They bore only one child, Susanne.

Susanne's childhood memories were captured on celluloid, but left behind in a dresser during a hasty retreat. The getaway was another chapter of lost memories, another moment of impulse that Junior inflicted on his wife. It tore at Susanne that all her sweet memories of the Leishmans and Petersons, aunts and uncles, with great names like Augusta and Adolph, were gone. Only fragments and glimpses of people and places remained. Susanne often thought of her family and the photos left behind in the dresser Junior forgot. She learned to keep a box of letters and cards hidden away, but easily found if needed.

It was during one of those hasty retreats when the tuberculosis in Susanne's lungs erupted and caused her to be sent away to a place called Norton. Susanne was sent away twice—once when James was a baby, and again after the family had grown to include Patrick, Katherine and Elizabeth. Junior couldn't care for the children and keep his job on the railroad so the family was broken apart.

Each child was sent to a relative who particularly favored them, all except Elizabeth who hadn't had time to become a favorite. Katherine lamented from time to time, "The foster family wanted to adopt you, but Dad said no. You were the reason we left and Dad took mom out of the hospital." It seemed reasonable to Elizabeth. She had seen the photos of herself as a baby, being held by some unknown woman, and she recognized she was indeed a beautiful baby. The report of the Service League noted that the baby first came to foster care malnourished with a small hernia, unable to do what other babies her age could do, but Elizabeth never saw the report and would not have believed the observations.

Katherine and James, the oldest son and oldest daughter, went to the 0'Sullivans, and Patrick went to Oklahoma to live with Junior's favorite uncle (married to Vena's sister)—a person not held in high esteem by the O'Sullivan clan. Junior, who enjoyed making his father unhappy, relished the idea that his son would live with a man his father disliked. It was as if Junior wanted to poke his father whenever he had a chance.

Junior developed diabetes early in life. His father accepted that his oldest son was doomed from the beginning, caught in a cycle of illness and near-death experiences. He was sure his son would not accomplish much, but he believed there would be other children he could place his dreams on. The feeling of disappointment displayed by the father, in a look or a small comment, was always noted and never forgotten by the son.

Junior never felt his father's hand in anger. His mother saw to that. Junior was her son, and he was perfect. He knew how to make her laugh and how to gain forgiveness. This was a son who would later buy a music box with a ballerina swirling on the top for his wife in the hopes of finding forgiveness. Such actions had worked before to show his regret, and he was sorry. He was always sorry.

Susanne slid the ballerina into the box as she thought back in time to the quiet and austere home of her youth. Her father's smile brightened her day just like her voice lifted his spirits. Her speech came at age two after infantile paralysis in 1923 raged in her body. She survived, but there was evidence of the disease—her left leg was smaller than the right leg.

An experimental operation during the early 1930s had slowed the growth in her good right leg to allow the left leg to grow and catch up to the other, so now there was nothing visually to set Susanne apart from being normal. Elizabeth often asked to see the scars that looked like railroad tracks. She ran her fingers over the scar, thrilled but equally repelled. This was her mother's leg, but it made her seem something other than a mother, like she had a history that Elizabeth didn't understand. The scars made the leg look tortured.

Susanne moved toward the bed. It would be morning soon and she would have to ready the clan for church.

Chapter 3

Elizabeth loved being Catholic—all those saints, all those stories, all the drama, the great robes, the mystery, the incense. She often wondered why anyone would be a Protestant; that was beyond her understanding. The Protestants in Elizabeth's neighborhood didn't have very many children. They didn't have any beautiful saints to pray to, and they were definitely going to Hell. However, she learned from her mother that somewhere along the way, while crossing the American heartland, the Catholic religion had been kidnapped. The religion of beautiful statues was abandoned and left on the frontier (a parting gift) as the family moved west. Thank goodness! Elizabeth thought when her mother described her own upbringing in a household of Protestants. She was happy that her father had converted and chose incense, chants and a foreign language that only Catholics sort of knew. It was the only time she thanked him.

The saints died for their beliefs with horrible deaths, some upside down like St. Peter. The thought of it made Elizabeth's head swirl. She would give anything to have just one holy card (a perfect replica of a saint). A holy card was small, not even as big as an index card. It would fit right into Elizabeth's pocket. She could take it with her everywhere, but there was never enough money for things like holy cards.

As an alternative to buying, Elizabeth only had to be especially good and smart to receive a holy card from the church. She tried hard to be good, and that was the only challenge for she knew she was smart. But there was just one thing that stood in her way—Mary Paul, whom she considered to be the meanest nun to ever don a habit. Elizabeth chastised herself each time she had bad thoughts about this monster who looked more like a Penguin, an image Elizabeth could not shake no matter how hard she tried. Mary Paul, with her squatty body dressed in the black and white habit, waddled around squawking, never smiling. Elizabeth never used the word "Sister" when she thought of Mary Paul.

None of the children ever used the word Catholic around their father's mother Grandma Vena. She was an Episcopalian, a "pretend Catholic," Elizabeth's father would say. Grandma Vena was saddened when her oldest and dearest son became a Catholic. It drove her crazy. Just the word "Catholic" would send Grandma Vena into a tizzy, and Grandma Vena knew how to throw a tizzy.

Aside from the fact that her grandmother was Protestant, Elizabeth thought her Grandma Vena was the greatest grandmother anyone could ever have. They all loved her. She made the best chicken and noodles that were thick and gooey. She rolled the noodle dough out and cut long skinny strings with a paring knife. The strings of dough would be left to dry, and then mixed with chicken and creamy stuff. This was food Elizabeth loved to eat; there were no beets at Grandma Vena's house. She also made great pinto beans and tortillas, a skill she developed when she married Elmer.

Elmer was a man motivated by hard work with a recipe for success based on the number of hours that a man could possibly toil. His job was to maintain the rail bed that supported the trains. For the family, pinto beans and tortillas became a staple and a connection to a place and time where hard work justified all actions and made a person whole. A job meant you were worth something, and it was a joy to be worth something when there was so little. They lived, worked, and ate with the Nationals, recruited from Mexico as cheap labor.

Vena's first home was the last car on the train. When it came time for her to give birth to Elizabeth's father, the first of her five children, Vena got lucky and so did Elizabeth's father. She was assisted by Elmer and a railroad worker who only spoke Spanish, but had delivered several of his own children.

The stone structure was simple. Stained glass windows depicting the journey of Christ to his crucifixion allowed a muted sun to enter the chamber and lay across the faces of the worshipers. The place was packed with mostly railroad families. The O'Sullivan family, dressed in their Sunday best, took up half of one long pew. Over the altar was a life-sized carving of Jesus Christ hanging from a cross. Statues of the Blessed Virgin Mary with a cherub Baby Jesus in her arms, and St. John the Evangelist, patron saint of the Church, bookended the altar.

Elizabeth looked around the church. It seemed the same but different somehow, or maybe it was her. Maybe she had changed. They had been gone for over a week, a last break before school started. That's how it was explained to the children, but they knew it was to protect the sinner.

All the families looked alike and were white. There were no brown faces in the crowd although the city had been populated with workers from Mexico who broke the ground that allowed the train to move west. The Mexicans had their own church, much more ornate than the lily white church, and a priest who spoke Spanish from the old country.

The people weren't so far apart economically because they all worked at the railroad. They had built the railroad, brown and white together, but once the sun went down, the brown people lived in a different part of town, went to a different church and attended a different school. The old brown people spoke only Spanish and lived with their children in these houses. They made the best enchiladas and sold them from their back porches. At least once a week, Elizabeth was summoned to fetch two dozen from Mrs. Rocha.

Church was different for the white Catholics and the brown Catholics. It was more casual in the Mexican church. Mexican mothers opened their dresses to feed their babies during Mass. Elizabeth had seen it one winter when she went to a Christmas Mass with her mother who had been asked to sing. Once a year, the two churches exchanged services, but there was no breastfeeding in the white church. Elizabeth felt a little out of place with no screaming babies. She liked the image of a mother breast feeding; it seemed right and she was mesmerized. Elizabeth was certain she would never have breasts. What would a nun do with them? She didn't remember her mother breastfeeding John, but maybe she did. Katherine was maturing that way, sort of, which made sense to Elizabeth because her sister would have her own baby one day and would probably breastfeed like the brown mothers. Katherine would be a good mother; Elizabeth knew that.

The parish priest, a huge man in his sixties with gray hair and a booming voice, genuflected and turned to his flock and said, "Dominus vobiscum." The parishioners responded with "Et cum spiritu tuo."

Elizabeth loved that response, it made her want to laugh saying too-too, and she would say it over and over in her head. She thought of a ballerina in a tutu, and then imagined the big priest wearing one. It was almost more than she could bear. She knew what would happen if she laughed.

Although Elizabeth loved being Catholic, she didn't like mass, but she attended everyday before school and always on Sunday. She took communion because the nuns and most of the community were watching. She never felt very holy or special once the wafer was down her throat. Oh, there were lots of good words, all in Latin which she liked because she could pretend she was in a place far away, but at its core it was really boring. The music was good; she liked the music and knew most of the responses, but she would rather think about anything but Jesus . . . like maybe purses; she liked purses. She didn't have one, but she wanted one with all the mysteries they held inside. She also liked to look at the statutes of the saints placed in alcoves and on small altars scattered throughout the church, and then wonder about their lives. Most were nuns—and Elizabeth was fascinated with nuns.

Just a few more responses until Mass was over, then the priest would bolt out of the sanctuary with the altar boys trailing behind. No doubt there was a meal waiting for this very big holy man.

Elizabeth looked over at her mother who was watching the crowded choir loft. Susanne smiled at a young woman who waved back. Susanne longed to be in the loft singing, making her way with notes and chords among the friendly faces. Elizabeth knew when her mother was most herself—when she was singing. Susanne started singing at about the same time she began to talk. Although the Depression stole any chance for more of an education, Susanne was given singing and piano lessons through the Works Progress Administration. Due to circumstances beyond her control, she could only use her talent in places like weddings, war bond rallies, and Sunday services.

As the doors opened, the parishioners exited with the O'Sullivans making their way among neighbors and coworkers. Just as the family reached the last step leading down from the church, the young woman from the choir loft grabbed Susanne's arm. "Susanne, it is so good to see you. We can't wait for you to come back. I was so sad to hear about your accident."

Susanne smiled and just as quickly looked at Junior. He pretended not to see the young woman or hear what she said. Susanne reached out and touched the woman's arm as a show of appreciation before she was pulled in the other direction.

"I need to get something to eat," Junior announced—the artful act of the diabetic. Maybe he had not eaten and his sugar was low, or maybe he already had a bite before they left for Mass. The truth wasn't important; he just needed a way to maneuver Susanne away from prying eyes. It also wasn't important to the children. They would rather he lie than make a scene. And then they were gone.

Chapter 4

Elizabeth took her turn helping out in the kitchen. Her jobs were minimal and nothing close to cooking or what might be asked of Katherine. Elizabeth peeled potatoes and set the table, but never had to read a recipe.

She watched and marveled at her mother's skills. The hands that flew across the black and white keys of the piano worked as well whipping up potatoes or batter for pancakes. There wasn't a recipe she avoided. Elizabeth wondered where her mother learned so much. The other things like laundry or house cleaning happened because everyone had a chore, but Elizabeth hardly noticed those. It was food that was important because a missed meal meant something different in this family. Everyone knew that a diabetic had to avoid sugar and eat on time. Being on time for the family meal was a rule that couldn't be broken. The family routinely gathered before the father went off to work the night shift at the railroad. Meals were almost always a high alert time, especially for Elizabeth. Would her father like what Susanne had cooked? Would he be in a foul mood? Would they have sugar beets (which Elizabeth hated), and would Elizabeth be required to sit until everything on her plate was eaten? This was the time Elizabeth had most of her bad thoughts about her father.

Junior sat at a long wooden table with benches, reading the paper with a cigarette dangling from his mouth, his fingers yellow from the tobacco. The table was much more like a picnic table than a real table, not like the table of Elizabeth's O'Sullivan grandparents.

The kitchen was well used with circa early 1940's appliances and cracked, stained counter tops. A damaged sink, filled with cooking utensils, sat under a window that faced out onto the backyard, in view of a small space with a dilapidated shed off to the side filled with junk. It was a treasure chest generally off limits to the children. The back door opened onto a small screened porch.

Each child had their place at the table. As luck would have it, Elizabeth's seat was next to her father, and Patrick across from her. She didn't really understand how she got that spot and wished she sat in another room as far away as possible. Susanne sat directly opposite from Junior, next to John in his high chair. At three, John was not much of a baby. He was big for his age and way too big for the high chair. His role as the baby was to provide cover for Susanne, at least at mealtime.

Junior, intent on the paper, didn't notice as the children filed in and found their spots—James next to his mother and closest to Elizabeth, Patrick next to Katherine. Junior looked up, and as if on cue, put the paper down. Without commotion or fanfare, he brought his hands together and bowed his head. Susanne and the children, even John, followed his lead.

Junior prayed, "Bless us, oh Lord, and these thy gifts which we are about to receive from thy bounty through Christ our Lord."

The children looked up but Junior kept his pose.

"We are especially thankful to have the family back together, and we are thankful that Susanne has recovered from her fall. Amen." He then raised his head with a genuine smile on his face as a quiet encompassed the room. Junior looked to Susanne for recognition and she smiled tentatively, just enough. Junior's smile widened as the children exhaled.

"Hey, pass that chicken," he commanded.

The ritual began and the platter and bowls were passed. It was a good Sunday meal with chicken, mashed potatoes and gravy, green beans, and rolls. The father was happy.

And then the sugar beets arrived causing Elizabeth to balk. She knew this would be bad. Maybe he wouldn't notice, she hoped. Maybe he had something to do and would leave the table before she finished. She knew she would gag if forced to eat the sugar beets that Junior seemed to love. Sugar beets, there was nothing sugar about those beets. Whoever named them probably couldn't tell the difference from eating dirt, she thought.

As the bowl of sugar beets were passed to Elizabeth, she hesitated before taking one and putting it on her plate. She quickly looked over at Junior who was distracted by the platter of chicken that came his way. She was saved for the moment, if only she could outlast him.

Junior, with his mouth full, chewed, and then looked over at Susanne. The children watched his every move. "I bought Mom a special gift, a music box, because she loves music so much. It's pretty, if I do say so myself," he proudly announced.

Quiet. Do they acknowledge and break the silence, or do they ignore? They knew it would probably be Patrick who would make a remark—he had the least to lose and was the best at making conversation. Patrick didn't look as much like an O'Sullivan as the other children, but more like the Peterson side of the family, more like Susanne's father.

"Yeah, we saw it, Dad. It looks real nice," Patrick replied. Junior smiled and took a big bite of chicken. Patrick was also a good storyteller and Elizabeth liked that about him. He brought to life images almost like a camera taking photos, and then he spit out the tales to thrill his audience. There wasn't much he couldn't do: math, science, and even history. Most importantly, he knew how to handle his father.

"Now that you kids are home, it's back to business. I want this house clean when I come home, no stuff lying around. I don't know what bad habits you might have picked up at Grandma's," he smiled.

That was a really stupid comment, Elizabeth thought. Grandma Vena ruled her house with an iron fist, but equally important was the fact that the home Elizabeth lived in didn't have much stuff to lay around. The house was as sparse as a job during the Depression. She had heard Grandma O'Sullivan make that comment. Was her father trying to be funny? Yes he was, she concluded. That was a good sign. Her encounter with the sugar beets was looking like a thing of the past. This day might turn out just fine.

Junior pushed his plate away. Just a little bit longer, Elizabeth thought. She was hopeful. Maybe he will go lie down for a nap.

"Susanne, how much insulin do I have in the fridge?" No such luck, Elizabeth realized. Susanne got up from the table and stepped over to the fridge. She pulled out a vial of insulin and held it up for him to see.

"It's full. Good. I might need some later," Junior remarked. Hmmm, what does that mean? Elizabeth wondered.

Patrick was always on his toes, assessing, "You working the second shift later?"

Junior looked over at Patrick, "No, I'm going to head down to the Flood Room for some cards."

Patrick nodded.

Elizabeth knew there was something else about Patrick, especially when it came to their father. It was as if he were a step or two ahead. Elizabeth admired that about her brother. She saw his skill just as James and Katherine saw it, but neither she nor the others had Patrick's capability. They were always on guard, but not prepared. Patrick was on guard and always had a plan. He didn't always act; sometimes he just waited.

Junior leaned back in his chair and looked over at Elizabeth. Elizabeth moved the beet around on her plate with her fork. She was stalling, hopping he would get up and move away.

"You don't like beets do you?" he said, looking sharply at Elizabeth. Her hand slipped with the words, "Do you?" and she accidentally pushed the beet juice off her plate onto the white table cloth. A dark stain immediately appeared. Somewhat frightened, Elizabeth quickly looked up, hopeful that somehow he overlooked the misdemeanor, but he had not.

She knew what was coming. There was nothing she could do—the monster was about to arrive. She saw the familiar steam sneaking out of his nose, and his eyebrows growing thick formations like an awning over his eyes. His front teeth protruded causing his lips to disappear. The Monster finally brought up his hand that now appeared to be a paw with claws that could rip her face off. She hunkered down while he slapped her hard. She'd had worse, but it still hurt. It was a premature assault, but at least he wasn't fully a monster…yet. James attempted to stand, but Susanne was right behind him to reach out and gently restrain him with her hand placed on his shoulders.

"Look what you have done," Junior said, his voice distorted. "All I wanted was to have a nice meal. Is that too much to ask?"

Elizabeth watched closely as the monster struggled to get up from the table. He had grown so tall that his head brushed the ceiling while his toenails, sharp as a butcher's knife, cut through his shoes leaving them in shreds. He arose and took one big step to grab Elizabeth's plate from the table and deliver it to the cracked sink, slamming it down with force. It was as if he were auditioning for a movie, but the audience had seen it all before. Quietly, he stood at the kitchen window while no one else moved. What would he do? Everyone wondered. Was this the last of it or just the beginning? This time he hadn't been drinking; he was stone cold sober. He had plans and needed to calm down so he could return to human form before he left the house. Elizabeth wasn't going to wait to find out what he would do next.

Patrick caught Elizabeth's attention and discreetly moved his eyes toward the kitchen door. Elizabeth knew what that meant. She eased off the bench, trying not to make the slightest bit of noise. She rounded the corner of the kitchen and then looked back to see the shoulders of the monster's frame burst through his shirt. Her tiptoe exit sped up, and she flew across the living room, up the stairs into the bedroom.

The door closed gently behind her as her face flooded with tears. The bedroom window was open. Good, she thought. If he comes looking, he will think I made my way out the window, onto the roof, then onto the tree and away.

Elizabeth was lucky. She had a place no one else had; it was hers alone. Through the tears she found her way past the neatly made beds to a small closet. Behind the dress up clothes, worn only on special occasions and Sunday Mass, she pushed a small panel that opened to reveal her sanctuary. It was a place so small it would hold only Elizabeth and maybe a toddler like John, although she would never invite him into her special place. She crawled in, pulled her legs up against her chest, and rocked. The routine of an abused child; it was automatic. First she cried, then pulled at her skin, and then at her eyelashes. The pain must equal the anger or she would burst.

Chapter 5

Susanne awoke to the rising sun and the small sounds that announce the day, a soft bustle. The first day of school held excitement and dread. She knew the children would move about and ready themselves, but not wake him.

She slid out of bed and went toward the window and glanced down at the cement path that led to the sidewalk. She knew the boys would be the first to leave. Katherine always dressed quickly as she was always prepared. Her uniform, which included the blue jumper, white shirt, red handkerchief, white socks and plain black shoes that were laced and not attractive, would have been laid out the night before. She'd help Elizabeth comb her hair and make sure she wore good socks, and then get John ready for breakfast. Yes, she thought, Katherine makes up for what I don't have left inside.

Susanne hated herself for thrusting Katherine too far into the future and taking away her childhood, but Susanne needed her. Katherine was good at many things. She knew how to cook and sew, all things a woman should know, Katherine knew. She learned quickly; it was just second nature to this young girl. All the children counted on her, and it was expected. It wasn't meant to be that way; it just was and was never talked about. Katherine never really asked for care for herself. It was as if she was an old soul and had eclipsed her own mother. Susanne sewed, cooked and did the laundry. The things a mother did. She knew how to love her children, but she didn't know how to protect them. She didn't even know how to protect herself.

In Susanne's childhood family, life was hard because a bigger world made it that way. There wasn't any person that Susanne could blame for her father's arthritis or her mother's frail health, or the Depression that made them nearly homeless. Susanne didn't blame anyone for her life now but herself. She had met him and married him too quickly. A price was paid. She could have lived her life playing the piano and singing, and she would have been happy. The children widened her world, but she didn't know what to do with them. She had no brothers or sisters, no way to compare. She would just love them the best that she could.

As expected, James bolted out the front door with Patrick close behind. Katherine, with perfectly combed hair pulled back into a pony tail and wearing a clean uniform, hustled after them. She had done all she could to help Elizabeth be on time, and she could do no more.

Elizabeth, with toast in hand, paused before exiting the front door. A window pane provided ample reflection and she saw a glimpse of herself. Her school uniform, recently pressed by Katherine, looked smart—the uniform of a good Catholic school girl. Elizabeth often thought of her father's friend who had led them to the Catholic Church. She wanted to thank him for the Saints, and the uniform. She certainly liked her uniform. No one knew how poor the family was when everyone looked the same. Oh, the nuns knew who paid tuition and who got free tuition. It was important to the nuns, and they measured the children's behavior by that fact. Katherine had told Elizabeth that she needed to behave because they really didn't belong there; the nuns looked for reasons to expel them.

Elizabeth looked back at her mother who had joined John at the table. How pretty she was. How happy she seemed. She smiled at John and lightly ran her hand over his head. Elizabeth is reminded of her grandmother, Susanne's mother, who had been shelved away in a hospital for Tuberculosis. There wasn't money to travel to see her, and the one time they managed to visit the outpost, Elizabeth held back. Her grandmother looked like a witch. A very pretty witch with a close resemblance to her mother, but a witch just the same. The woman was frail and dressed in black with white hair pulled up into a bun. She had long fingers, just like her mother's. The Witch reached out and it was all Elizabeth could do not to run screaming. The woman didn't look angry or even sad, just hungry.

What a difference from her other grandmother, Elizabeth thought; Grandmother Vena Ethel, with the fat arms, grand laugh and dark brown eyes. She wondered how this could be. Were each of these women really somehow a part of her? It seemed impossible. She remembered her mother's sad face when word came that Isabelle Leishman Peterson had died. Susanne saw to the arrangements with burial in an unmarked grave at the State Hospital for Tuberculosis. There was no money for a headstone.

But that was then and the now was John giggling, chewing cereal and squirting out milk, which made Susanne smile. It was the best part of the day for Susanne. Although John was spoiled, that Elizabeth knew for sure, he brought joy to her mother, and through his antics he brought "Gary Cooper" into her life.

It happened on one of the police occasions when John ventured out just two minutes after arriving home from a visit to Grandma Vena's. He took off and rode his tricycle across the highway, went into a store, stole a toy and then took a walk. He left his tricycle unattended which was not smart for a family that had no extra money to buy a new one. The boys who were under order to keep their eyes on John felt no compunction to keep track of John, even though Susanne asked them to watch him; they were good brothers, but not all that attentive. When John came up missing, the police were alerted. There wasn't a phone in the house so Susanne had to run across the street to use the neighbor's.

This became routine. John would take off, and a few hours later the police would bring him home. Everybody at police headquarters knew where John lived. He would ride up front with the officer, usually with a Tootsie Roll pop in his mouth. Elizabeth really hated that he got special treatment for doing something bad. Not often, but occasionally when he was brought home, Elizabeth's father would be waiting. He would not be happy. The children would wait outside listening at the door, certain he would get the whipping of his life, but it never happened. John was always spared.

On one special occasion, Elizabeth met the man that she believed was Gary Cooper stepping out of her living room. He was the police officer who delivered John back home. He walked out of the house right past her; tipped his hat, and said, "Hello." He was a tall man so she couldn't see his face, but she heard something in his voice—a soft but strong voice, a little questioning, with just a hint of a resonating lilt.

It came to her. She had seen the movie "High Noon" and there was a poster advertising the movie in the window next door to that wonderful, but generally off limits place where magic happened—the movie theater. She remembered standing and staring at the movie poster. Gary Cooper's beautiful blue eyes made her smile. It was as if he were looking directly at her.

So what was Gary Cooper doing in her town? Simple really, she reasoned. He must be practicing for a movie. She was sure he was "on location." She knew that movie stars sometimes came to small towns to shoot movies—she saw it in a movie magazine at the beauty shop one time when her mother got her hair cut. He certainly would make a great father, Elizabeth thought. He seemed a little tough, but not too tough. He could protect her; he would be perfect. She knew it was a sin to wish for a replacement for her father and highly unlikely to happen because her father would have to die first.

Out the door and onto the sidewalk, Katherine waited for Elizabeth, anxious as usual. "Elizabeth, we can't be late. It's the first day of school."

Elizabeth made a feeble attempt at running then was distracted by the O'Brien clan down the street that came out in squads. Each child was clean, but poor looking. The younger children's school uniforms were real hand-me-downs, worn by at least two other siblings. Elizabeth's hand-me-down came from her sister so it was only a one-time hand-me-down.

"You think this is funny? You know how much Sister Mary Paul dislikes you," Katherine said.

"Katherine, she hates me," Elizabeth responded. "She hated me last year and I don't know why I have to have her again."

Exasperated Katherine looked at Elizabeth, "I have told you this whole summer that Sister Mary Basil left, and I mean left. She is not a nun anymore. They had to find a replacement for the fifth and sixth grade. Sister Mary Paul moved with your class, fourth into fifth. Besides you don't know that she really hates you."

Elizabeth knew that Mary Paul actually did hate her. It was easy for Elizabeth to see. The word hate was very strong and Elizabeth knew this was an indictment of great proportion. The nun would stare at her with a hint of rage just under the surface. She would take her pointer or a ruler and whack the knuckles of any child that seemed to be bored, but most often it was Elizabeth. The students could see the intent and the target, and it had nothing to do with being bored. The nun might mumble about sitting up straight, then whack, whack. No one, not even a nun, was allowed to hate, but Elizabeth knew that Mary Paul hated, just as she herself did.

Elizabeth liked saying "Mary Paul from Gaul." It reminded her of her Great Aunt Grace (a married woman without children, which was strange) who had gotten her gallbladder removed. Elizabeth once heard her Grandma Vena talk about it. Gallbladders were disgusting, green things that really mean people had. Grandma Vena had said that was why Aunt Grace had been so nasty, her gallbladder was acting up. It made sense to Elizabeth. Just like Aunt Grace, nuns didn't have children. Perhaps there was a connection. Mary Paul Gallbladder was a perfect name for the half monster, half penguin. The name changed when necessary, but she would never be Sister Mary Paul to Elizabeth.

The hardest thing about hating Mary Paul was that Elizabeth adored the saints and a good many of the saints were nuns. Elizabeth reminded herself that the nuns she saw on the holy cards were special. St. Theresa of the Little Flower, Catherine of Sienna, didn't look crazy or mean. None of them could be like Mary Paul. If they had been, they never would have made it to Heaven, let alone become a saint. Elizabeth was very sure of that.

Her fear of Mary Paul led her to hope every day, in this her eleventh year on Earth, that Mary Paul would disappear. How unfair, Elizabeth thought, that Mary Paul would be her instructor two years in a row. At the end of the last school year, her box of bad thoughts was overflowing with images and words. It was a good thing she had found a lid, a way to keep those from coming out. Just merely thinking those thoughts would require a confession. She chose not to disclose all of what was in her box. In the confessional she would simply say that she had bad thoughts or that she had been mean. If the priest pursued and asked her what bad thoughts she had, she would usually make something up—not a good thing to do for sainthood. The confessional was problematic but essential. People kind of knew who had not been to confession for a long time because they would be in the confessional for what seemed forever, right before Mass. Elizabeth often wondered what in the world these people could be confessing. No one went to jail in her town, at least none that she knew. Not even her father.

On days when she felt particularly strong she could rationalize any indiscretion. Other days she felt bad about her thoughts, and she often found herself agreeing with Mary Paul that her chances of reaching Heaven were slim to none. To be sure, she never had bad thoughts about her mother—not even when her mother delayed curling her hair and worked on Katherine's instead, then ran out to the store to pick up something she needed to make dinner saying, "I'll be right back and we will do your hair later, Elizabeth."

Elizabeth only heard the word later, as in being never. She found the scissors, climbed up on the sink in front of the mirror, and cut chunks of her hair off. Susanne was aghast but never raised her voice; she merely shook her head. How could Susanne explain this? She wouldn't and neither would Elizabeth. There were no real questions or real understanding, only love. The curious dance of a mother and daughter when the dance card was full, too many children. She never expected much from her mother because she had Katherine.

Lucky for Elizabeth it had been summer and there were no nuns around to say something mean. Elizabeth knew they couldn't really say anything as they didn't have any hair under those habits—they were as bald as peacocks. This thought always brought a smile to Elizabeth's face.

There weren't any commandments that said honor and love crazy nuns. She was definitely off the hook with Mary Paul, but her father . . . now that was another thing. She didn't really know him, but he scared her more than any nun ever could, except for Mary Paul. She knew she should love him, but she didn't. Jesus had died to keep her from going to Hell. He showed the way. He loved everyone, even the ones that had tortured and killed him, and she took this to heart. She tried very hard not to hate her father and felt incredibly guilty when she did, which was quite often, especially when he slapped, whacked, or punched her, her siblings, or her mother. She did hate him—a cardinal sin—but she chose to never confess that sin, never. The saying of it sent shivers of fear into her body.

The cardinal sin of hate wasn't born in Elizabeth, she knew that. She felt it coming on when there was no way to stop the craziness that her father brought into the family. His targets changed, but mostly he lashed out at Susanne and James. A late dinner resulted in a slap to Susanne's face which would prompt an evil eye from James, and the games would begin.

On one especially ominous night, Junior went after James with such a torrent that Elizabeth froze in place. Katherine moved to the corner with John at her side, the tears flowing. Susanne pleaded James' case, but Junior was determined to teach him a lesson. He took James down to the floor and was choking him when, out of nowhere, Patrick appeared with a broom and quickly broke it over his father's head, knocking him out. That was a night full of bad thoughts. Perhaps, Elizabeth believed, if she prayed hard enough, God would hear her prayers to replace her father.

"Your father works very hard," Susanne reminded the children after a night filled with terror—cold comfort and she knew it, but what could she do? She couldn't leave. The job at the railroad was quickly filled when the men returned from war. Her life was scripted like most of the women of her time and place; she could only be a wife and mother.

The children knew that Junior never missed work, which was a good thing because they had nowhere to go if their father didn't work. They would be split apart. No, it was important that their father stay healthy and working. They knew what to do when the sugar was low. They immediately went to the fridge and got the orange juice. One of the boys or Katherine would help Susanne, and they would force the liquid down him. It would take just a few minutes and he would recover. He then just needed to sleep it off. The reactions usually came after he had thrown some sort of fit.

It was routine, a drill, and they knew it. The house was never without orange juice. For Elizabeth, it seemed like a silly game because a monster can't be killed. His fits were just his way of showing his strength. He could bring them running back, strike terror in them and keep them close, all at the same time. Elizabeth had seen it too many times. Her best antidote was to stay out of his way.

To Elizabeth, Mary Paul and her father were like one very ugly monster, tethered together with a long rope that extended for miles. One was short and fat, the other tall and skinny. Each had eyes as black as night and could invade her soul to steal it away if she wasn't careful. If one appeared, Elizabeth knew for sure the other was just around the corner, lurking somewhere in her mind. They were like the wrestlers at the fair, a tag team. One was in her home at the dining room table, on the back porch, or in the yard with a beer in his hand and cigarette dangling from his mouth. The other was at her school, in the church, or on the playground. There were few places where at least one of the monsters did not appear.

Elizabeth wished that she didn't hate Mary Paul because she strangely felt a bit sorry for her. She seemed to creak when she walked, when she wasn't being mean. Elizabeth wanted to be a nun, her ticket to Heaven, but how could she be a nun when she had so many bad feelings for this closer-to-Jesus person? She thought she would look good as a nun, and even practiced their special way of walking. She could envision the nuns, before they were really nuns, practicing. They bowed their heads and stuck their hands under their garments, which were like very long aprons, and then floated. At least to Elizabeth they looked like they were floating.

There was one nun who gave Elizabeth hope. She had never spoken to Sister Mary Rose, but she could see her kindness peeking out from the starched white coif that surrounded her face. It was the way she talked to the children, her smile. That was the litmus test. Elizabeth could call her Sister. She laughed a lot and even played baseball at recess. She liked everything and was always humming, and most importantly, she was the best floater. When Elizabeth became a nun, she would be just like Sister Mary Rose.

Katherine and Elizabeth arrived at church as the bells, high above in the steeple, began to ring just minutes before Mass. Children gathered into a single line with James and Patrick in the front. The children were expected to be lined up when the Penguins arrived. Nuns with their leader, Sister Mary Agnes, who was also the principal of school, entered the church first and the children followed.

Mary Paul had her eye on Elizabeth throughout Mass. It wasn't until they were in the classroom that the nun made her move. The room was bleak; no special anything on the walls except, above the blackboard and underneath the clock, was a crucifix.

"Elizabeth O'Sullivan," Mary Paul said. "Would you please lead us in the morning prayer?" Oh no! Here it was the first day of class and she had been singled out. Elizabeth looked across the room at Katherine. It was a combination class of fifth and sixth graders. Katherine was taller than most boys or girls in her group and could easily be spotted. Elizabeth liked that— she was only a few feet from her sister, a lifeline.

Elizabeth approached the front of the classroom and noticed a beautiful, new, holy card of Joan of Arc placed below the crucifix in the center of the wall just above the chalkboard. Elizabeth's confirmation name was Joan, selected with a purpose in mind, although she was not especially fond of the name. She didn't like the way it sounded when she said it, but Joan was a star in the dictionary of saints. She must have it.

She saw the small stick in the nun's hand. Mary Paul tapped the stick gently on her hand, turned her back and left Elizabeth front and center. This was Elizabeth's worst nightmare, in front of the classroom with Mary Paul, aka *the monster*, observing her. Since this was the first day of class, Elizabeth needed to ponder her choices. The nun held the stick while Elizabeth began, "Our Father," and the children joined in with, "who art in Heaven, hollowed be thy name, thy kingdom come, thy will be done, on earth as it is in Heaven."

The nun turned around and walked up behind Elizabeth. The children, sensing that this was not about prayer, grew silent. Elizabeth continued, but her heart was racing and she broke out in a small sweat, "give us today, our daily bread, and forgive us our trespasses as we forgive those who trespass against us."

Suddenly, Mary Paul brought her stick up and smacked Elizabeth hard on the back of her legs, not once but twice. A loud gasp filled the room as Elizabeth flinched. Across the room, Katherine closed her eyes while Elizabeth continued the prayer. It was, for Elizabeth, the moment when she understood irony with the words, "and lead us not into temptation but deliver us from evil. Amen."

Her punishment for being late was a good excuse to teach humility. It won't be the last thing I teach Elizabeth O'Sullivan, Mary Paul thought with confidence.

Elizabeth knew what Amen meant because a priest had once told her. It meant "I agree." Oh yes, deliver us from evil. She knew exactly what evil was. She didn't know how she would make it through the year. Perhaps next year she could go to public school, but at the moment she needed to make it back to her seat. Tears welled in her eyes and she fought them with all the strength she could find. She looked up again at the holy card, at Joan of Arc. The Saint began to shift a bit and the noise of clanking armor in Elizabeth's ears was deafening. Quickly, the helmet that was safely in the Saint's hand, is thrown down like an invitation to fight. Slowly, Joan smiles and waves at Elizabeth who smiles back.

Elizabeth with head high, slowly walked to her seat. She is Joan of Arc dressed in armor, tall and strong. While difficult to negotiate the desk and chair with the clanking of imaginary steel in her ears, she gently lowered herself into her seat.

"Elizabeth, perhaps this will help you understand how much you hurt Jesus when you come late to Mass. You will stay after school and clean the boards and erasers." Turning to the class, "Fifth graders, work on your math assignment. Sixth graders, open your book." She says with a smile.

Elizabeth opened her math book and looked back up at the holy card, "Thank you," she whispered.

Elizabeth knew that Joan of Arc was not much older than she was when they burned her at the stake. It broke Elizabeth's heart to think of it so she chose to think only about the saint's heroics on the battle field.

Before recess, as the children assembled to leave the class, Elizabeth slipped a white index card from the crafts table into her pocket. She had already taken a lead pencil. She looked around to see if anyone saw, and to her relief, no one paid attention to her except for her sister who was busy at the reading center finishing her work. Each child spent time weekly at the reading center picking out stories, reading them, then taking a quiz. It was how the children prepared for comprehension tests. Elizabeth's comprehension was tops best in the class.

Elizabeth surveyed the room. The Penguin stood at the front preparing to waddle her way out the door with her chicks following in a perfect line. No one was allowed to break the line until their feet hit the pavement of the schoolyard. Elizabeth would have to bolt around the building, get the job done, and get back before the bell rang. If there wasn't enough time, the deed would have to wait until after school.

The classroom was empty as the Penguin sat at her desk grading papers. Slowly Elizabeth took the erasers to the window.

Without looking up and in a stern voice, the nun directed. "No, take the erasers outside. I don't want any mess in the classroom. I have to leave for a meeting at the church so shut the door when you are done. Make sure you do a good job. I will check, you know." Yes, Elizabeth was sure she would.

Elizabeth smiled. That should have alerted the Penguin, but her thoughts were somewhere else. The Priest had called the first meeting of the nuns for the school year, and not one would be late—it was not allowed. It didn't matter what the nuns had planned or how they would fit an extra hour into their day, which irked the Penguin. She didn't like him; she didn't like many priests.

Without much notice, Mary Paul was up and out the door. Perfect! Elizabeth drug a chair over to the blackboard, grimacing when a screech shattered the quiet. She looked around the room to make sure no one was watching, but better to make sure. She went to the door and looked into the hallway. No one. Good. Stop stalling, she thought, it is now or never. She hurried over to the chair, climbed up, and did a quick look around. She pulled out a newly minted Joan of Arc. The replacement looked good. Maybe she would be an artist, it was possible, she thought. Just below the window, a few feet away in the bushes that circled the school, a pair of eyes watched.

At the end of the day, children filed out of the school and scattered in all directions. Katherine sat on the school steps close to the front door while James and Patrick, eager to get going, paced.

Katherine knew what would make Elizabeth feel better—something sweet. Perhaps James had some money from his bowling alley job. If he did, she knew he would give it to her because he was just that way, generous. If he didn't, maybe Patrick had money. Patrick on the other hand, would say, "If you ain't humming, you are a bumming. Lean me, loan me, let me have." It was all a ruse. Patrick was always good for a few pennies or an occasional nickel. Although it was usually Elizabeth who did the pleading, today it would be Katherine's turn, and it would be more like demanding. The punishment for refusing would not be mentioned.

Sister Mary Rose came to the school door hoping for a chance encounter with Elizabeth but it was too late. She felt anxious and unsettled. She watched as Elizabeth, Katherine, Patrick and James crossed the street onto Strong Avenue. Sister Mary Rose knew it was unlikely they would hear her, but she had to try. "Elizabeth," she called. Several young girls looked around because Elizabeth was a popular name.

Sister Mary Rose didn't have a direct connection to Elizabeth. She knew the family since she had Patrick in her class. She knew, too, that the family barely eked by each month which was common for many in the parish. There were stories of violence at the home, of the father's drinking at the local bar, but there were other stories of the father, who would at times, also show great charity. The mother, whose voice should have been heard in Carnegie Hall, sang in the church choir. Sister Mary Rose was often brought to tears with the sheer beauty of the voice—God had touched this woman.

Although there was a time or two that a hole in a sock would show itself, the children were always clean and cared for. The Sister knew there was little she could do about what happened at the O'Sullivan house, or even at school. She certainly could never go against a Sister. That was impossible, but she still worried.

She heard about the punishment from Mary Paul's own mouth. "I would think that Elizabeth O'Sullivan would have learned what I expect from my students," she said. "She didn't learn from last year's teaching, however, I think the switching today will do the trick. Vain little girls grow up to be vain women." Sister Mary Rose remembered the conversation and felt her stomach turn just a bit as a feeling of nausea washed over her. She wanted to reach out and say something comforting to the child. "Elizabeth O'Sullivan!" Sister Mary Rose yelled again, but it was too late.

As they moved further from the school, Elizabeth stopped. "Katherine," she began, "You know that holy card should be mine. I picked Joan of Arc for my confirmation name. No one in the class picked that name." Her defiance on such a hard day made Katherine proud of Elizabeth.

"I think a piece of candy would be good right now, Patrick." Katherine said while looking hard into his eyes. The signal was sent. He had heard about the event with Mary Paul—everybody in the school had, and he knew it was important. He dug into his pocket and pulled out several coins which would buy a piece of candy for each of them, including one set aside for John. Where did he get his money? Katherine often wondered. In the end, it didn't really matter because the world would be good again with a piece of candy and a walk home with a detour through the woods. It didn't take long for Patrick to return from the five and dime with Tootsie Roll Pops for everyone.

Katherine was confident that Elizabeth would be tired and sad from her ordeal, but she was wrong. Elizabeth was upbeat and happy as if nothing had happened.

The last time a nun hit an O'Sullivan child, her father threatened to tear the building down, and he had to be restrained. However, Mary Paul had missed that episode.

Katherine put her arm around her sister as Sister Mary Rose stood in the distance and watched the girls grow smaller. The Sister would pray, as she did every night, but tonight she would make a special prayer for this family.

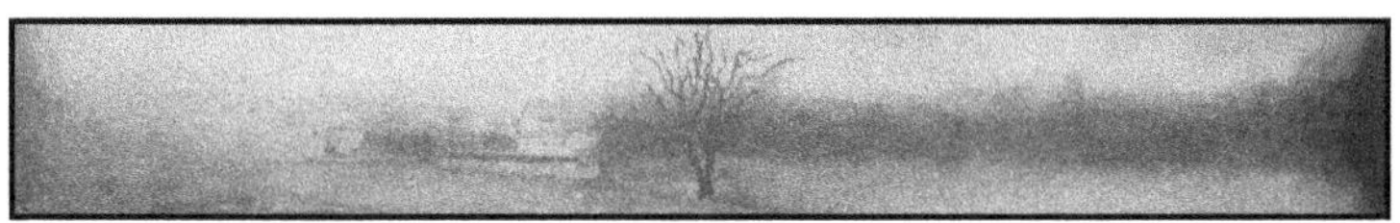

Chapter 6

Elizabeth joined her siblings as they marched in a silent but not orchestrated cadence—each with thoughts of their own, each one a different character from a distant place and a different time. The neighborhood changed and slowly the woods unfolded with James in front, (he was always in the front), Patrick and Katherine fighting for second, (a common occurrence since birth), and Elizabeth bringing up the rear.

Once inside the maze of trees and undergrowth, the children ran straight toward a large oak tree. At the foot of the tree, a large female squirrel lay dead as a door knob. The sun peeked through and cast a glow on the four children as they solemnly looked at the dead animal. Patrick got as close as he could without touching the squirrel with his nose.

"Yep, she's dead. Looks like her neck is broken," he reported.

Disgusted, Katherine stepped away and pulled Elizabeth back with her, but Elizabeth resisted and got closer to the squirrel. As she and Patrick pondered the carcass, James stared at a nest high in the tree and began to circle around. He made his assessment. "I bet she has a baby squirrel in the nest," James offered.

With that, Elizabeth dashed to a nearby tree, not as large or foreboding as the oak, and climbed it with ease—she could master most trees. There was only one that caused her injury, the small apricot in their back yard. Last summer she fell and landed squarely on her rear-end. She could still remember the pain and the instant shock; it took weeks before it healed. Susanne said there was no way to fix a tail bone, and it was in those moments that Elizabeth resented her mother. She wanted to be comforted, she wanted her mother's smiles, but her mother had none to give.

"Well, we have to do it," James said.

Katherine knew exactly what James was going to say. She jumped in and launched her verbal assault. "What are you going to do with a squirrel? What are you going to put it in? You can't make a squirrel a pet. Besides, how do you share a squirrel?"

James had seen her do this before and he knew this was his territory, not hers. She was the emotional center of the family; she cared for the clan when things got rough. Patrick kept the monster at bay, a big job. James' part was the physical world. He was the oldest and when he made a decision, it was settled.

"We will each take a turn with the baby squirrel," James declared.

Katherine was disturbed. She would do what he wanted, but she didn't have to like it. They didn't need another baby; they had John. Besides, she knew who would worry about the baby squirrel the most... she would.

Elizabeth surveyed the activities on the ground, and she interrupted the discussion. "I think that is a grand idea."

Oh great! Katherine thought. There were times she wanted to shake her sister-child.

"Come down and we will say a prayer," offered Katherine, confident that Elizabeth would do one of her imitations, and pronounce that she was Saint something or other. But Elizabeth didn't budge from her perch this time instead putting her hands together as if praying, slipping and catching herself.

"I'll be a saint in Heaven," Elizabeth said, looking down at the small cabal assembled below.

Perfect! Katherine shook her head, but her frustration went unnoticed. Elizabeth was in Heaven, being up a tree—her perfect place.

James took some leaves and put them over the dead squirrel. Katherine, James, and Patrick bowed their heads.

"Our father in Heaven, hallowed be thy name, thy kingdom come, thy will be done, on earth as it is in Heaven, give us our daily bread as we forgive those that trespass against us, and lead us not into temptation but deliver us from evil, Amen."

The children crossed themselves, in a robotic action, with little or no feeling. Elizabeth on the other hand crossed herself as if she were using sign language, an embellished dramatic gesture.

Katherine, nervous, paced, "Mom told us not to be late. Dad is gone tonight."

Patrick, hearing a challenge in Katherine's voice, kicked rocks off into the creek, "I didn't hear her say that."

Elizabeth chimed in because she hated to be left out of the conversation. "Patrick, you don't have to sit next to him," (meaning the monster, her father).

"I'm not afraid of him" Patrick said with pride.

True, Elizabeth thought to herself; Patrick wasn't afraid of their father. He was the smartest person in her family, and he knew that, Elizabeth knew that, everybody knew that. However, Elizabeth thought he should still be afraid. She knew that Katherine was afraid, and James, too.

James circled the tree. "If we're gonna get it, we had better do it quick."

"I sure hope we don't have sugar beets again," Elizabeth offered. "I don't know why they call them sugar beets, nothing sugar about them." No comments. They had heard this tirade before.

Katherine was done arguing. She turned and made her way through the trees with Patrick close behind. She wanted no part of his stupid decision. Patrick was bored; animals bored him. Oh, he liked them, but he did not trust a wild animal like a squirrel. He wouldn't mind having a dog, maybe, if they were well-trained, but he didn't really know any dogs that were well-trained. They had a dog once, but that was before the animal was sent away for biting any brown person who walked by their house, in a town of multiple generations of Mexican railroad workers, that happened several times a day and required a fee to get the dog out of jail. There were no pets allowed in the O'Sullivan household now. "One more mouth to feed," his father would say. Maybe if they lived on a farm and had cattle to herd it might be okay, but just having a pet was not part of the landscape.

As far as Patrick was concerned, James was on his own with this project; he had no interest. He decided instead to challenge Katherine to a race home. Elizabeth watched as the two siblings disappeared. It had a been a long day and her legs hurt as a reminder of Mary Paul's stick, but she would quickly forget again. Today she was an acrobat walking a tight rope.

She looked down and saw James. He could do in the physical world what Elizabeth was forced to do in her mind. One day he would escape this place, this home, because he knew how to do things and make things. He was quiet most of the time, but Elizabeth knew he was always thinking. He wasn't a great reader, or writer for that matter. Books didn't interest him much, but pamphlets did, especially if they showed him how to construct something. Today he would scale the tallest tree, with ease, and rescue the baby squirrel. She would watch with amazement and wonder at his confidence.

Elizabeth, mesmerized by the brilliant sunlight, dangled from a branch by her knees, her uniform over her head. It was then James noticed the back of her knees and calves. Clearly, someone had taken a switch to her legs—a switch that had a shard, a tear in the wood that cut her leg. She swung and flipped to the ground. James rushed to her as she landed somewhat unsteadily, and then bounced up.

"Elizabeth, are you nuts? You could get hurt."

Elizabeth assumed her pretend role, "James, you need not worry for I am a trapeze artist." She curtsied, never losing her character.

Patrick burst through the living room door, out of breath with sweat bubbles forming on his upper lip and holding his side. He crossed the finish line just a step or two ahead of Katherine who was winded and collapsed on the couch.

Soon after, Katherine paused to give John a kiss on the top of his crewcut hair as she strode into the kitchen. John, content with a green plastic dinosaur adorned with *Texaco* written on the side, didn't notice.

Big Band music filled the house. No rock and roll, no Elvis. The only music was from men named Dorsey, Ellington, and Miller, all from Susanne's past. The children liked the music; it made their mother happy. Katherine knew where her mother would be—at the stove. She liked the image of her mother cooking, a moment held for all time.

Most evenings Katherine assisted, but Elizabeth was the clean-up girl. It wasn't a position that Elizabeth liked, but one she understood. This was Katherine's and her mother's time together—the minutes when the roles were clear, unfettered, just mother and daughter. Katherine was mentored and taught, and treated like a daughter, like a kid.

Elizabeth never felt shortchanged. She had two mothers and felt good that she did. The old tin measuring cup, the one Susanne always held close because it was her mother's, would pass to Elizabeth's sister. Elizabeth had no illusion she would be the one who would cook or sew. That place was reserved for Katherine. Elizabeth's dreams never resembled the life her mother had.

The smell was familiar; it was fudge for sure. Susanne stirred and stirred the hot concoction of cocoa, butter, milk, nuts, and then poured the mixture out on wax paper to cool. When completely firm, the fudge would be cut. It was a treat beyond measure, but dinner came before the fudge.

Quickly, Katherine began to gather all the utensils, plates, and condiments needed to set the table; her turn tonight. She missed the preparation time just to see that stupid squirrel, but she knew there would be a million more opportunities to help her mother in the kitchen. Everyone took a turn setting the table except John; he was too little. Elizabeth doubted he would ever be required to do any house work, the perk of being the youngest.

Tonight's menu was macaroni and cheese with chunks of ham left over from another meal, and hot rolls, a simple dinner that made Elizabeth feel good and full. And thankfully, no beets.

Susanne glanced over her shoulder and smiled. She guarded the pan, careful not to let the children see its contents. It was too late; they knew the moment they entered the small house. She turned, displaying the contents of the pan as Elizabeth came into the room. "Heaven," Elizabeth pronounced sliding into her seat at the table with her hair a mess and in her eyes. Susanne smiled and returned the fudge to the stove as James sauntered into the room with the squirrel.

"Look what I found," he said. Susanne, aware of the joy in James voice, turned and came over to see the squirrel.

Katherine stopped suddenly and automatically recited her prepared, deadpanned speech loaded with sarcasm, "She was all alone. She needed a family."

James shot Katherine an annoyed look. He knew she disapproved, but it was not her place to voice an opinion. He was the leader of the pack. His word, like their father's, was the last and Katherine knew this. It was the way they got along. There had to be discipline and order in their pack, and loyalty was paramount. They could argue in the quiet of their bedroom or in the forest, but never in front of anyone not a part of this clique, and that included their mother. They could play and tease, but never were they to share the conversations that made them endure.

Susanne reached over to pet the baby squirrel and smiled. She was always proud of her children, but it was the unexpected, silly things that brought her the most joy. James was certain she was pleased, and that pleased him. Without thinking, he announced, "We need a cage for her."

At that moment, Susanne recoiled. The word, like a sharp knife, punctured her. Cage, a place she knew very well. She stepped back looking past the children into the living room and spied the gift, the gift that was intended to heal the wounds— the music box perched on the side table. A daily reminder of her confinement.

Katherine watched her mother's eyes and saw the pain that the words caused. Something bigger than a sword had just pierced the armor that protected her mother. What Susanne could never say was always found in her eyes. Katherine knew that, and she also knew she must do something."Well, we better make her a great home," Katherine said as she smiled at her mother. Susanne, recovered and went back to the stove; the pain was diverted. Very quickly, Susanne again checked on the hot fudge which was now a brown, golden treasure.

"Mother, do we have time before dinner to go to the shed and get what we need to make our pet a home?" James asked. Susanne nodded as James started out the back door with Katherine at his heels.

"I can go it alone, Katherine," he said a little sarcastically. Katherine knew what James meant and what he would say if he could. She ignored him and stood her ground. Actually, she had something to talk with him about. There were too many things popping up, and it was never a good omen when things began to pop up, or unravel. First, the incident at school, and now the squirrel that will require her time and the time of her always tired mother. They needed a plan. The two, sister and brother, continued down the porch steps with James walking briskly as if to say, "You are not welcome," to which Katherine's gate seemed to say, "I don't care."

The shed was filled with boxes, old furniture, a metal shelf and a workbench covered with carpenter tools that made it look like a regular maze. A small light hung from the rafters. There was barely enough room to walk. James pulled on the cord lighting his way through the cramped storage.

"There has got to be something we can use in here," James said.

"What are we going to . . . ?" Katherine began, then became distracted as James pulled a box full of odds and ends off a small metal shelf spilling the contents onto the already cluttered floor.

"Name her?" James asked.

"No. What are we going to do about Elizabeth?" There was frustration in Katherine's voice.

James was focused; he didn't look up. "Yeah, I know, I saw her legs," he replied nonchalantly.

"What . . . are . . . we . . . going . . . to . . . do?" Katherine's voice raised.

"Nothing. We are doing nothing." James answered as he completed his evaluation of the clutter that surrounded him. Finally, he announced, "This should do nicely."

"What if . . . ?" Katherine started to say as James finally stood up with a collection of wire, half of a bird cage, and string. "What if he finds out?" Katherine forced herself to finish.

James knew he needed to pay attention because she would not stop until he offered something plausible. Her nagging was a curse and a blessing. She kept him on his toes, made him a better brother-father.

"We'll just keep her out of his way for a few days. It will all fade," he said confidently.

Katherine was having no part of this apathetic kind of thinking. It was another one of James' stupid plans of denial —don't think about it and it goes away, and that never quite worked out. *Fade! As if anything in this crazy world they inhabited would ever fade.* Her anger exploded, "She has more than welts; there are scratches and bruises."

James was uncertain; he didn't know what to say. He had to pretend he was not just older, but wiser and willing to compromise. He must be an adult, although in his heart, he didn't really want to be one. He wanted Katherine to take care of it, he wanted Elizabeth to stop getting in trouble, he wanted to have fun, build a cage for a squirrel, and forget about a damaged mother and a father who knew how to hurt.

He knew that Katherine was right about what would happen if their father found out about Elizabeth's injuries. There would be an explosion, an event, and everyone in his path would feel his "justified" wrath. No one could touch his children, not even a nun. After it was over, James and Katherine, aching with embarrassment would go back to school and feel the shame that occupied those kinds of events. Patrick could move through those moments and know he was not in any way responsible. He also knew he would never be his father. As for Elizabeth, she would retreat, let the rain wash over her, and recover.

"Well, what do you want to do? Well . . . ?" Katherine, sat down on a box of junk, and pondered.

"I don't know."

James, with his arms full, reached down and offered her his hand, gently pulling Katherine to her feet. They were a team. He pulled the cord and the light went off, ending their conversation. The evening sun cast a bright orange hue across the backyard as the two silhouettes made their way back into the house.

James later fashioned a cage out of wood that the squirrel, although fond of the children and their gifts of oranges and nuts, would quickly chew through and disappear.

Patrick, busy setting the table, didn't notice James and Katherine. He didn't seem to care and kept at his task. One by one, they all took their seats, but the dinner table was especially quiet. Even Elizabeth, the talker, was silent and she seemed distracted. Normally, they laughed and made jokes—the cornier the joke, the better. It didn't matter who told the joke, or if it was as old as Methuselah. That's why the quiet now was alarming, almost like a weather alert.

After dinner, Susanne retreated to the piano, an old upright wooden box of magic. It was another gift salvaged and brought home after an event by an again remorseful father. The music lifted the mood, a welcome addition to the night. Susanne's fingers flew across the worn keys of the piano causing a carnival-like atmosphere rushing through the house. The girls cleared off the table and the boys washed the dishes. Each one had a duty, just as each one had their place at the table.

James had been eyeing Patrick. After the meal routine was complete he made his move. A quick look and the game was on.

James handed Patrick the last dish in the sink and let out the water. He turned and grabbed a wet dish towel, twisted it and flipped it at Patrick, pellets of water spraying the room. James wound the towel again, ready to deliver another pop, when Patrick grabbed the towel. The match was on, and they tussled.

Patrick yanked the damp towel from James' hand, but James knew what was coming and dashed into the living room, stopping just inches from Susanne who was now playing the piano with great enthusiasm and abandon. He turned and avoided Patrick's snap of the towel. Quickly, Patrick rewound the towel for a second pop at his brother, but lost control with the towel flinging out of his hand and onto the floor. Out of nowhere, Elizabeth picked up the towel, danced around the room, and taunted the boys. She suddenly stopped, and with a grin, popped the towel. Elizabeth was back to her old self, and the boys were glad.

Their sister was an annoyance, but she added a fun dimension to the struggle. Thrilled, she did it again—pop and pop again. The boys ran for the front door with Elizabeth in pursuit. Accidentally catching her foot on the end of the sofa and slamming into the side table, all in the room watched in horror. The music box sitting on top of the table wobbled, and in slow motion, crashed to the floor. The figurine on the top of the music box broke loose and rolled under the sofa.

The music stopped. The shock of the moment engulfed the room and no one moved. Susanne looked at Elizabeth, and in the smallest of voices, uttered, "Oh, no."

Pandemonium erupted while Susanne darted from the piano straight to the sofa. She lifted an edge slightly, and Elizabeth slipped her small hand under to retrieve the figurine. Out of nowhere, James quickly grabbed the pieces and disappeared as Elizabeth slumped to the floor. Within minutes, James was back with a small tube of glue and began to mend the broken piece. Elizabeth closed her eyes, and felt a darkness.

Later, small mounds of children outlined by the shadow of a full moon, lay in their beds. Their thoughts raced in competition with the quiet of the room. Katherine lay in a small twin bed that she shared with Elizabeth who was struggling in her sleep. James and Patrick, close by in the narrow room, hugged the edges of their double bed; while John, deep in slumber, took up most of the space in a very worn baby's crib.

"She's really done it this time," James pronounced in a low and cautious voice out into the darkness.

Katherine sprung up in bed and wanted to scream, but her whisper was as thick and hard as her feelings, "You should never have been fighting." She knew that the pieces were falling into place: the incident at school, the squirrel, and now the broken figurine. There would be an event.

This whole incident was just one more reason James couldn't wait until the day he could build a boat, take it to the river, and sail away. For now, he just reasoned, "She shouldn't have gotten in the middle." He wanted to be right.

"Then you could have been the ones to break the music box instead, all by yourselves with no help from Elizabeth." Score one for Katherine.

There was no way to control Elizabeth. They all knew that. Her realities were softened by the moments where she left the present and watched from another place. In contrast, their realities were grounded in the hard cement of life and they knew how much danger was lurking around the damaged music box.

James, clad in underwear and a tee shirt, and already sporting a physique that telegraphed potential to future football coaches, went to the bedroom window and looked up at the moon.

"It will hold," James said, referring to the glued figurine on the music box. His declaration was mixed with hope and confidence, and a need to make a petition. Katherine, in her outgrown nightgown, got up and joined James at the window.

"For Elizabeth's sake . . . for all our sakes, it better," she said.

Patrick sat up on his elbows, looked over to his siblings, his friends. He knew he was needed; his keen sense of purpose would never let them down.

"It only needs to hold until we can buy another one," Patrick stated without emotion or fear.

"How are we going to do that? We don't have any money," Katherine lamented.

Getting money was never a problem for Patrick. It wasn't as if he had a lot, but he always had some.

"I have an idea. I know this kid at school," he offered.

Elizabeth rolled off the bed onto the floor causing a heavy thud for such a little person. Katherine quickly turned from the window and tiptoed over to her. She attempted to pick Elizabeth up, but it was a heavy load for a bean pole like herself.

Quietly, Katherine told her brothers, "Help me."

James stepped away from the window and reached over and lifted Elizabeth up with ease. He gently lay Elizabeth, half asleep, onto the bed. He pulled her nightgown, large for her, down to cover her legs, then the coverlet over her small frame. All the movement finally awakened Elizabeth. "Where am I?" she asked.

Katherine got into bed with Elizabeth and smoothed her hair. "Go back to sleep," she said. Elizabeth snuggled with Katherine, and within moments, she closed her eyes and returned to her slumber. Patrick, in pajamas, another contrast in tastes to his older brother, got out of bed and joined James. Katherine noticed and slipped out of bed again, leaving Elizabeth alone. She knelt down between Patrick and James, her normal spot. The three hung out the large window looking into the darkness. Their features were clear and easy to read; they were handsome children.

The whistle of an approaching train, the music and life blood of a railroad town, sounded. They didn't jump or move; it was a familiar and welcomed announcement. They stared, listened, and felt comfort while Elizabeth rolled over and felt for Katherine. She sat up and looked at the three older siblings silhouetted at the window.

Later, Elizabeth quietly slipped out of bed into her awaiting sanctuary. She pushed the door panel and entered the darkness. Her hand searched and found a heavy and substantial treasure—a flashlight taken from the shed. She knew her father would not be happy to know she stole one of his flashlights. His anger was the price she would pay if he found out, but she needed it in moments like this. It didn't take much to make him mad, so what difference did it make? Every chance she got to take what was his, and everything was his, she would. This was her way to replace the lost eyelashes she pulled out in despair. It was her style of deliberation and justice, handed out in her small world.

She first acquired an old cigarette lighter left on a table. There wasn't any lighter fluid in it so it didn't work, but she loved the mechanics of the tool, particularly the sound it made when the top was popped open to reveal the flint, fire starter. Then came tobacco and rolling papers, and a partially used jar of hair cream. She especially loved the day her father prepared for an evening out playing cards. She remembered him standing in front of the bathroom mirror combing his hair and looking for his jar of hair cream. He was sure he had more. He needed it because his hair was heavy and thick, and never stood on its own without help; it fell down onto his face.

Watching her father from behind a crack in the bedroom door was a thrill. He looked and looked in the bedroom, in the bathroom, upstairs, downstairs. It could have turned into an event until he remembered that James had a jar. James was summoned and a replacement was found. It was the uncertainty on her father's face that she liked the most. Had he used it up? What could have happened? Who would take his hair cream? The confusion and desperation made him seem weak, and she loved that. She knew it was wrong to take things, but it was one of those sins she would never confess.

The moment was broken when sounds from the next room came through an air vent on the wall. A door opened, creaked, and Elizabeth had to be very quiet. She could hear the halting footsteps of her father. Intoxicated, Junior stumbled, but regained his stride. Elizabeth didn't need eyes in the room to know what he looked like.

Susanne lay still, but awake in the bed with just a thin sheet covering her body. The windows were open with a small breeze lifting the curtains as Junior undressed, revealing a thin almost gaunt body as he slid under the sheet. Susanne closed her eyes, continuing to make no movement. Junior came close, his face next to hers while she held her breath. The moon deployed a small fragment of light through the window.

"I know you're awake," he said. Susanne didn't move.

"You think you are so smart, too good for me, but you're not. You are a nobody . . . I try . . . I work hard." There it was; Junior drew his fist to Susanne's face.

"Say something so I can hit you." The words pierced the quiet, but Susanne simply opened her eyes and stared at him. He slumped down on the bed as he turned away from her. He had done it again. The rage he felt inside, he pushed out onto Susanne.

For Elizabeth, with her ear up against the wall, it began again—her father's tears and words of regret.

"I am so sorry, Susanne, so sorry . . . I didn't mean . . . please forgive me."

The shuttering sobs soon engulfed him and his body heaved with emotion. His cries were deep like a wounded animal. Susanne wiped away the tears that streamed down her own face, and reached over to stroke Junior's arm. It was a protective move learned and cultivated throughout the years. Slowly she moved closer and pulled him near her. The crying lessened as Junior's breathing became deeper and deeper until he fell asleep. Susanne did not.

Elizabeth grimaced knowing what her mother was doing and it disgusted her, but it also taught her. In the part of her that allowed such thoughts, she catalogued the capacity to conceal and manipulate. She knew that was how her mother survived. She felt the back of her legs, the scabs left as a reminder that evil comes in all shapes and sounds, and realized her own transgressions were simply like her mother's.

Elizabeth was sad for her mother. The remnant of childhood, a wish, delivered a single tear that rolled down her check. She brought her knees up to her chest and rocked. The rocking always helped and soon the sadness faded, and she didn't feel the need to tug at her eyelashes.

There was a light coming from the corner of the space, but it was not her flashlight. A smile slowly crossed her face. Joan of Arc, dressed in her military armor, jostled with her sword, lunging in and back out again. The clanking was clear and loud in Elizabeth's head.

Chapter 7

Sister Mary Rose, the nun with the Mona Lisa smile, bowed her head to a crucifix that sanctified the space, her hands folded tight, as if concrete had been allowed to bond the fingers in place. The profile of her face was interrupted by a white coif—a cotton cap secured by a bandeau and white wimple of starched linen that covered her cheeks and neck to frame her face. A black veil, the last piece of the headdress, fell from the top of her head down to meet her tunic. The light from a small table lamp illuminated the features of a woman totally unaware of her grace and beauty.

It was the same routine each night. She prayed she would be humble, kind to her sisters in the Lord (especially the one she didn't understand), and be fair to the children and not pick favorites. But she did have a favorite—a little girl, full of life, not in her class but part of a family known to her. She watched the little girl make her way through the halls, always touching very lightly something or someone, connecting. She was at times other worldly, someplace else, especially during Mass. She didn't squirm; she seemed to lift and fly, to hover just out of reach.

"For Elizabeth . . . and Sister Mary Paul," she said as she made the sign of the cross and rose to leave. She felt a presence and turned to see in the doorway a very portly boulder—Sister Mary Paul herself. She was immediately overcome with a deep sense of darkness. Her feelings frightened her, but she recovered quickly. She could be startled but she always knew how to regain her composure. She was fully aware that the Sister was blocking her retreat as she took up most of the doorway. She smiled sweetly, but the other nun returned the gesture with a hot stare which sent a chill through Sister Mary Rose.

"Sister . . . " she began with her best imitation of calmness. It was the obligatory greeting of two women with the common understanding they were all brides, married in the work of the Lord.

"Who do you pray for this night, Sister?" asked Sister Mary Paul.

Sister Mary Rose was caught, taken aback. Lying was a sin and she wasn't very good at it. She was always able to finesse the truth, or more accurately stretch the truth, but this required more. The boldness of the older nun to ask about a private prayer was disturbing. How could she tell her inquisitor her prayers were for own deliverance? Deliver Elizabeth from Sister Mary Paul, and Sister Mary Paul from herself. It sounded conceited, a cardinal sin, to think yourself so much better.

"I . . . I pray that we may know God's purpose in our lives." The word "purpose" stuck in her throat. She was sort of praying for that; it wasn't a total lie, just a little finesse.

Sister Mary Paul knew Sister Mary Rose did not approve of her approach to teaching and discipline; she had seen it in the younger nun's eyes that very day.

Finally, Sister Mary Rose looked away, trying to avoid Sister Mary Paul's eyes. She would give herself away if she lingered too long.

Her prayers were never answered when it came to Sister Mary Paul. She thought it was perhaps because of her own righteousness. Sister Mary Rose's mind was working overtime. There was an uneasiness that existed between the two nuns. She felt it the first time she met Sister Mary Paul at the Motherhouse in Atchison. In most cases this sort of unease would trigger a response to do something, not let it rest until she found some way to reach out. But this woman meant to smother so they were never friends.

The Sisters never spoke ill of one another. However, suggestions, especially by a veteran Sister to a younger Sister who had not yet taken her final vows, were acceptable. It was a very grand assumption for a young Sister to comment or suggest she knew better than a wiser, older Sister, but Mary Rose had a gift. She could see into someone's heart, and most often she found goodness and love. The trouble was that she could also find fear and darkness.

The children were sometimes exasperating. Even Sister Mary Rose occasionally had to take a deep breath, so she understood the reaction of the other nun when she met her limit. But it was more than that; it was the delight Sister Mary Paul took in her bone-hard approach.

Sister Mary Rose often thought that Sister Mary Paul's rigidity might just be her way of keeping body and soul together when she felt that her own life was slipping away. Perhaps the vows that were taken so many years ago, were more for the Sister's family at home on the ranch. Sister Mary Rose knew many of the Sisters had come to this place for that reason, actually someone else's reason—the pride of a Catholic community to have one of their own in a religious order. For some it was a safe place with food, but Sister Mary Rose was not one of those. She loved children and had a need to serve. She experienced God as a feeling, not so much as an entity. She always knew she wanted to be a Sister, always.

Although her own home had not been a place of light and love, the church meant that to her. Her mother was a decent cook and housekeeper with daughters to help. She was always busy with baking bread, cooking meals, and darning and mending clothes, and she liked her life and didn't expect much more. Sister Mary Rose worked in the fields to get a crop in when it was needed, but that wasn't often. Four boys filled that role.

Sister Mary Rose's ancestors came from Sweden to America at the time the Russians arrived in Kansas with Turkey Red Winter Wheat. Sister Mary Rose's great grandfather took a wrong turn and never arrived in the Smokey Valley where the enclave of Swedes was his intended destination. He took up farming further west next to German Russians and learned their language. Although not Catholic, he took up the religion the moment he set his eyes on his wife to be.

Sister Mary Rose's father was a hard worker. He rarely smiled, and worried constantly about the weather. He never kissed or told his children he loved them, and neither did their mother. It wasn't done, but the children knew their parents' hearts.

"No, Sister. I think you pray for me. Why do you pray for me?" Sister Mary Paul continued her prying.

Sister Mary Rose tried to step around the boulder of a nun, but she stepped with her. Here was the "dance" that she had avoided all her life; she thought there must be a way to talk around the moment. She hated confrontation and she didn't learn it at home. There were rules, and people followed them or the crops wouldn't be harvested, the food wouldn't be prepared. It was easy.

She learned to laugh from her siblings and to talk. Their parents, stoned faced, loved to watch their children banter as if they were speaking in another language. It was a joy that came with a big family. She watched her older siblings debate and quickly learned that people, who kept calm and did not lose their temper, often won the argument. She liked winning and she liked being liked.

"Sister . . . I . . . " the Tango continued.

"You think I was too hard on Elizabeth O'Sullivan today?" Sister Mary Paul delivered the statement posed as a question.

"Sister . . . " Sister Mary Rose was without words, a first. She thought to herself, "What is happening to me? It was as if her words were choking her. She was beginning to panic, a knot was swelling in her stomach. She didn't like being out of control. She was always able to reason through kindness and find her way out of most situations. She knew that the older nun resented her, and she admonished herself many times for not figuring out what made this woman tick, to get past the darkness.

The closer Sister Mary Paul came, the faster Sister Mary Rose's heart raced. She felt something very ominous from this woman. Soon the feeling was more like a smell—a rotten, sickening gut smell like a dead animal, and it was overwhelming—it was fear covered with anger. She wondered why this woman was afraid of her, and why did she hate her?

"Elizabeth O'Sullivan is a willful child. She will learn." Sister Mary Paul liked the declaration, the summon to disagree. What would the good nun do? The nun with the beautiful smile, and the kind voice.

Sister Mary Rose could barely breathe. Fight or flight? She chose to step around the menacing figure.

"And you are her protector," Sister Mary Paul declared.

They slid by each other, a bare inch apart. The young sister was sick to her stomach. The war was on. She had seen it before when Sister Mary Paul decided she didn't like someone.

It was clear that the older sister had let the sweet Rose go around her. Tall and lean, the flower was no match for the rock that stood in front of her. Sister Mary Rose hesitated as Sister Mary Paul watched her closely. The older nun had never seen the young nun act so jittery, and her self-imposed independence, and years of experience inflicting intimidation, made her very aware of her effect on others.

Sister Mary Paul was a woman raised on the Plains. A place women got married early because every man needed a good partner, and she could have worked as hard as two men. Her feet were big and her torso as wide as her shoulders—there had never been a waist line—and her bust was small.

Unlike the other young women, she didn't try to find a partner at the Harvest Festival that drew eligible farmers and ranchers from the surrounding counties. Several of her peers also came from German stock with exactly her same masculine body type, and they found husbands at that very dance, and made good life matches.

With her hair pulled up into a bun and her facial features on display, Sister Mary Paul still presented herself a sufficiently handsome woman. But, she had a hard time giggling at the stupid jokes a lonesome rancher might spit out as a means of courting. It was plain to see that she didn't like the feel of a large hand on her back when the time came for a waltz. She didn't want to be told, through a touch, which direction to choose, and each man who tried could see his efforts were misplaced. Her no nonsense disposition put men off. She did not see the value in being told what to do by someone who knew less than she did, but thought that he knew more.

Still, Sister Mary Paul might have been willing to take a husband if it meant staying close to the land and the animals, but none had come calling. Her parents with twelve children to feed decided to make her an offering to the church. She would be given room and board, an education, and eternal grace—all that in exchange for her life. No one bothered to ask her what she wanted. They never asked her what she would do with the ranch, even though it was evident at a very early age, she had the skills to run the place with or without a man at her side. She knew cattle and wasn't afraid of tangling with them when it was needed. The elements also never slowed Mary Paul down. She always completed her chores, and many times finished the work of a lazy brother. No, the ranch would go to the boys and she would go to the convent. She never forgave her parents nor did she ever return home.

Sister Mary Paul was determined to teach and be happy, and at times she was. There were several Sisters throughout the years who wanted the comfort of her friendship and attention, but she was limited. It wasn't as if she didn't like these women. She just never understood how to comfort and be close because she had never experienced the feelings herself, so she pushed them away. There were several others who ached for sexual intimacy. Sister Mary Paul considered their nature a curse, but she came to understand that they had no way to change no matter how much they prayed or promised that the last touch would be just that. Sister Mary Paul stayed clear of these women; she simply was not like them. Sex was what the animals did on the ranch, it never seemed to be anything that interested her. For Mary Paul the vow of poverty and chastity worked just fine.

Sister Mary Paul's life was simple, structured and dependable until she met the charismatic Sister Mary Rose. The desire to befriend this Sister was overwhelming, and she was delighted just to be near her. All who met Sister Mary Rose felt that way. She was a magnet who pulled people to her.

Sister Mary Paul envisioned friendship with the younger nun as like being with her own family again, working on the ranch beside her brothers, making fun of their stupid jokes. She could feel the joy of living that emanated from the sweet young nun. Sister Mary Rose was like Christmas morning all year long, and maybe her friendship would be an elixir to the tired woman who had never stopped yearning for home—a place with animal smells and snorts, harsh wild weather, and prairie flowers that bloomed on rolling hills. She missed the crispness of the fall without colorful trees, and a sky as big as any mountain with a broad reckoning. She missed home, and something about Sister Mary Rose recalled the essence of that happiness.

At the first meeting of the two nuns at the Motherhouse, she reached out to Sister Mary Rose and was greeted warmly, but it became clear Sister Mary Rose greeted everyone with warmth and kindness. When Sister Mary Paul came to the current parish, the third one in as many years (she did not stay long anywhere), she was happy to see Sister Mary Rose, and thought maybe they might still enjoy a more family-type of friendship. But she was immediately reminded Sister Mary Rose was close to everyone, yet no one in particular, except for one of Sister

Mary Paul's students, Elizabeth O'Sullivan. Sister Mary Paul could see it when Sister Mary Rose's eyes landed on Elizabeth. There was a special bond between them, and it stirred anger and jealousy, a close ally of hate, inside her.

Sister Mary Rose considered delaying her departure long enough to defend Elizabeth and herself, but was overpowered by her desire to just breathe—she had to get farther away to do that. While Sister Mary Rose made her escape, the older nun watched the half bird, half flower sail down the hall. It took so little to unnerve this hybrid; it was almost too easy. Sister Mary Paul always tried to rationalize her own behavior with substitutions for what she really felt. She was only concerned for the immortal soul of another wife of Christ who was taken in by a little hellion.

Sister Mary Rose didn't look around. She could feel Sister Mary Paul's eyes piercing her back. She finally opened the door to her austere, but comforting room where she felt safe. She ripped off the heavy outer garments and headdress; she was burning up, sweat ran down her forehead.

Dressed only in her slip, she walked to the bureau. There were no mirrors or tools to distract. She pulled off the skull cap that kept her hair in place. She moved her hands through her short, curly, and matted hair, and they began to shake. She made a conscious effort to focus. She finished removing her slip and under garments, revealing a firm body with ample bosom. She fumbled through the small bureau and pulled out a plain night shirt. She dressed with eagerness, a fear that she might be seen naked. She suddenly felt vulnerable; there were no locks on the doors. Why would a convent need locks? she reminded herself. It was an open place, filled with love. She stopped and her head was spinning. She had to think, but slowly, very slowly. She put her arms around her body and held on, just so; she would eventually be able to reason through her unsettling feeling. How did

Sister Mary Paul, with her benign question, elicit such an emotional commotion?

She dropped to the floor, overwhelmed and made the sign of the cross. She was confused. What do I pray for now? she wondered. Do I pray for safety, for understanding, or simply because I always pray?

What was it she felt from this woman? Was she horrified by the darkness, the fear, the hostility; or was it sadness she felt from Sister Mary Paul? What must Elizabeth's life be like to be the target of this storm?

The words of prayer finally came to her. "Dear Lord, please help me. I am a sinner, a conceited sinner. Help me find the way."

She again made the sign of the cross; her hands trembled as she rose. The bed, once a place of comfort from a long day, seemed distant and very cold. There will be no sweet, soft, sleep tonight. The small light was extinguished and darkness fell all around. Her eyes were wide open and she questioned her life while holding her body close.

Chapter 8

The classroom, full of children, was as quiet as a church without parishioners. Books were neatly stacked on desks while the children awaited instruction. They dared not move.

The Penguin stood at the front of the class. The older children, with heads down, studied. Katherine looked up and over to the younger children in search of Elizabeth and found her. Elizabeth sat in the last seat in the first row, and appeared quite calm. Katherine was suspicious. Elizabeth was extremely content as they made their way to school. Content was not an emotion that Katherine equated with Elizabeth—happy yes, content not likely.

Elizabeth began to feel anxious and knew the Penguin would soon begin to change. She imagines a long cord coming out from beneath the bottom of the nun's habit that would run the length of the building out onto to the street and down the many blocks to the monster that lived at her house. She closed her eyes, and tried to get the image out of her head; it was hard, but she had to try. She must not think of the two-part monster, and she must stay calm.

"Today we are going to see who will take home the holy card. Sixth graders, read your English assignment," Sister Mary Paul directed. "This is a competition for the fifth graders today."

Elizabeth was suddenly focused and the images were gone. She could just be herself, her smart self, and she listened intently for more instructions.

"The student who answers the most questions correctly by the end of the day will take the holy card home. Richard, can you tell the class the rules?"

Richard, a slight boy with greased back hair stood up slowly, his face twitched, and he took a deep breath.

"We...we...we, well, Sister, if you are called upon and answer correctly, you get a point. If you don't kn, kn, know the answer, the student behind you can take the question. If they answer the question correctly, they will receive the point." His sigh signaled the class that he was finished and they were all relieved.

Elizabeth thought the boy looked miserable. He stuttered and no one in the class ever felt comfortable when he began to speak.

"I will keep track of each child's correct answer," the Penguin said as she planted herself directly under the crucifix which was close to the now replaced, but unnoticed, holy card.

"Students, keep track of time. We have only one hour for the contest."

Students raised their hands, including Elizabeth, who felt especially confident. The Penguin ignored her which Elizabeth knew would happen. So it went, each round Elizabeth tried to answer a question, but was ignored. She finally gave up and let her mind wander. It was never a fair playing field with this hybrid Penguin. She looked at the old nun and immediately saw the word "gallbladder" stamped across the top of her habit which sat precariously on her face. It made Elizabeth giggle, and she couldn't help herself. She looked at the holy card and giggled even more.

Just then, Sister Mary Paul noticed Elizabeth. Everyone in the room noticed Elizabeth, especially Katherine who slumped in her seat—strike three for Elizabeth. She knew something was brewing and it was just a matter of time before a major event occurred. First the switching, then the broken music box, and now this (whatever it was to become, and it would become something, she was sure). Whatever it was, Elizabeth was squarely in the middle of it.

"What is so funny, Elizabeth O'Sullivan?" Before Elizabeth could recover, Sister Mary Paul came close to her. "You think you are so smart that you can giggle through class? Well, you can just teach class once the contest is completed and music is finished. I won't have you ruining choir for the rest of the children."

"Students, find your seats for music. You should know your parts."

Elizabeth always shared a seat with Maria, whose dark skin isolated her, for music. Elizabeth was bothered she was not a soprano like her mother, but she didn't sing high. Neither did Maria.

There was shuffling as the children moved around and found their seats. Elizabeth sat down next to Maria, not sure what to say. She was supposed to teach and be humiliated after music, and Maria probably would think she had cooties. What a day! Before Elizabeth barely landed, Maria smiled. "Don't worry about later. You will do fine; you are very smart. You can do it."

A small tear came forward, but was washed away with the quick brush of Elizabeth's hand. She was overwhelmed. She felt something she couldn't identify, something she had never felt before, not even with Katherine. She felt gratitude as Maria smiled.

The music started. Voices rang out, even Elizabeth's, but inside she was considering the new feeling and hoping she would have it again someday. She was calm, and she began to digest the events.

The Sister's punishment was a punch in the stomach, for sure. People would make fun of her forever. She would be known as the girl who thought she was so smart she could giggle at Sister Mary Paul. However, in her own way, she sort of liked the idea of teaching, and she liked being connected to the word giggle, which made her giggle again. She would get to practice being a nun and that was definitely a good thing. If she could wear a habit, she would be ecstatic. She knew the habit was out of the question so she would just call up a pretend image and feel it. She would wrap herself up in the black, heavy and course material that constituted the tunic, and listen intently to the cracking of the rosary that would dangle down her side. But how could she do it? She didn't know how to teach. Although she had a million butterflies in her stomach, she was still excited and happy. She doubted she would even be able to eat her lunch—an egg sandwich her mother had assembled the night before and one she might trade for a cheese sandwich. No peanut butter and jelly for her. She hated peanut butter almost as much as she hated sugar beets.

All around her, the routine of the day was being played out. The bell rang for lunch to finish which meant a quick recess and time to think. It seemed so normal. The comfort of the traded sandwich soon vanished and her sense of calm faded.

Strangely, every time she saw something that made sense, she felt more out of whack. Even a group of girls from the neighborhood, playing Jacks on the sidewalk leading into the school, made her feel a little less calm. Another group of children, led by Sister Mary Rose, played baseball with James on first base. James was intent, ready for the action. Sister Mary Rose laughed and threw the ball high over the plate. She floated with exuberance when the ball was hit by a lucky someone and her black habit flowed, swirling around.

Elizabeth was definitely feeling out of place, and she wanted to grab hold of the garment and fashion it into a kite—a strong kite that would lift her up and away. Elizabeth could see herself flying high into the clouds, disappearing. The only thing better would be to hide herself in her secret place. She wanted to shut down, close down, slam the door. Oh, how she wished she was in her special place! She began to rock, totally unaware how close she was to the action of the game which was just a few feet away. Sister Mary Rose suddenly noticed her behavior, and so did James.

"Elizabeth, move. You are right in the way of the batter. You could get hurt," James yelled. The words returned her to the present. She walked out of view toward the side of the school building.

I have some serious problems, she thought. The most immediate one was how to teach the class. There was also the broken music box and the need for a replacement. And then, of course, the holy card. She had stepped over the line with the holy card, and she knew it. Now things were beginning to really swirl. Why, why, why, did I do it? she wondered, as she banged her head with her hand. When the monster realized the holy card was missing Elizabeth would be the first one accused. She wished Maria would join her, but standing next to the building holding your head was not a sight that would entice people. She could see herself. It was as if she was outside her body watching.

No, Maria had been kind and done her part, and now she was back with her other friends. Elizabeth looked over at Maria and hoped they would someday be friends, too.

For Elizabeth, the best part of taking the card was the eventual discovery. She couldn't wait to see the monster's face when she realized there had been a theft, and then she was equally afraid of what would happen when the deception was uncovered. The anticipated joy of seeing the nun distressed had clouded and camouflaged her own ruin. It was a deed done in the way that Elizabeth understood: taking things, hiding things—a way to fight back to make herself seem more in control and less unanchored all at the same time. It was thrilling. This game of hide-and-seek was exactly what she did with her father, the other monster in her life.

Another switching was in her future which made her spirits sink. She paced while biting her nails and thinking. Finally, she climbed on a swing-set. Okay, who can help? she wondered. Her mind was whirling—zip, zip, zip, a wild ride at the county fair.

"Well, seems you find yourself in a tricky spot, Sis," Patrick said as he rounded the corner of the building. Elizabeth snapped to a dead stop.

He wasn't there to judge her, or even ask how or why she had to teach class. He wasn't interested in that. He was interested in the excitement it would provide, and it would be a challenge. He loved a challenge. He came behind Elizabeth and pushed the swing.

"I have a plan," he said.

The school bell rang, startling but not unexpected, which prompted the children to run and stand in line at perfect attention.

Elizabeth bailed out of the swing and landed near Patrick. She blew out a big breath of air, and quickly realized she was glad he was there. One problem at a time she thought, or she might just burst out crying and tell him everything. She found it almost impossible to hold back when it came to her siblings, but she had to try. No, get it together, she told herself.

"How am I going to teach the class? I'll look so stupid," she said sadly.

"Not the first time or the last," Patrick answered. He was blunt, but never mean.

"Elizabeth, the kids have been taking bets about whether you can do it, and I am betting on you. I'll make some money on this one," he said confidently.

Elizabeth stopped suddenly, "You won't make a dime because I won't know the questions, let alone the answers."

Patrick placed his hands on Elizabeth's shoulders. "Of course you will . . . with a little help," he smiled a knowing smile.

"What are you talking about?" Elizabeth stepped back dislodging Patrick's hands. "How do you know I can do it, and with what help?"

A little frustrated and for very different reasons, Patrick took a deep breath and blew it out, exasperated that she would even question him. "I have my ways, Elizabeth, and you have to do this. You don't have a choice."

Elizabeth studied her shoes. The clock was ticking. Patrick knew the biggest challenge would be to get Elizabeth ready. He knew about the mechanics of the situation; she just needed to perform. He knew she could do it—he had seen her step up to the plate to meet challenges a thousand times. She just had to act.

"Elizabeth," Patrick began in a way that let her know he was serious.

"I am not Elizabeth. I am Sister Mary Teresa. Mary T for short," she said with a grin the size of a carved pumpkin face. She resolved to be the best nun she knew how to be in the tradition of Sister Mary Rose.

"Well, Sister Mary T, or whoever you are, it's go time. Get the workbook. It will be right under the hardcover book on Sister Mary Paul's desk. There is a lesson plan with questions and answers so slip it into the book." Elizabeth was stunned.

Patrick trotted off, like a pony in a parade, proud and confident. Elizabeth walked slowly and steadily toward the group of assembled children. She stood erect, her hands folded at her waist. Her head was held high, and she floated.

Recess was over and children were all in their places. Here it was—the moment. The workbook was exactly where Patrick said it would be. She only had to do a quick switch; she was focused.

As the Penguin, on the brink of monster-hood, turned to walk down the aisle that separated the students, Elizabeth slipped the workbook into place, done. No one seemed to see except Katherine who was pretending to be busy with her own work. She had made a career out of watching without being noticed.

Elizabeth looked at the Penguin and thought that today the nun looked more like a Penguin than ever. It made the situation less dangerous. She was simply a Penguin, a very benign sort of animal that Elizabeth had only seen in magazines. There was nothing dangerous about a Penguin; she had only to remain calm.

Sister Mary Paul found an empty desk and squeezed in like a sardine in a can, an image that raced through Elizabeth's head. Her father loved sardines and ate them with relish, she thought to herself with amusement.

It was time for action. Clearing her throat, Elizabeth opened the book and looked at the questions and answers so perfectly displayed on the page, just as Patrick stated. She smiled, but the smile was wiped away the moment she looked into the Penguin's eyes. They were black, no speck of color. Elizabeth shuddered and told herself: Penguin. Penguin. No monster. She staggered back, almost losing her balance. She recovered and looked for anything in the room to concentrate on. At last, there she was—Maria, the skinny, little girl who was kind to her. Elizabeth would look at her and the fear would go away. It was her kindness that was so real.

Once her composure was restored, Elizabeth turned and smiled at Beatrice, not a girl she really liked or thought was very smart. She was the Penguin's pet. Her friends called her "Bea." She was perky, very perky, played the piano, and her parents paid tuition. She definitely did not have a good saint name. Although Beatrice was a saint, she never fought for the church. She was nothing like Joan of Arc or St. Teresa. Elizabeth decided to give her the first question. For just a moment she looked at the Penguin; sparks started to fly and she looked away.

"Beatrice, you will have the first question today. What is the capital of Canada?" Beatrice stared at Elizabeth and went blank, but quickly and sweetly responded, "Toronto."

"No, Beatrice, I am afraid you are wrong," said Elizabeth with restrained relish. Beatrice slumped down into her chair, and for a moment, Elizabeth felt both sad for her and a little ashamed of her own pleasure because she knew Beatrice was not very smart.

Beatrice, on the other hand, was not at all like Alice—the girl who wore hearing aids. Her voice sounded different when she was forced to speak. The Penguin took little or no mercy on her and often wrote a large F on her papers for everyone to see. Elizabeth cringed whenever the Penguin called Alice to the blackboard; the sheer evil of it all made her sick to her stomach. Elizabeth felt lucky to be smart.

Moving on, Elizabeth continued, "Richard will move ahead if he knows the correct answer." She hoped he would get it right even though he was a favorite of the Penguin. He could conquer any math question and also knew a lot about rocks, but a profound sadness followed him like his stuttering. She felt sad for him. He didn't have very many friends, just like her.

"Ottawa," he said with clear diction. Good for him, Elizabeth thought. She harbored no ill feelings toward this favored one. He had it much worse than she did. The kids made fun of him when the Penguin stepped away. It was cruel and she wondered how he managed it.

A quick look back at the Penguin and an unexpected smile crossed Elizabeth's face. She wasn't afraid anymore. The monster was trying to come out, but the Penguin's face was a frozen glacier of hate with steam coming out of her ears. It was as if a bucket of tears, collected throughout the years from all the children she had hurt, had been thrown on her head cascading down into her ears, eyes and mouth, melting away the monster underneath. No, the monster would not come out today and Elizabeth had nothing more to fear.

So it went—Elizabeth asking and children squirming. By the end of the hour, it seemed Elizabeth had grown twelve inches and stood taller than she ever thought possible.

The Penguin struggled, nearly landing on the floor, as Elizabeth switched the workbook again. *How did she do it?* The Penguin wondered. I will find out!

"What a grand day we have had," Sister Mary Paul remarked, the anger just under the surface. "Now we have a surprise. Father Wagner will be conducting a practice session for confirmation. You need to know your catechism backwards and forward before Bishop Sheehan comes to town. Line up and head to the gym, and please find your seats on the bleachers."

"Elizabeth, stay behind," the nun directed.

Elizabeth flashed a quick look at Katherine who had a smile the size of the Grand Canyon across her face. The smile was disrupted when Katherine suddenly wondered how painful the punishment would be for succeeding. She could see that Elizabeth didn't care. It was the great dichotomy of Elizabeth that would call Katherine to both love, and at times, be exasperated by her sister. She would burst with pride for her young sister's daring, and then dread the fear and chaos that would follow.

The children filed out while some looked back. They knew Elizabeth had won, but none of them wanted to be in her shoes. Katherine lingered but was dismissed by the stare tossed at her by Sister Mary Paul. She hesitated for only a brief moment more before leaving Elizabeth alone with the nun.

"Well, you have had quite a day so far."

Elizabeth prepared for the assault: the deluge of words, of accusations, and the fire that would pour out of Sister Mary Paul's mouth. She steadied herself; there was no turning back. There was also the holy card to consider which Elizabeth had almost forgotten. She'd had such a banner day that the thought of the holy card had just slipped away. It was a capital crime to steal, so she would just consider it another borrowed item, much like the other borrowed items Elizabeth found in her hands when she went to the grocery store or rummaged through her father's bureau. Round two was coming up.

"Don't try to apologize," the Penguin said. That thought never entered Elizabeth's mind and she almost laughed out loud. Control, she remembered. She must control herself, no giggling.

The Penguin waddled up, with her short leg, limping. Elizabeth wondered what it looked like; it was the scientist bubbling up inside. She had thought about becoming a scientist, just once, when they learned about Marie Curie. But changed her mind when she realized there was only one Marie Curie, only one woman scientist. She decided instead to stick with being a nun and then a saint. There were lots of saints.

Elizabeth did love looking at the railroad tracks on her mother's leg. As grotesque as it was, it was also thrilling to think that her mother had another life. She loved touching the scars. Maybe the Penguin had had the same disease as her mother, but it was hard for her to consider there could be any connection between her beloved mother and the Penguin. She really wanted to see the leg first hand even though that seemed impossible.

"Talking to you is like pouring water over a duck's back." Elizabeth almost burst out laughing at the nun's comment. She still had the vision of steam coming out of the Penguin's ears.

"You apparently will never learn. I had hoped you would change your behavior." Her voice was getting very hard, very close to the monster's voice. A moment of caution filled Elizabeth. She knew when to be quiet; she was experienced in that department. It was always good to keep her thoughts to herself when her father was about to erupt. She had learned what untimely words could mean.

The Penguin came up to Elizabeth, toe to toe. "I have seen your kind before. You are insolent—too smart for your own good, and one day you will get in trouble with boys."

What? she thought. *What did she mean about boys?* The Penguin was crazy. Elizabeth knew all about boys, and their stinky socks and underwear. She had three brothers. She loved two of them and tolerated, treasured, and yes, even loved the last one. She was not confused about boys. She would never get in trouble because of a boy, but perhaps a boy would get in trouble because of her. Her mind started to wander, but she pulled herself back. She would save for a later time the thought of a young man throwing himself at her only to be rebuffed as she left for the convent.

"Perhaps a parent-teacher conference?" the Penguin said as she brushed by Elizabeth toward the door.

"Now get to the gym. You don't want Father to notice your tardiness," she offered. For a moment, Elizabeth thought father as in her own father. No, not my own father, thank goodness! but Father like in a title. A funny thought entered her head. Men who wear dresses during mass called Father!

Elizabeth stood immobile. The Penguin had no idea what Elizabeth's father (the evil twin) could do at a school conference. A knot grew in her stomach and she felt sick.

The events were piling up: a school conference, a holy card discovered missing, an interrogation, an investigation. Did anyone see her doing what she shouldn't? She didn't think so, but she was very proud when she took the holy card. In fact, she was almost smug, she admitted to herself. Would she break and admit it? No doubt she would. The Penguin, if she were not a monster would be a Nazi; she probably had techniques of torture.

Elizabeth learned all about World War II, Nazis, and Japanese Kamikazes in her favorite class—history. She loved history because that's where all her favorite people lived, outside of her family. Her head was spinning now. What was she thinking? The rumination began. Who could help her? There was no way Patrick could help this time. He played his winning hand earlier that day. Katherine, oh Katherine, how could she face her?

Elizabeth figured Katherine would be mad at her for at least a year. As for James, he was always the target of her father's wrath. She couldn't bring him into it for any reason. He was the topic of the last school conference, an explosion that nearly sent the family to public school.

Public School, Elizabeth thought. That could work. But what would she do without the black tunics, white headdresses, clanking beads, the incense, the daily Mass with music, the statues of Saints, and the tortured children she really liked but would be fine leaving? She would miss it all. Then instantly she knew what she would do. She didn't need to leave them entirely. She would take them with her, sort of. She would dress all the teachers like nuns. Every time she passed one in the hall, they would be wearing the garments, even the males. She would remember Maria for her kindness, Richard for his sadness, and Alice for being even more sad than Richard. She would even remember Beatrice, whose life had been blessed with perfectly combed hair, fresh and bright red neck scarfs tied under her white shirt uniform, and most importantly, for her fancy lunches.

Problem solved. She would go to public school after they kicked her out for stealing, and her father would be sent to jail for doing whatever it was he would do during the school conference: throwing fists, screaming, etc. Equally important, she and her siblings would find a way to replace the music box while her father did his time.

The study session was over and the children were back in their places. Most importantly, Elizabeth found peace. There was no reason to panic. She had worked it out, and all would be good. Relax, she told herself. The fun will soon begin.

The Penguin was at the blackboard diagraming a sentence. Elizabeth liked to diagram sentences. It was a little like a puzzle and an art project all rolled into one exercise. Turning to the class, the Penguin, almost like a robot, said in a very emotionally deprived voice, "Students, before the end of the day, I will announce the winner of the holy card."

The children wiggled in their seats. Sister Mary Paul slapped her hands, casting off the excess chalk from her work at the blackboard, and turned to picked up her favorite object—the despised pointer. She tapped a spot just below the holy card and glanced up at the object. Elizabeth held her breath; Here it comes, she braced herself. She wondered if Penguins could fly because a lift off was about to happen.

A look of bewilderment came over the nun's face. She looked away and back again, and just as quickly was stricken. The card had changed. The force of the realization pushed her backward. The holy card had been replaced with a crude reproduction. Shaking, she threw the pointer to the floor and reached for her hard, wooden chair for balance, which Elizabeth knew was just another extension of the monster. The students envisioned the portly nun falling onto the floor. However, the chair was sturdy, not unlike the nun. It held.

Elizabeth had another thought. Maybe if she fell, her leg would be visible. Would it be like her mother's, or not? If it looked like her mother's, there was a chance the nun had something in common with her mother, which would almost make her seem human. Although Elizabeth knew it took more than a leg, an arm, or an eye to make someone human. There was no explanation for all the meanness that spewed from Mary Paul. Elizabeth did not want to believe that a human could be that bad. Diseased leg or not, the nun could not be human.

Elizabeth caught a glimpse of Katherine's face. She looked petrified, but Elizabeth smiled. It was a smile of delight and confusion. Katherine knew this face, a cover up for the fear that was hiding just below the surface. She mouthed, "Elizabeth!"

With her nose up against the card, Sister Mary Paul removed her glasses. Elizabeth never understood why people took off their glasses to look at objects that were right in front of them. There it was again, a hint that the Penguin might be like other people. Suddenly, she began to look at the nun a little differently.

Sister Mary Paul paced back and forth and then retrieved the pointer, gently tapping the palm of her hand with it. She whirled around, the long wood rosary around her waist clipping the pointer. Slowly she limped down the middle aisle that separated the older children from the younger. While she stood at the back of the room, the children stared straight ahead. No one moved.

Approaching without a sound, the nun walked up and stood behind Elizabeth. "It seems we have a thief in our class. Someone who finds it humorous to mock the saints, a sin against the church," she declared. Then a gentle tap on Elizabeth's desk. Creepy how that Penguin can just sneak up, Elizabeth thought.

"If anyone knows who took the holy card, they are obliged to stand now and report who did it."

Yeah, right, Elizabeth mused.

"Very well then. If no one confesses, I will have to conduct an investigation during recess."

A collective groan from the children spread across the room, but Elizabeth was already a million miles away. If the Monster was just a dressed-up Penguin of a person, how was she tied to the Monster on the other end? If she were human, what was her father? She was getting dizzy. She would think about that another time.

Mary Paul continued, "After you are interviewed, you will go back to the classroom and work on your math. Someone will come in to monitor."

Chapter 9

Wow, what a day! Elizabeth thought. She would never forget it. She looked down the long hallway at the children from her class, both fifth and sixth graders, who took up most of the space on one wall.

Elizabeth stood at the end of the line, right behind Katherine. There was a silence that occupied the moment. When Katherine was especially put-out with Elizabeth, the moment could last for at least an hour. There was no use in trying to talk to her.

"Why did you take it?" Katherine whispered into Elizabeth's ear.

What? She talked to me? Surprised, Elizabeth looked away and stepped back. "I know nothing," Elizabeth replied, never looking Katherine in the eyes.

Katherine was on edge as she moved closer. "Elizabeth. It's a sin to steal."

"It's sin to lie. Will you do that for me?" Elizabeth crossed her arms and glared at Katherine. *There, take that*! Elizabeth thought, a real act of defiance. She was putting Katherine in an awkward position. Would she go down the path of righteousness, or would she stand with her, or just leave?

"Tell the truth, Elizabeth."

There was an anger in Katherine's voice that Elizabeth had not heard before, but she was not afraid. She had grown a foot today, and she was not going back, plus she had a back-up plan.

"You tell the truth," her sister again commanded.

The door to the office opened, and Richard followed Sister Mary Rose into the hallway. He walked past Elizabeth and stared. The stare was lost on Elizabeth; she didn't realize he wanted to help her.

He knew she took the holy card, not only because he saw her but because there was not another student who would be so bold, so strong. So he lied. For the first time in his life, his speech impediment was a gift. They would not want to wait through his contemplative silence, waiting for the right breath to come into his throat and mouth to make the words work. He waited. They waited, and then he shook his head. He had lied with just one nod because he admired Elizabeth. He too felt a foot taller—a day he would never forget.

So it went with a different child entering and exiting the cold, bare office at three minute intervals. Elizabeth couldn't care less. She didn't try to read their faces. She figured they were all saying she had done it, but none had. When summoned, Katherine stepped forward, turned and scowled at Elizabeth. They locked eyes. Then in slow motion, or what seemed like forever, Sister Mary Rose ushered Katherine into the office.

Elizabeth, alone, began a game of pretend hopscotch. She mentally jumped from floor tile to floor tile until she reached the end of the hallway. She turned and went back again, twice. She was flying. She was fully exhausted but willing to go the length of the hallway again to break the record she had just posted in the Olympic game of hopscotch when she heard her name.

"Elizabeth." There was no hint of kindness in Sister Mary Rose's voice as Katherine emerged from the inquisition.

Katherine passed by and gave Elizabeth the evil eye—a good sign for sure. If Katherine had told the interrogators the truth, there would be a hurt look on Katherine's face, not anger, Elizabeth decided. She was done with hurt and silly feelings, she knew she needed to toughen up. She already started today with her performance. She might have been hurt when she looked into the eyes of her classmates, but no, she didn't care. She was someone else, a better version of herself. Yes, she knew about hurt; she had seen it, felt it. She knew she had to throw up a roadblock to hurt when it started to come. She was working on fear, but that was a heavy chore. Hurt came when she least expected it, based on some unknown feeling, and popped up like a jack-in-the-box. Hurt and fear were tied together.

Anger intrigued her. Just a mere spoonful was enough, nothing like the gallon of anger that morphed when heated into the rage that propelled the twin monsters. She would have to find anger and use it when necessary, like Katherine, with the evil eye as she passed by. Just once she would love to give someone the evil eye as an exclamation at the end of a sentence. She had never given it to anyone, not even her baby brother whom she knew needed the occasional evil eye. He would probably just laugh and mimic her, and look cute.

The Penguin sat on one side of the table, Sister Mary Rose next to her. Elizabeth looked around the room. She had never been in the office; it was a private place just for nuns. A large cross, minus Jesus, hung on the wall behind the interrogators, forming a trinity. Off to the side of the metaphorical triumphant, and above a file cabinet, was a picture of St. Therese of the Little Flowers. Elizabeth always liked the way St. Therese looked with flowers all around her. The other St. Teresa, with a different spelling, was also a Carmelite but less glamorous. The Carmelites were heavy duty; no fluff for them. They were cloistered. Elizabeth didn't really understand the word, but it reminded her of a closet and she knew something about closets. She hoped there might be a wink coming her way from the saint with all the flowers, but the little saint was silent. Another time, maybe.

Sister Mary Rose cleared her voice, hoping to get Elizabeth's attention. The child seemed indifferent. Did she not get the gravity of the situation?

"Elizabeth, Sister Mary Paul seems to think you know something about the missing holy card. Do you know anything about the holy card?"

Elizabeth looked first at Sister Mary Rose, then at the cross, the Penguin, and finally the picture of St. Therese. It pained her a little to lie to a woman she loved so much, the nun with the perfect smile and kind eyes, but she had no choice. She would defeat the Penguin which was becoming less of a challenge with each passing moment.

"Do I know anything about the missing holy card? No, Sister, I do not."

That was a nice big lie, Elizabeth knew she had slid down a slippery slope. She could sense it—a new feeling. It was easy to lie when you weren't afraid, and she was just getting warmed up. Throw another one her way; she was ready.

The Penguin fumed, but the steam had lessened and turned into sweat on her upper lip. She was changing right before Elizabeth's eyes—monster to Penguin to nun. It was working. The less she feared, the more real the nun seemed. She could match her evil with her own.

The squatty nun glanced at Sister Mary Rose and then leaned across the table, lifting herself out of the chair as the chair slipped back. "Your sister says she knows nothing about the holy card, but I think she does. I think everyone knows." She looked over her shoulder at Sister Mary Rose and then back again at Elizabeth.

"You are not fooling me, you little devil!"

Perfect! Elizabeth was ready; this was too easy. Katherine was nearly a saint and everyone knew that. Elizabeth twitched to make it look difficult to answer. Here it comes—salvation, she mused.

"Well, Katherine never lies. If she says she knows nothing I would take her at her word." There it was, the truth turned upside down. Elizabeth smiled.

Mary Paul turned to Sister Mary Rose, but Sister Mary Rose didn't acknowledge her. The sweet Sister was intent and watched Elizabeth with concern. She was worried for this little girl's soul. It was apparent she was lying, and enjoying it.

A rush of anger rose in Sister Mary Paul. Elizabeth could see it, but not feel it. Then it dawned on her that Mary Paul's anger was at Sister Mary Rose. She was simply a bystander.

Even at this moment, Sister Mary Paul thought, when the Sister should be my partner, she is more interested in what this little liar is saying. Well, this will get Sister Mary Rose's attention.

Sister Mary Paul turned and bent down so she was eye-to-eye with Elizabeth. She reached out to slap her face, but Sister Mary Rose blocked her hand and pulled hard, jerking her back. Instinctively the irate nun resisted, but she liked the tussle and connection. She liked the other nun's hand on her arm. Sister Mary Rose then pulled harder, almost shoving the nun away from Elizabeth, which sent the older nun sailing backwards.

Sister Mary Paul hit the wall with a crashing smack sound, her head bouncing off the wall hard onto the floor. The momentum flung her body under the table leaving her feet, in laced up shoes with a slight heel, sticking out from below. Elizabeth noticed and immediately thought of the Wizard of Oz, her favorite scary movie.

Sister Mary Paul's habit was up around her knees, revealing heavy black stockings on unequal legs. One leg was definitely much shorter than the other. Elizabeth peeked over the table and there it was—the nun's leg, very much like her mother's.

Elizabeth gasped and covered her mouth. The monster was really a human after all, but what about the monster who lived at her house? That monster came out when the sugar was too high or not high enough, or if he was just in a nasty mood. Her mind whirled, the scene a blur. Was the disappearing monster, now slightly Penguin and mostly nun, really hurt or just pretending, preparing to leap up and grab her? She steadied herself, quick into the survival mode. She grabbed her body with her arms. Sister Mary Rose looked at Elizabeth and recognized the maneuver of self-protection.

Sister Mary Paul's anger had simmered, but had lost its heat like the dying ambers of a fire. She was now pathetic with her small leg and pale face joining the remaining lifeless lump. The change was complete—the monster was dead.

Sister Mary Rose dropped to the floor, felt for a pulse, and listened to Sister Mary Paul's breathing. She was breathing, thank the Lord! Sister Mary Rose looked up at Elizabeth. "She's unconscious. Get help." She had a very worried tone in her voice.

Elizabeth pondered, and then a smile crossed her face. Sister Mary Rose caught the look, cringing inside; but Elizabeth knew exactly who she would get, and with that she was up and out the door.

Katherine stood against the wall and waited. She could not leave until she was sure Elizabeth was not expelled. The behavior was risky because she could be sent home for disobedience, but she didn't care.

She reached for Elizabeth the moment she saw her, but Elizabeth never looked back. She was on a mission—her ears closed to the voice that cried out her name, and she was excited. It seemed like something out of the Joan of Arc legend. She was on her white horse, galloping across the field into battle with her armor clanking and her sword held high. She leapt down the stairs that led out to the playground, and to the castle just down Main Street.

Stunned and torn, Katherine peeked into the office. What would she see? What had Elizabeth done? She heard the muffled words and the scuffle. Elizabeth must have really done it this time! Sister Mary Paul's feet stuck out from under the table and Katherine's mouth dropped open.

Sister Mary Rose spied Katherine with dread and apprehension, the look of "what do I say?" in her eyes. Katherine crept silently to where the injured nun lay and knelt next to Sister Mary Rose.

"Did Elizabeth . . . ?" she started to ask.

A sadness came over Sister Mary Rose as she shook her head, and with a small voice answered, "No. No . . . she . . . " How would she explain this? Her own complicated feelings toward the Sister had surfaced. She realized that. Had she pulled so hard that she caused it, or had Mary Paul in her reckless way contributed? Either way, there was no acceptable explanation for the actions of the two wives of Jesus. And, had Elizabeth enjoyed the moment? Sister Mary Rose saw it—the smile, and that scared the good nun the most.

Elizabeth stopped abruptly and looked up to see the police station, a small and unassuming brick building. She went in the front door, and there he was—Gary Cooper, so handsome, so strong in a silent kind of way. Elizabeth trotted up to him out of breath. She could barely speak, holding her side.

Gary Cooper, in slow motion, turned and saw Elizabeth. He smiled immediately and he recognized her as the sister of the boy who always took a trip on his tricycle at the most inconvenient time of day, shift change. And most importantly, she was Susanne's daughter. In turn, Elizabeth only saw Gary Cooper's eyes.

"Hi," he said in the softest of voices.

Elizabeth was frozen. She wasn't really prepared. Yes, she did know who she was looking for, but she wasn't completely sure she would find him so quickly, and she was out of breath. Of course, he was an actor and not really a police officer, but training was training, and he was standing right there, exactly where he should be. It was a sign.

She exhaled very dramatically, closing her eyes, hair in her face. She swiped it back and let her arms go limp. He quickly flashed to another little girl he knew a long time ago, somewhat less dramatic, but just as pretty.

"I know you are probably practicing, but I need your help."

Officer Mike smiled at the thought, "The Captain might call it practicing . . . what do you need?"

"Well . . . Sister Mary Paul . . . fainted or something. Maybe she's a diabetic and needs juice." There was no way she would report what really happened. This was Gary Cooper. He would have no part of anything sinister. She had to talk fast. The crazy old nun's head might be exploding. Yes, she was a nun, not a monster, but still dangerous.

"That's what we give our dad when he has a reaction... juice. We always have enough juice at home, always, and we know exactly what to do. It's important to do it fast, no lollygagging around. We never panic." That would prove she knew something about medicine. Of course she knew that the Sister wasn't having a "reaction" to anything.

Officer Mike signaled for help, heading for the door. "You have to stay here. Someone will take you back to school."

She was only slightly disappointed because John always got to ride in the front seat when they brought him home. The truth was that she was relieved. She would let Sister Mary Rose explain what happened and then she could conveniently forget everything. It had happened fast, and the last thing she remembered before the Penguin slipped, losing her balance and falling, was

Mary Paul's hand coming at her face. She didn't want to talk about a stolen holy card and maybe, just maybe, Mary Paul might lose her memory, too.

A small crowd of onlookers, students and nuns, gathered around the ambulance as a gurney with Sister Mary Paul on it was carried out by two attendants dressed in white. An old and infirm nun got into the ambulance to ride with her, and the ambulance took off with sirens blaring.

Elizabeth arrived just as the ambulance left the scene. She had waited for a ride, but then decided she could make her way back to school without any assistance. She made her way to the police station on her own so she knew she could make her way back. Officer Mike looked over at Elizabeth and smiled. He had a pen and notebook in his hand.

"Elizabeth, we won't need anything more. Sister Mary Rose explained everything to me. I will file a report, and if I need you, I will let you know. A fainting spell is not a crime. You can head home. You have lost your teacher for the day."

Too bad it isn't a year, she thought, but then it dawned on her—he knows my name! *Oh, perfect,* she sighed. She realized she had not mentioned her name, so how would he, Gary Cooper, know it? No matter, she thought.

She turned and ran in the direction of Katherine, who stood across the schoolyard. Her school uniform fluttered up and down in response to each stride she took; red stripes could be seen on her legs as she ran. There was an uneasy moment when Sister Mary Rose tried to look away, acting like she was not watching Elizabeth, but it was too late.

"I wonder what happened to her legs? Looks like a switch might have been used," Officer Mike observed.

What a day! What could she say? Another lie to cover up? Sister Mary Rose was exhausted. She looked at Officer Mike and thought, what beautiful eyes he has, but finally uttered, "Well, I don't know."

A quick glance resulted in seeing Sister Mary Rose not as a nun, but as someone he wanted to know in another capacity. That was strange. Why would he want to know a nun? Get back to Elizabeth, he thought. "I have an idea how she got them."

He heard about the confrontations at the Flood Room. He knew the man had a temper. He remembered seeing Elizabeth's father fight his way out of a conversation. Maybe they were in different high schools in adjacent counties, but close enough to hear stories, especially if you were paying attention. Yes, the man had a reputation long before he visited the Flood Room and moved to this town, Susanne's hometown.

He knew Susanne. She was shy, a product of a small family with few distractions, and a love of books. He watched and admired her from afar, all through high school, which was not exactly the recipe for courtship. He too was shy and quiet, but the war changed that, and when he came back injured with medals, Susanne was a mother with a husband. He heard that opposites attracted and maybe that was how they found each other.

"I'm sure it's nothing," Sister Mary Rose replied. Officer Mike turned to her, and the uneasy moment lingered. He looked away as they both held their thoughts—one was wrong and the other was hiding. They watched again as Elizabeth ran and disappeared into the distance.

Chapter 10

The four children ambled down the street which quickly turned into a wooded area with James and Patrick in front, and Katherine and Elizabeth behind. Katherine was stiff; she was steaming. She wouldn't look at Elizabeth who had stopped to tie her shoe. The boys continued on and disappeared into bushes while Katherine automatically waited for Elizabeth.

"You don't have to wait on me."

"I do. I really don't want to. Not after today."

"Wow, Mary Gallbladder looked goofy today. One leg was so much shorter than the other. Maybe that's why she's not a very good floater." Finished talking, Elizabeth jumped up ready to go. She felt great.

"Elizabeth, that is not her name. Be respectful—she's a nun. She could have died. She hit her head really hard."

"She's too mean to die."

That was too much; Katherine grabbed Elizabeth's arm. "What you did was wrong."

"I didn't do anything." This lying stuff was really getting easy.

"I know you stole that holy card. I know it in my bones."

Elizabeth, feeling her own strength, yanked her arm away. "You don't know for sure. There's lots that you don't know."

"That's what I told them, that I didn't know anything, but I do know something. I know you."

Katherine turned and walked away. Elizabeth stood alone and watched Katherine disappear into the overgrowth. She hated herself. This was worse than twenty switches. Removal from her sister's favor, no matter how short term, was an eternity, but she needed that card.

Elizabeth crawled through the dense undergrowth which opened into the clearing where James, Patrick, and Katherine sat on the forest floor. Once all were together, Patrick handed out Tootsie Roll pops. He smiled at Elizabeth and offered her a treat which she gratefully accepted. He'd made a killing on the bet of whether Elizabeth could teach the class. Of course that was with his help, but Elizabeth had come through. He would use the money to help finance a new music box.

"So, Elizabeth, you were at it again, I hear."

Elizabeth ignored James as she headed to her favorite tree and scaled it with ease. She perched herself above them, took the wrapper off the treat, dropped it on the forest floor, and began to lick her favorite flavor, cherry. She couldn't wait to bite into the chewy middle of the chocolate tootsie roll.

"Don't believe everything you hear, James," shouted Elizabeth from above. She had survived a very difficult day, and the loneliness that she felt from the absence of Katherine's connection turned into staged disaffection for the others. James had seen this before. He was not interested in encouraging her.

"I call this meeting to order."

"Why do you get to run all the meetings?" Katherine said, having had a bad day herself. James and Patrick simultaneously gave Katherine a look, and thought, *not her too*. Katherine could be a pill, but usually she just wanted what was best for the tribe; they knew that. She was right when she called them out. They needed to solve a problem—a problem they knew they created, but blamed Elizabeth. "Okay, Patrick, tell us your idea," James said with authority.

Ever watchful, even when she was mad, Katherine kept her eyes on Elizabeth as she climbed higher in the tree.

"Look," Patrick gave his suggestion, "you can hunt for pop bottles and turn them in for money. Some boys from school do that, but I think we can do better."

Katherine gave her twin a look, "Patrick, we aren't going to steal anything!" She looked back into the trees, but the glare of the sun blocked her view. She couldn't see Elizabeth.

"No, Katherine, we don't need to steal anything. We have a treasure just blocks from our house, down by the tracks." James was interested. How was Patrick going to make taking something into not stealing?

"Copper. It's in an old plant with lots of junk. We can take it to the salvage center; it's in the wire," Patrick said with great satisfaction.

"Salvage?" Katherine asked.

"I like this," James offered, knowing full well that they were taking something from one place to another without permission. It was still stealing. He tried to rationalize that perhaps the owners wouldn't mind. Maybe they wouldn't bother with the wire anyway, too much trouble. He didn't need much convincing, but they did need a plan.

Patrick reached for a stick on the ground just as Elizabeth descended the tree. The conversation was getting interesting now, so she quickly grabbed it and handed it to him, an indication she was ready to be part of the group.

Patrick drew a rough map of the neighborhood. "Okay, we live here." He drew an X to mark the spot. Next he drew lines and squares and pointed to one of them. "The train tracks run this way next to the stock yards. And the other square is the spot we need to get to on the other side of the stockyards close to the railroad tracks."

Katherine squirmed. "That's far," she noted with apprehension.

James got up and walked around the tree. "Yep, we'll do it."

"How much copper do you have to find to make a dollar?" Katherine was not convinced, especially when Patrick admitted, "I don't know." She finally got up to walk away. She didn't like junk yards because there were always dogs around—frightening, mean-looking, hostile animals.

"Let's head downtown. See if we can find another music box. See how much it costs." Patrick was ready to make decisions; Katherine was not.

She gave James a disapproving look as she made her case, "It's too late. Dinner will be ready soon. Let's go tomorrow."

But the decision was already made. They were going downtown.

James then looked at Elizabeth, who sat with legs crossed, and avoided his glare. "Stay out of trouble." He meant it. No turning back now.

The first day after the event at school, Sister Mary Rose was asked to substitute teach for Mary Paul who had a severe concussion and would be in the hospital for several days. At first Mary Paul didn't know her name. Next, she knew her name but not where she lived. Finally, she knew her name and address, but not what happened in the office.

Sister Mary Rose's class was covered by an ancient nun who stayed at the convent, but did not teach. The children didn't even know her name (Sister Mary Ruth) until the day she showed up, but there was no problem with her substituting since these students were the easiest, smartest and best behaved in the school—Patrick's class. If only the good nuns knew, that for a quarter,

Patrick did homework for those who lagged behind and needed a little extra help.

The Principal thought it better to bring Sister Mary Rose into the classroom for Mary Paul. She was calm, level headed, and was part of the holy card event. The young nun was the perfect replacement: she played baseball with the boys, four square with the girls, and basketball in the winter in the small school gym, taking turns with the girls and the boys. She could also spin a story right up to the edge of falsehood.

Sister Mary Rose learned to play games of all kinds from her brothers on days when the crops were in and the leaves had begun to fall, and while it was still not too cold to stay out until the sun set. They had a basketball hoop attached to the barn, and she was a good shot. Those were the times when she wished she were a boy.

The Principal had seen how children of all ages responded to her, and she needed the children to be reassured. But most importantly, she needed the parents who were asking questions, to be reassured. This was a serious matter. The altercation in the office had left a nun on the floor unconscious, and a child running from school was viewed by anyone tall enough to see out the window.

Sister Mary Rose walked up and down the aisle. "What a great day we have had. Sister Mary Paul will be back soon." A generalized shudder went through the classroom. The good nun noticed but said nothing.

The school bell rang, and within seconds, the books were placed on desks as the children stood at attention ready to bolt. Elizabeth was last in line; she wasn't in a hurry. She was tired, her sister was barely speaking to her, and there was the expedition to find copper. She would try to be happy for the outing with her siblings, but she struggled. She wondered what adventure she could craft out of it. Maybe it could be like a treasure hunt. Patrick said there was treasure. She could be a pirate, a female pirate. She had never heard of that, but perhaps she could be the first.

She wondered what would happen when Mary Paul came back. Would she keep asking about the holy card? Would there be a school conference, and would the father-monster come out and wail, and end up in jail? Was public school in her future? It seemed so inevitable until Sister Mary Rose pulled on the Penguin's arm and she went flying.

She mulled over the moments before the Penguin hit the deck, but it happened so fast. Elizabeth tried to slow it down in her mind, and the more she replayed the event, the clearer it became. Yes, the Penguin wanted to hit her (she had been hit before), but somehow the anger didn't really seem directed at her this time. It occurred to Elizabeth that Mary Paul only wanted to hit her because she couldn't hit Sister Mary Rose. There was something between the Penguin and Sister Mary Rose that had nothing to do with her. She felt it. Her heightened sense for feelings and emotions had been fined-tuned from her earliest days, like knowing when to come in the house and when to stay away.

Sister Mary Rose looked out at the students from the front of the class and paused. "Elizabeth O'Sullivan, could you stay for just a moment?"

Sister Mary Rose looked over at Katherine. "It won't take long, Katherine. I need Elizabeth's help with something." She knew Katherine always waited for Elizabeth; it was her job.

Elizabeth hung back as requested as the children filed out. The nun wanted to talk privately, "Elizabeth, will you help me?"

Elizabeth moved slowly; she really was tired. Sister Mary Rose tossed a blackboard eraser to her and she began to capture the daily chalk. She stretched as high as her arms would allow, right below the missing Joan of Arc holy card. Sister Mary Rose moved over to her. "Elizabeth, you must do what is right."

Sister Mary Rose, tall as a mountain, squatted down by Elizabeth. They were eye-to-eye. Elizabeth backed up and looked away grimacing. Her face was the map of guilt, and she walked to the window, her back to the nun.

"Elizabeth," the kind nun said with the tone of a determined woman. "If you have it, you must return it. Everything will be all right."

Elizabeth turned around to see Sister Mary Rose now at the door, waiting and hoping she would do the right thing.

"Why does Sister Mary Paul dislike us so much?"

"Us?" Sister Mary Rose heard it, but was stunned. She felt the blood leave her face and pool at her feet. *How does she know?* She hesitated and then turned and floated away, but the float was less precise, a little less smooth, almost a stumble, as if her feet were tangled. Elizabeth noticed.

There he was, standing alone, waiting, hoping. Elizabeth needed a friend; he was sure of that. She'd had a few rough days. Elizabeth lumbered out of the school—lying by avoidance to the good nun was tough. Deep in thought, she passed Richard. Here was his chance. He had to act; he hoped his voice would not betray him, sputter, and stop. He took a breath.

"Elizabeth," he said, anxious for a response. He could feel the sweat in the palm of his hand. He didn't know what to expect.

Elizabeth heard her name and slowed. Who was calling her name? She turned around and there he was. Richard. What does he want and why is he here? she wondered. All the other children were gone except for the kids who got in trouble and had to stay after, chalk on their hands, a tale-tell sign.

"Hello, Richard, what are you doing here?" There was no pretense. She really did want to know what he was doing there. He was the teacher's pet; no chalk on his hands.

"Oh, just here, waiting." He wanted to be strong.

"For what, Richard?" She didn't get it. Why would anyone stay after if they could leave? Nobody liked school except maybe Patrick.

The words were stuck. He took a deep breath and it cleared the log jam letting the words burst out. "Sister Mary Paul had it coming. She's mean. I'm proud of you."

She stopped. No one had ever said they were proud of her, no one in her whole life, not even her mother. This comment from Richard surprised Elizabeth greatly, especially coming after the kindness Maria had shown, and when she needed it most. She wondered how she ever deserved this special treatment or care. What could she say? She looked at him with disbelief.

"Why?"

Another deep breath and he halted. She waited while he just stared at her and she wondered how long this was going to last. What a puzzle! Richard, who had never spoken a word to her, was standing there looking like he was lost and wanting to say something. Her life certainly was getting interesting. Perhaps she should help him out.

"Well, Richard, how about we walk and I talk and you nod?"

Not a mean bone in her body, he thought.

"I had a couple of banner days. I think you must have noticed. I got to teach class, which I did very well." Richard nodded agreement.

"Although you don't know exactly what happened in the office, I did save a life."

Richard nodded again, flashed a smile, and thought, there she goes, being Elizabeth. He knew she had a great imagination and really didn't care if she was lying or not. He wanted to hear more. Of course that would mean he would have to eventually speak, but before he could muster the courage, Elizabeth jumped back in with a jolt.

"I don't expect the nuns would want me to tell you this, but since I guess we are friends now, I think I can trust you."

Richard was about to collapse with all of this sudden intimacy; he was actually learning about her life.

"Well, Sister Mary Rose and Mary Paul were about to get into a fight over whether or not I took the holy card, which I don't think is really all that important."

Holy smoke! They got angry? He never even thought about nuns in that way. It was as if Elizabeth were opening a door to a new world of emotions and frailties. Nuns having fights. His mouth dropped open and Elizabeth couldn't help but notice the astonishment on Richard's face. Where had this boy been? Probably in a nice family where they never throw things or hit people, she thought.

"Sister Mary Rose was defending me, sort of, because Mary Paul was going to slug me right in the face, but Sister Mary Rose pulled her away. Well actually, she shoved her."

Richard stopped abruptly. He had several questions. First, why didn't she call Sister Mary Paul, Sister? Secondly, why wasn't Elizabeth surprised that the nuns were fighting? He would have to ask another time, but right now, he was aghast.

"You know what? I don't think Mary Paul really wanted to hit me. I think she wanted to hit Sister Mary Rose." Now stunned even more, Richard couldn't move.

"So, what do you think of that?" Instantly she wished she could take the question back. The poor kid couldn't walk or talk, she realized. She would have to slow things down and change the subject.

"Hey, let's go down to the Five and Dime. I need a Tootsie Roll pop and you look like you could use one too. You got a nickel?"

Richard was relieved he could just nod, and so he did, which signaled his legs to move. They sauntered, and he began to feel relaxed.

"So, they got into a little wrestling match which was really funny to see—two Penguins tussling." Elizabeth laughed, forgetting how tired she was. She felt better now, and she had Richard to thank for that. She liked Richard.

He didn't notice the change in Elizabeth because he was still stuck with the vision of two Penguins "tussling." Where did she get these descriptions? Nuns as Penguins, although it did make sense. Who cared? She was sharing them with him and that was all that mattered.

Elizabeth proceeded to talk and talk while Richard nodded and nodded. She felt great and so did Richard. She talked about her siblings, each one in detail. Richard knew Patrick, had seen him win the spelling bee, and avoided James because he looked scary. He knew that Katherine was Elizabeth's keeper, as he saw her always watching Elizabeth. If anyone had been watching as he had been, they would have seen the confirmation of Elizabeth's guilt as the thief when Katherine mouthed, "Elizabeth" just as Sister Mary Paul noticed the missing holy card.

Elizabeth described her mother as a beauty who could sing and play the piano, and cooked the best meals. Surely he had heard her sing during Mass. She even mentioned John, the last of the O'Sullivan crew.

She conjured up words to describe John as if she were using a dictionary—words that hid his outrageous behavior, his aptitude for getting away with murder, or plainly speaking, that he was a bit of a brat. She would never speak ill of her siblings. John was "adventurous, destined to do something amazing and would probably become a world traveler," she offered instead.

When they got to the Five and Dime, Elizabeth knew exactly where the candy section was. Richard was not so familiar because his mother made candy at home. They did not splurge on things like store-bought candy. He didn't really care much, and didn't feel the slightest bit of neglect.

Elizabeth never mentioned her father, and Richard never asked. In fact, he never spoke until the end of the walk. He was relaxed and happy. His house came first on the journey home—a house very different from hers. It had a grand front porch with large baskets filled with flowers hanging from the rafters, and a yard with lots and lots of trees. A perfect place to live, Elizabeth thought.

"I'll see you tomorrow," Richard's words were sweet and smooth. There were no pauses or repetitions.

"Yes, unless I die in the stockyards," Elizabeth laughed—a comment he could not possibly understand.

What kind of life did she live? he wondered as she lifted and floated away. Yes, she could float, just like the nuns. He wished they could walk and talk forever. He had found a friend, and so had she.

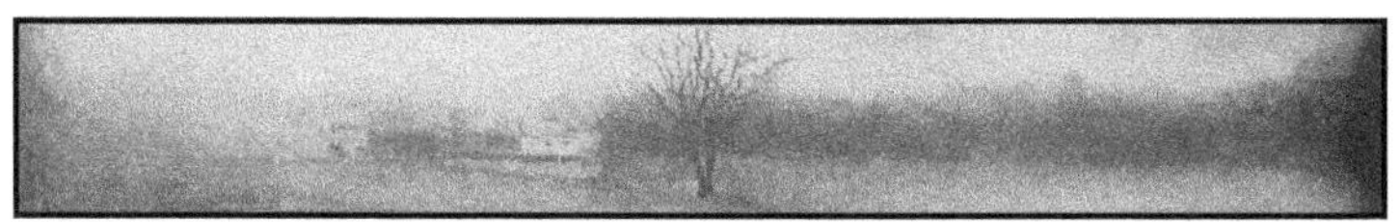

Chapter 11

A small stockyard, with wooden holding pens half-filled with snorting cattle, ran parallel to five sets of train tracks. The O'Sullivan siblings stood and stared at the pens.

"We need to get through here, then climb over the empty pens and onto the railroad tracks," Patrick directed with just a hint of concern.

"I won't do it. This is stupid," Katherine said defiantly.

Patrick let out a long sigh. Not now, he thought. "It will take too much time to go around. We need to climb into this pen right here and go out the other side, then onto the landing, go around the building, and down onto the tracks."

Katherine folded her arms with determination. This was too much, too dangerous. Was she the only one with any sense in this family? "That is too dangerous. We could fall in and get trampled to death."

James smiled and looked through the slats of the fence. "There is just one dumb cow in this one."

Patrick surveyed the area. "Katherine..."

"I won't do it." she resolutely replied.

James knew what he had to do. "I'll go first." He was the leader so he climbed the wooden cow pen with ease, dropping into the pen while a large animal slept in a corner. He quickly crossed the pen, scaled the other side, and reached the landing.

"I'll go next, just a dumb cow." Before James could say a word, Elizabeth scaled the side of the wooden pen.

She perched herself on the top of the stall and waved as if she were a homecoming queen in the annual parade. She leapt down, landed softly, and quickly righted herself squarely in front of the once sleeping animal. To her surprise, it wasn't a cow but a large bull that pulled himself up and stood heads above Elizabeth. He snorted with fragments of soft moisture coming out his nose, lingering in the air and slowly drifting away. It was as if everything was in slow motion.

Elizabeth did a double take. The eyes of the bull were mean and red, almost like they were squinting and trying to get a bead on Elizabeth. She moved very slowly, inching toward the other side of the pen. She tried to focus as the bull snorted again.

I can do this, she said to herself. She began to shake inside like a volcano, ready to erupt. She knew she must get control, move and get out of the way of the gargantuan—a scary, fire-in-the-eyes creature. What saint could fly? she tried to imagine. None. There were none; but angels fly, she thought, so she would just have to be an angel.

James knew he had to think of something to distract the bull, but all at once Elizabeth jetted up the side and over the top with the speed of a Chuck Yeager fighter pilot. At least that is how James thought of it as he watched her make her way to safety.

She breathed hard, trying to catch her breath, and keep the tears in check. She said nothing, but James saw the momentary slump of her very small shoulders. She was just a little girl and he was the father/brother. He should not have let her go. A moment of guilt, like a giant wave of water swept over him. It was his job to protect her, but he had a lapse in judgement. He could never let that happen again, he vowed. A small knot swelled up into his throat. He trembled and turned to avoid the eyes of the others.

He never wanted Elizabeth to be anyone other than who she was. He knew the day she stopped pretending, or living in another world, would be the day that he should begin to worry. He looked at Katherine and Patrick, but still couldn't speak.

Katherine wanted to get a better look at the animal in the pen, so she came as close as possible and peaked through a space between the wooden slats of the fence. Patrick joined her.

The twins shuddered inside, but never uttered a word. The animal was a beast. They lost track of James and Elizabeth as they pondered what could have happened. As twins, they often had the same thoughts and really didn't need to say a word.

Slowly, a small gate near the pen opened. Elizabeth and James had left the perch just above the bull and found the opening that had been there all along. "What are you two waiting for?" Elizabeth said, recovered.

Katherine gave James a stern look. "Next time we should probably just use the gate," she said, feeling very vindicated. James and Elizabeth joined the two accomplices at the fence, their eyes focused on the bull. The bull turned and snorted. He moved toward the four sets of eyes peering through the fence. They had seen this fire before.

A nervous, excited, laugh rang out from Patrick before he commented, "Holy cow! That was close."

"Need I remind you, that was not a cow?" Katherine replied.

They enjoyed the moment then James gave them the signal to head out and they ran as fast as they could, giggling and laughing. It felt good.

The sun high overhead was bright and blinding. The siblings looked down the train tracks and saw movement in the distance, an approaching train. James stepped inside the tracks with Katherine close behind. There were five sets, each several feet apart. Rail cars sat, ready to be called up and put into action, partially blocking the view. Patrick stopped just over the last set of tracks and looked down at the ground. He saw something shiny.

"Hey, it's copper." Patrick was genuinely surprised.

Elizabeth, at the rear, fell behind and stopped midway across the tracks. She looked down and also saw several long threads of the bright, shiny metal. "I see some, too. Wow!"

Elizabeth was excited and didn't look back up. Her eyes were glued to the ground, picking up as many of the threads as she could. It was beautiful and she wondered what she could make with it. She gently picked each one up and laid it across her palm. Maybe she could fashion a tie-back for her hair, or better yet, a tie-back for her mother. It would take lots of the copper strands all tied together. They were similar in color, but still a little different from her mother's hair. A tie-back would stand out, but not too much. She could see her mother proudly walking into church with her hair shimmering from tiny pieces of metal.

Patrick was past the tracks where the train would soon travel. He looked back and saw Elizabeth, and knew that she was somewhere else, lost in thought.

A loud, hot whistle came out of nowhere. It hurt Elizabeth's ears causing her to look down the track. What was coming at her? It was the size of a dragon, fire coming from its mouth. The blackness grew bigger, shifted, moved from side to side, leaping off the ground into the sky and back down. She tried to make sense of what she was seeing. Mesmerized, her eyes stayed focused on it and she didn't move. She couldn't. She was consumed with fear—the train was coming straight at her.

Katherine looked back and saw Elizabeth stopped in the middle of the tracks. "Elizabeth, come on! Stop fooling around." But Elizabeth didn't move. The fear was too big and she couldn't think it away.

Fear also ripped through Katherine, and she screamed again, "Elizabeth!"

"Elizabeth! Come on!" James cried with panic.

In a very quick assessment, Patrick looked up and saw Katherine and James gripped with terror, but in the clear. The train, just nearly a block away, was bearing down. It couldn't stop. He took out like a bullet racing toward Elizabeth.

The train's warning blared. Patrick was just moments ahead of it as he dove for Elizabeth, snatching her up and bringing her close to his body as if they were one. He held on tightly. Katherine cried out in horror as James grabbed her and pulled her to his chest. The train sailed by with an earth-shattering noise. The brakes of the train suddenly screeched, trying to stop the behemoth with its load of new automobiles heading to the next big town. Brightly colored Chevrolets, carried piggyback, stormed by with flashes of light stabbing through the pieced together train, time after time. It was hypnotic. The weight carried the train down the tracks, blocks, before it stopped.

James searched through the landscape for two figures. His eyes filled with tears and blurred the scene. Katherine slumped like a rag doll, all her senses gone from her body. It was the first time James ever held her so tight. He had to hold her upright; she couldn't stand by herself. He shook like a worn-out washing machine with the rag doll moving in his arms. The motion brought Katherine back to the present, but she wasn't ready to open her eyes. She didn't want to see. She felt out of control. The terror was heightened because she knew James was never afraid—not of their father when he should be, and not even of mother nature. He loved storms and he never hid from anything. He was big, so other boys never bothered him. But this time, he was afraid.

Katherine realized there was nothing she could do if Elizabeth and Patrick were gone. But first, she would pray. If God let them live, she vowed never to complain about her sister again, ever, or at least she would try not to. She would also do a better job of protecting Elizabeth.

And she would be a better Catholic. If God let them live... She started to cry and couldn't finish her prayer.

"Katherine, Katherine," James said gently, not wanting to instill more panic. Katherine opened her eyes as the words and tears brought her back. She was ready to learn the fate of her two siblings.

There they were, two lumps; James could see them. Relief washed over him although the stillness was not a good sign, but at least the train had not taken them. There was hope.

"We need . . . " He couldn't say more and his voice cracked. He waited a moment until the terror left, freeing his vocal cords. "Come on, let's go get them." He was trying to be confident, but Katherine could hear the doubt.

James and Katherine worked their way across the tracks. The few unsteady steps they took that lead them to the lumps, seemed like a mile. There they lay silent—lodged next to the metal tracks. Elizabeth, facedown on her stomach with Patrick's arm under her, moved slightly. Slowly James turned Elizabeth over. Her eyes opened, and she tried to focus. What was James doing? What just happened?

Katherine moved toward Patrick and put her ear to his chest. His heart beat, air blew out his nose. She scanned him from the top of his head to his toes. He had a large scratch on his forehead, and a bump was starting to emerge. He had taken most of the force from the fall that occurred when he tackled Elizabeth. He shielded her and protected her, slamming himself on the ground; now a broken rib was crying out. Patrick, disoriented, opened his eyes to see Katherine. What a beautiful sight! He was alive, but where was Elizabeth? That was quickly answered.

"Where do you hurt?" Katherine said. There was no answer. "Elizabeth?" Patrick's voice cracked as pain crept into his consciousness.

"Here. She is here, with you, exactly where you put her," James said with just a hint of fun. Patrick closed his eyes. His voice stuck; a lump bigger than the one on his head had settled in his throat. He turned his head and saw the profile—she was safe.

For a moment they rested, but only a moment. Patrick then realized the heaviness he felt on his arm was the weight of Elizabeth's head. He swallowed the lump in his throat. "Well, I kinda hurt everywhere." That was an honest answer.

James reached down and picked up Elizabeth who rested her head on his shoulder. She was confused. One minute she was admiring the strings of copper on the ground, and the next she was stuck in cement and couldn't move. Then this. Her arm hurt where a big bruise surfaced, and the noise from the train filled her head. A numbness took over and she couldn't speak.

Patrick was still a little shaken, legs wobbly, side hurting, head throbbing. Katherine grabbed his arm and tried to put it around her neck. A pained contortion overtook his face. He needed to lean on her, and she would have to guide him. He couldn't lift his arm.

"We've got to get out of here before the crew gets us," James said.

They scrambled over the tracks and disappeared down a tree-lined dirt road that led to a small bridge across a creek. The salvage yard was out of the question; they were going in the wrong direction. It would have to wait. They had to get home.

Off in the distance two men ran toward the children.

A row of trees served as a large canopy, shading the area. Small scrub trees and bushes outlined the creek below providing coverage for the fleeing siblings. James carried Elizabeth on his back while Patrick, stunned but mobile, moved with Katherine's help. The children traversed the upper level of the embankment, then down to a rock overhang and into a small cave. The cave was dark, craggy, with trickling water, and the children were now enclosed. They felt safe.

James stood next to the opening of the cave, looking, while Katherine held Elizabeth close to her. Elizabeth was quiet, not sure of what happened. There were things she just couldn't take in at the moment.

Patrick sat unsteadily on the rock covered floor, braced up against the cave wall. His head hurt, a lot. He felt sick to his stomach and didn't say a word. He couldn't say anything because his thoughts seemed to be frozen. He tried to form words, but they wouldn't come. He was just as overwhelmed as the rest of his siblings, maybe more. He saw the train face to face—another near miss. It was too much. He might cry, might begin to doubt himself so he stopped thinking.

"They're gone by now," James said, almost as a wish. He looked over at Patrick and could see the knot on his head was growing. They needed to get him home, sneak him into the house, get some ice, and hope for the best.

"How's your head?" James asked, hoping that Patrick wouldn't say something awful like he hit his head so hard he couldn't see.

"It's just a scratch." Patrick knew the truth wouldn't matter. If his head kept hurting like this, he would have to go to a hospital. He knew about stuff like concussions. He looked it up at school after an event at home when he took a broom to his father's head. He would wait it out, but he had to have a plan, just not now. His head hurt too much.

James saw the pain in Patrick's eyes. He diverted his gaze to Elizabeth. "Elizabeth?"

Huddled together, Katherine watched her sister closely, trying to find some reaction, but the face remained still. No motion, just quiet.

Inside, Elizabeth relived the moment over and over. The fear she felt when the train was bearing down was the greatest that she had ever experienced. She had become immobile, her feet hard and heavy. She believed if she thought about the noise, the smell, the whistle enough times, she would be immune to the fear she now felt. She repeated the image over and over again, and the more she thought, the more she realized that the fear of the train which immobilized her, was a different kind of fear. It was unlike the fear of her father's rage, or the nun's switch that stung and embarrassed her. The train—the thing that could have sent her sailing five thousand miles was something new and different, and truly non-human. There could never be negotiations with a train. Her father, although just as dangerous because he could take her life, was not made of metal. He could be tricked, he could bleed, he could die. He was human.

It was not a good thing that just happened. Katherine knew it was another red flag. Everything was churning out of control and she held Elizabeth even closer. There was no need to taunt, "I told you so." Katherine could see the feeling of failure in James' mannerisms, especially his eyes when he looked past her.

"Let's go home. Mom will be waiting," she said.

"I'll go first and make sure the coast is clear."

James needed to make up for his part in this fiasco so he came out of the cave first, and purposefully, slowly climbed the embankment before pausing. He waited until it was perfectly still.

Patrick opened his fist, revealing a small piece of copper. He started to shake his head in disbelief, then stopped. It hurts to do that. Stupid, was his first thought. He paused, took a deep breath and waited for the pain to recede, no more shaking of the head. Even in the haze of pain, he knew he couldn't give up the plan; it was still a good one to make money. Okay, that was a positive. They just had to find a better way to get into the salvage yard. He would work out that plan; that's if he didn't have a blood clot and die in his sleep. The conversation with himself was headed to a dead end. He laughed at that thought...dead end. Patrick was not one to roll around in self-pity.

"Guess we'll have to come back tomorrow," Patrick was talking to himself. No one else was listening.

James looked around. The coast was clear; he waved for the rest to follow. Katherine pulled Elizabeth up and took her by the hand. She was moving, but mostly lifeless; the lights were dimmed. Patrick inched up the side of the cave, mimicking the downward spiral that took him to the spot.

Out of the corner of James' eye, he saw two men approaching the embankment. He could see them, but they couldn't see him. He didn't know the men, but he had seen them in church. They seemed like all the other men in town—nondescript, average, nothing stood out, but one was just a little bigger, more muscular than the other. They could have been twins, but they weren't. He motioned to his siblings to hit the dirt, lie still, be silent, all done with a one-hand gesture. They knew what he meant.

"Those damn kids are lucky," said the one man who was just a little bit larger than the other. "What in the hell were they doing playing on the tracks? They stopped just feet from James and looked around. Their sight-line was too high.

"Dumb kids. One of them looked familiar." James hoped they were as nondescript to the men as the men were to him. "I think one was O'Sullivan's kid," which drew a grimace from James.

"O'Sullivan? I sure wouldn't want to be that kid when the old man finds out. You hear about his wife?"

"Some kind of accident."

"An accident? I am sure that is his side of the story." The man's wife had her suspicions and had told him so—too many bruises, and the fear in the O'Sullivan woman's eyes when she thought she might be late. "She had the voice of an angel. My wife sang with her in the church choir. She can barely talk now. No, the guy choked her."

The harshness of the moment descended upon the children. Each knew the truth of their lives, but they didn't know others knew it too. Katherine wasn't sure how much Elizabeth was taking in. She hoped her sleep-walking state would keep her inoculated.

The men turned away from the embankment. The smaller man stopped. "You know what? I didn't recognize anyone today."

The men hurried down the dirt road and out of sight. The children sat, their emotions trickling out dry tears. They all wanted to cry, but none of them would. What would a few tears do anyway? It was clear; they all felt the same. They were numb.

The road home would be slow. Patrick's knot was too big to ignore, and they knew he would struggle to explain it if his parents asked what happened. He would have to avoid both his mother and his father. Elizabeth wasn't talking, almost a first for her, but she was thinking.

When James finally gave them "the coast is clear" sign, the gesture to rise reminded Elizabeth of the parish Priest during mass. Sit for the scriptures and stand for the Gospel at the Alleluia verse. Some things never fade; they hang in the air, dangling within reach.

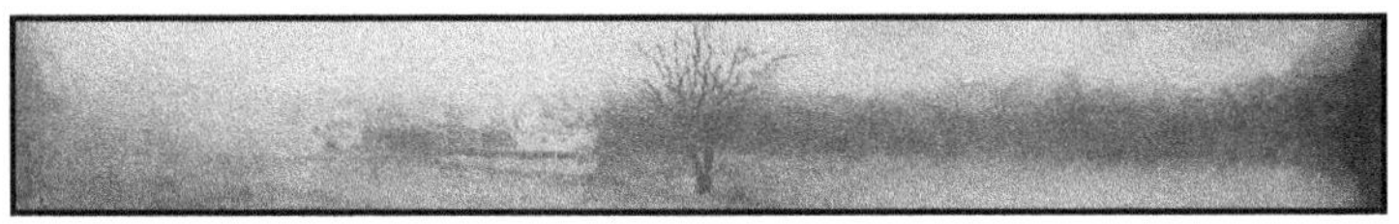

Chapter 12

I think we need a big garden this year. I better get to it tomorrow, too late today," Junior said. He took a swig from his beer.

The sun was setting and there were several empties on the table. He looked out onto the yard from the back door. The lawn needed to be mowed, but the pork chops would be ready soon, green beans flavored with bacon, and apple sauce on the side. One of his favorites. Yes, it can all wait, he thought.

It was his day off. He was feeling good, happy almost. He always thought of himself as a farmer removed from the land, untethered, adrift in a hard mechanical world. The beer helped with that feeling. It would be a matter of a couple of hours before the beer high would mean a beer descent. It just worked that way. The alcohol was metabolized and then there was a crash.

Dinner time on his day off was a little later than on work days. As usual, Susanne stood at the stove. She barely moved, intent on watching the chops to make sure they cooked just as he liked them—done, but not dry. Just as predictable, Elizabeth smelled the chops, went directly to the stove and her mother, and put her arms around her waist. She stretched up to give her a kiss.

Junior turned and watched the scene at the stove, then noticed the scabbed-over stripes on the back of Elizabeth's legs.

"Elizabeth," more a command than an acknowledgment.

Elizabeth jumped back, startled. Since the near miss with the train, she was edgy and reacted more strongly to noises. She had not seen him at the back door. If she had, she would have stayed away, basic survival.

James entered the room as the indictment came out of Junior's mouth. "Hey, what happened to your legs?" Elizabeth had forgotten about the switching. It seemed like a different lifetime. She, like the rest of the tribe, was more concerned about the bruise on her arm, the big knot on Patrick's head, and the stiffness that circled his abdomen.

Dead silence. Without hesitation, and with the desire to relieve Elizabeth of any responsibility, James explained, "She did it climbing a tree."

That almost worked. Junior knew Elizabeth broke her tailbone climbing the apricot tree in the backyard the year before. The fall caused little discussion: "Are you bleeding? No? Go play." It took weeks before she could ride the family bike. It hurt to sit down on the seat. She liked how grown up she felt when she rode down the block, her hair blowing in the wind. It was tricky because her legs barely reached the peddles. The bike needed to fit all leg lengths of the family.

Elizabeth, assessing the situation, moved away from her mother as Junior approached. He wanted a closer look. He lifted her dress just enough to get a good look. The anger started up his neck and exited through his eyes.

"How stupid do you think I am? Who switched her?" He looked directly at James as he slammed his fist on the worn-out kitchen table. Automatically, James moved back.

"At school." His answer, not a good one, was the only one to give. James prepared for the assault. He was the oldest; it was his responsibility. He waited for the pounding. Susanne never turned from the stove, her best response—act like nothing is happening, just normal family discussion. Besides, there was no way physically to get in between James and his father. She would wait her turn to act if he attacked. She had a pan nearby. She could do it, she told herself.

"No one hits my kids." His voice now a thunder, he looked around for something to throw which was better than landing a punch. A new twist to the family, James is getting bigger by the day, Elizabeth thought. It would not be so easy to wrestle the growing boy to the floor.

Junior stormed out of the room. Elizabeth heard his footsteps, almost a run, and the door slammed. The engine of the Hudson started up and he was on his way when James yelled, "Katherine." There would need to be a family meeting.

Elizabeth, with the front porch light directly above her head, stood staring out at the street. The police cruiser slowly passed by as Officer Mike looked intently at Elizabeth, attempting to read her face as she pointed. There it was, that moment when words weren't needed. Gary Cooper cruised by several times a day, something that Elizabeth noticed and cherished. He knew her name, and he was her friend. Her mother noticed the cruiser too.

The car picked up speed as Junior's face clinched. He slammed on the brakes in front of the Flood Room.

Sister Mary Rose was unsure. Was this wise? Yes, she must be the one. A plain bureau sat against a wall with a crucifix hung where a mirror might have been placed. The only other furniture was a small single bed.

The windows were covered with plain shades and white curtains, reminiscent of her own room at home. Yes, she resolved, she must make the first move.

Sister Mary Paul, in a dressing gown, sat in a small comfortable chair brought into the room for her recovery. She wore a white skullcap over her closely cropped hair, and held a rosary in her hands. She looked unsure as her hands trembled. There was a speck of white sticking out from under the cap; she was older than most knew. Maybe it was her weight that kept her looking younger, but her limbs ached and her joints squeaked.

Without looking up, she caught a glimpse of a visitor. Why had Sister Mary Rose come to see her? She could have waited. There was an accident of some kind, but she did not want to acknowledge her memory was not good. She thought it had something to do with Elizabeth O'Sullivan, but she simply could not remember.

Sister Mary Rose moved into the room, but not too close. "I wanted to see how you were feeling, Sister."

Stern-faced, it was the only countenance that felt comfortable to Sister Mary Paul as she looked up at Sister Mary Rose. "I'm doing very well, thank you. Not that you really care," she added before looking away. She wanted to cry. The sweetness of the other nun made her feel so small.

Sister Mary Rose sat down on the bed and forced the words out, "Sister, you sound angry." Immediately she knew she made a mistake. Was she just looking for trouble? Had she lost her mind? But Elizabeth's words hung in her memory, "Why does Sister Mary Paul dislike us so much?"

Sister Mary Paul closed her hand around the rosary. "All the children like you because you are easy on them. I am not easy."

Where did that come from? Sister Mary Rose steadied herself. Would she lose her composure like the last time when she found herself with this sad, dark woman? "I try to be a good teacher." That was okay. Keep control, she thought.

"I bet you were just like Elizabeth O'Sullivan when you were a little girl."

Sister Mary Rose stiffened, defensive within a moment. The old sister was right in a tangential way. Elizabeth reminded her of her own sister who had died in childhood. So full of life and just a little naughty, the little girl fell ill and never recovered. Sister Mary Rose missed her every day, and looked for those who could occupy that space in her heart. She would not be Elizabeth's friend, but she would love her like a sister from a distance along with all the other children. "What does Elizabeth have to do with this?"

"What really happened the other day? Did Elizabeth strike me? Like you strike me now with your false humility."

"Sister, Elizabeth did not strike you then, and I mean you no harm now." Finished and preparing to leave, Sister Mary Rose stood up.

"Don't call me Sister . . . " There! You can chew on that one! Mary Paul thought.

"Why do you say these things?" the young nun replied. She could feel the anger.

"I see how you treat her."

Sister Mary Rose knew jealousy when she saw it played out, or in the tone of voice. She was once jealous of her brothers and their trips to the state fair with a prized animal. All the fun they had at the arcade; they had something she wanted. But Sisters were there to teach, love and serve the Lord. There was no room for special friendships that could lead to jealousy.

She saw the sadness in Sister Mary Paul and could feel it. She wanted to reach out, but held back. Within an instant her feelings changed from sadness, to disbelief, to anger, and now back to pity. How could anyone be jealous of a child? Mary Paul now seemed like a juvenile, stunted. Sister Mary Rose knew she must leave before she said something she couldn't take back.

The street light made a silhouette of Junior as he stood near the lamppost. He watched as the lights in the convent began to turn on. He saw someone coming out the door. How odd, he thought, but how convenient. He might not have to break down the door.

Sister Mary Rose needed fresh air and rushed out of the convent straight into Junior. It was jarring. She looked up at first not recognizing him, but knew that men never stood outside the convent at night. Then recognition suddenly came with a small shiver through her body.

"Mr. O'Sullivan?

"How do you know who I am? I don't know you."

Sister Mary Rose, stepped back, wiped her face, regained her composure, and quickly extended her hand to Junior to shake with her eyes cast down. She didn't know what to do. Awkward. Even in the best of circumstances, she would never extend her hand, but it seemed important to appear formal, a completely insane gesture, she realized. It was night and she was outside with a man. Junior refused her hand.

She could smell alcohol, but she didn't think he was drunk. She withdrew her hand and stuck it under her habit. She had never had to deal with someone who was drunk, although she had seen plenty of railroad workers and the parish priest celebrate at the St. Patrick's Day celebration in March, and at Christmas time. Junior's words were not slurred. He was not swaying, but there was a heat that came from him. She recognized the force as anger.

"Well, I teach . . . "

"Do you teach, Elizabeth O'Sullivan?"

"Elizabeth?" Nervous, Sister Mary Rose backed up. She wasn't expecting that.

"Who gives you the right to hit my kid?"

Confused, unsure of what was happening, she stammered, "No, No, I . . . "

" Answer my question," he demanded.

Fear settled over Sister Mary Rose. Her throat was dry. She could barely get the words out. "I . . . I . . . never hit Elizabeth."

Agitated, Junior moved toward Sister Mary Rose. He could tell she knew something. Why was she hesitating?

"Who did? Who did, Goddamnit?" He was out of control.

"Maybe we could talk on Monday." Don't panic, focus, she told herself. *How will I get away if he comes closer*?

"I'm talking to you now." There was no hint of compromise.

"I teach Patrick." Divert. That might help, she thought.

"Patrick?" Success! He was diverted and stepped back.

Sister Mary Rose clasped a large rosary that dangled from her waist. "Yes . . . he . . . is a very bright . . . very creative child." She looked up and tried to smile. It wasn't working. So she looked away.

Junior looked intensely at her. Why was she trying to change the subject? Why would she do that if she didn't have anything to hide? Why wouldn't she look him in the eye? Oh, yeah, he thought, young nuns never do, just old ones. He played along.

"Yes, he is. The brightest kid in this two-bit school."

"Who's the brightest kid in school?" The voice was clear and welcoming. Junior turned as Sister Mary Rose exhaled. Immediately Junior recognized the man, Officer Mike.

"Well, if it's not the war hero," Junior chided. Officer Mike smiled in return, ignoring the sarcasm. Sister Mary Rose did a double take realizing there was history between the two men. How or what, Sister Mary Rose didn't have a clue, but whatever the connection, it was more than casual.

"Hi, Junior. How's it going?" Junior noted the superior tone in the voice. Real or otherwise, it was what Junior heard. Mike was always just a little bit better than the folks around him; a war hero commanded attention. Junior would give him that, but that was all he would give him.

Officer Mike maneuvered around and separated Sister Mary Rose and Junior, touching her hand, squeezing it. It always seemed strange to Junior that this soft guy had rescued his platoon and earned a Purple Heart. He had no hard memories of Officer Mike. A county separated them, but he knew from his buddies at the Flood Room that the hero had been smitten with Susanne during high school. They lived just blocks apart, but she never mentioned him. Junior also knew the other man had brought John home after an adventure to the town square. The war took Officer Mike away, brought him back a hero. Diabetes kept Junior at home and allowed him to meet Susanne, and sweep her away.

"Fine. Just passing by and ran into the good Sister. I had a question or two about my daughter Elizabeth."

"Kind of late for that, don't you think?" The mood changed quickly.

"It's never too late when it comes to your kids, but you wouldn't know about that would you?" The other man bristled a little at the comment, and Junior sensed the arrow hit home.

Officer Mike reached behind him and gently pushed Sister Mary Rose back just a step. "Why don't you head home?" This was his last appeal. He had to ready himself; Junior was wiry, but quick.

"Don't you think I have a right to know who switched my daughter?" That was the punch Officer Mike did not see coming. He knew from Elizabeth's pointed finger, telling him to go downtown, it had something to do with her. He was taken aback and realized, *so, that was the deal, the switching*. He felt a bit of shame at thinking Junior had done the deed. Yeah, the father had a right to be upset, but not now.

"Yeah, but, Junior, you need to go home. Talk to the good nuns tomorrow."

The moment passed with an acknowledgment and Junior started to crash a bit, beginning to sweat. He did not want the officer to see him tremble. The beer had peaked and was failing fast. He needed to focus, concentrate, and that took a lot out of him. He also had folks back home to deal with. He did not like being lied to, especially by James.

"Yeah, I'll take care of this another time."

Sister Mary Rose exhaled, turned, and looked up into the second story window. The figure of a woman could be seen, but not clearly; however, Sister Mary Rose knew who it was. The figure disappeared and darkness filled the space.

The drive home was not easy; Junior swerved down the road. The street was empty. Good, he thought. He had to make it home. The lethargic feeling was coming on, and it was hard to keep his hands on the steering wheel, just a couple more blocks. He was feeling his way like a blind man when he loses his cane, his hands on the ground, searching. He had to get home, get out of the darkness. He would teach the kid for lying to him. He stood his ground with the great Officer Mike, and he would not let a kid get around him. He finally made it home. The car pulled up, limping into its spot. He needed sugar.

The house was dark. He made his way slowly up the front steps with the help of hand rails, onto the porch, and to the front door. Not too bad; his legs were working. He felt stronger now that he was home, not so vulnerable. The front door was stuck when he tried to open it. Was it locked? No matter, he would break the window if necessary—it was his house. Instead he decided to give it one more push, and this time it opened. They had not locked it; they saw before what happened when he came home late and couldn't find his keys.

The living room was still and felt empty. Only ghosts of other late nights occupied the space. Junior flipped on the stairway light and looked over at the music box. If it was still there, then so were they.

His feet were heavy on the stairs until he reached the children's room and opened the door. The room was dark with just a sliver of the moon's light cast on the faces of the children. Junior searched for the light switch to turn it on, bringing bright lights flooding into the room. James opened his eyes while Patrick, already awake from the slam of the car door, crept out of bed and made a quick move for the door.

"Elizabeth," Junior called, "I met a nun tonight." He looked around the room. Where was Elizabeth? Junior twirled around and saw James instead.

"Don't you ever lie to me again." Junior grabbed James and smacked him across the face. "Do you understand me?"

It was beginning again. Elizabeth looked around the room from face to face. She saw rage, fear, and tears. She saw the monster; his face covered with hair and his nostrils flaring. His feet were heavy and thick, but he looked weak. She needed to run, get to her safe place. She moved back toward the closet and quickly disappeared.

Katherine's rage, once only fear, built up as she slid over to John's bed and quickly picked him up. He was heavy when he was awake, but like a sack of potatoes when he was asleep. Her anger gave her strength and she hoisted him up on her shoulder. His head landed softly next to her neck.

Driven by instinct, James smacked his father. He was shaking inside and couldn't make a fist. He'd often wondered how it would feel to strike back. There was no thrill, just a realization of what he had done.

Stunned, the monster paused. Slowly tears begin to fill his eyes. They all saw it. The Monster had tears. They had heard him cry tears of remorse through the thin bedroom walls, but none of them had seen the evidence.

Once the hand landed on his father's face, James knew there was a real reason for what was coming. Junior grabbed James around the neck, but his grip weakened and his hands began to tremble. His mind was empty, and he was fading.

Patrick returned with a frying pan and a glass of orange juice. He hoped Junior would get more disoriented, perhaps fall down—that would be perfect. A blow from the frying pan would not be necessary.

Elizabeth moved back toward the closet and quickly disappeared.

The struggle between son and father continued, but not fever pitch, more like a strange dance. Sweat spewed out of Junior's pores. Susanne stood in the doorway, her face stone, pale and bleak. She looked for Elizabeth and pulled Patrick back closer to her. There was not any need for a broom or a frying pan on the head tonight. They could use the orange juice once he started shaking.

Elizabeth sat and rocked in a quiet, stoic, rhythm. The rocking became harder and harder. She opened her mouth and let out a silent scream. Her small hands in fists, she banged her chest hard with the rhythm of the rocking. She rocked and rocked, until slowly the rocking subsided.

She found the flashlight and shined it on the holy card. She took the holy card down and stared. In that moment Elizabeth realized that the saint on the card was about as real as the Gary Cooper she had imagined coming out of her house. The real Gary Cooper would have stopped Junior from returning. He would have understood what she meant when she pointed, like in the movies. He would have pulled out his gun, put it to her father's head and escorted him to jail where he would sit until the end of time. No, there was no Gary Cooper in this town, or Saints that came alive.

Elizabeth wiped away the tears, tore the Holy Card in half, and stopped rocking.

Darkness covered the children as they lay in their beds. No one was asleep except for John. Katherine sat up suddenly calling, "James. James!" No answer. "James, you are only two feet away. I know you hear me."

"What do you want?" His throat hurt; he didn't want to talk. He recognized this night was nothing like what his mother had experienced, but it still hurt.

Katherine knew the event had taken a toll on James; he had to be afraid of what the morning would bring, but life went on and they needed to prepare.

"What are we going to do tomorrow?"

She won't stop, he thought. "Nothing. We are going to do nothing. Leave it alone."

"But the Sisters . . . "

Patrick knew Katherine was right, "They won't be happy," he said.

"They're never happy," Elizabeth said, somewhat surprising herself. She usually let the older three decide everything.

The talk, however low, had stirred John. He sat up and motioned to Katherine. She got up and went to him. "It's all right, John. I'm here. Go back to asleep."

"Sad," he said.

"It's all right now; go back to sleep." She gathered him close to her; snuggling. Just as quickly, John was back to sleep.

James sat up. His anger was strong, "Leave it alone, Elizabeth. Nothing is going to change." He blamed Elizabeth for the hurt in his throat, but just as quickly regretted his words and felt ashamed. She was not to blame; it was the ogre.

James felt his first pang of accomplishment for slapping his father, standing up to him. Yes, he had done it, and he would do it again if he needed to. The feeling was strong, but just as quickly, it disappeared and was replaced by a stronger feeling of regret that flooded over him. His youth was washed away. What son would hit his father? He couldn't find the thought to explain the feeling, but it was there.

Elizabeth rolled on her side, her back to her siblings. She had seen tears in the monster's eyes; he was human. Their world was changing and so were they. Why was James suggesting they pretend they didn't see what was coming? She had seen the future. She knew the holy card—that she believed would bring her relief—was nothing. No holy card. No Gary Cooper. No one to save them from the man. Yes, he was a man. There was no room or need for saints or high flying acrobats now. Her father could be anticipated. He was human. He had tears.

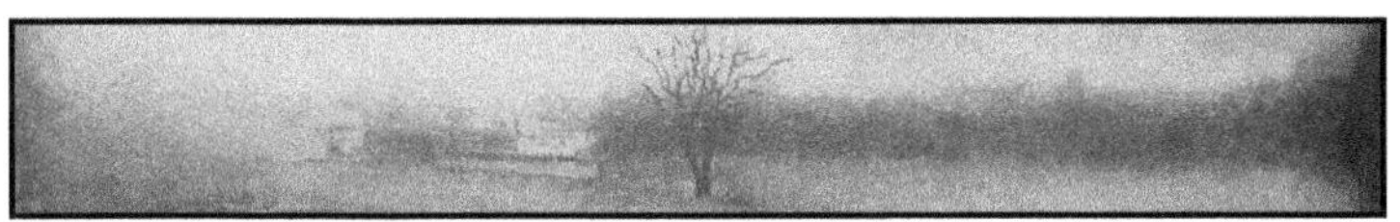

Chapter 13

Susanne was busy at the counter mixing up bologna and relish, a family favorite spread used on sandwiches. "Hey, make a picnic lunch and we'll take the kids out to the lake . . . a little cool for swimming, but we can fish. Patrick loves to fish." Junior was still reveling in the compliments from the good nun. Yes, Patrick was one of the smartest in the school—he needed to be rewarded. The events of the night before came back to him in bits, but some pieces would never return. There was something nagging at him just below the surface of what he could remember, something to do with James. Junior reached over and snagged the hem of Susanne's dress, but she did not turn around.

"Let's go, okay? Get the picnic ready, and I'll get the fishing tackle." Junior put his arms around Susanne's waist. He gave her a kiss on the neck and walked toward the back door, stopped and looked back.

"What color should I paint the house? Hmm . . . I think blue, yeah blue, lots to do before winter sets in." It was a rhetorical question. It didn't matter that her voice was nearly gone because he didn't expect or want an answer. Within a second he was gone.

Susanne looked into the soap suds and gritted her teeth. She pulled out a plate and crashed it against the faucet, dropping her head. Elizabeth stood in the doorway. She didn't need to see her mother's face. She knew what she was feeling, anger vented inward.

The lake, more like a small fishing hole, was quiet this time of year. Late summer—the trees still full of leaves, the grass not green, but also not brown. A good place, Elizabeth thought, for anyone other than her father.

Eyes followed the family as they unloaded the car and made their way from a small parking space next to the public access. Elizabeth's chore was to help Katherine carry the picnic basket. Their father had decided he didn't want their mother to have to carry it. He declared his expectations when he exited the car. He could be heard a hundred feet away. It was clear he was going out of his way to make up for what he couldn't remember from the night before when the sugar disappeared. What little he could remember was true, but somewhat twisted.

He remembered the incident at the convent—saying what he needed to say and being heard. The good nun and her friend the war hero, had backed down. He had sent a message that the switching event was over and there would be no more. He felt satisfied.

The well-used path, where Katherine and Elizabeth walked, led directly to the lake through a small growth of trees, the habitat that kept it clean. They carried the very large picnic basket. Elizabeth lagged behind Katherine, her arms lean and small were strained. Her meager start in life had never picked up any momentum.

"Elizabeth, keep up," Katherine directed. She was tired. The event last night took a toll on her, but she could never own up to it, never say a word. She must be strong. She saw it coming, knew it would happen; however, this time the result was more temporary. The switching, the missing holy card, the lie, the ambulance drive to the hospital, the broken dancing music box, the train, the revelations on the hillside from the railroad workers—all great ingredients for the tornado that was always brewing. She waited each day for Sister Mary Paul to make a move on Elizabeth, but it didn't happen. What did remain was the image of the angry bull as they raced away. She smiled each time she thought of the silliness of the moment.

Elizabeth was tired as well, but for different reasons. Her mind raced. It was as if she could not turn off the events around her. *No public school.* That was a pity, she thought. She imagined the tearful exchange as she headed to the local elementary school filled with Protestants; saying goodbye to all her semi-friends, and of course, Sister Mary Rose who had dropped a notch or two, but still meant something to her. Now, nothing. No change, just the same, except that she herself had changed.

"We don't want to make him mad," Katherine urged.

Elizabeth tried, but she couldn't keep up. Her pace slowed to almost a stop. She dropped her side of the basket.

"Elizabeth, do it for mother. Don't ruin the day for her."

"It's already ruined. He'll do it again! Nothing will change . . . or didn't you hear James?" She was being sarcastic, critical of her beloved brother. She knew it, but it felt good. Renewed, she picked up her side of the picnic basket.

They arrived as Susanne unfurled a blanket with the help of Junior; they found a pleasant spot under a tree. John ran underneath the blanket as it slowly drifted to the ground, and a large lump appeared under the blanket. Susanne reached down and tickled the lump and Junior joined in the fun.

John finally emerged from under the blanket, laughing. Junior grabbed him and twirled him around. He held John like an airplane and the toddler knew the drill and straightened his arms. They zoomed around, twirling, twirling and then fell down laughing. Junior reached over and kissed Susanne on the cheek. He rolled back toward John, and they started the game again.

Susanne smiled and ran her hand over her cheek down onto her neck. The smile disappeared for just a moment, then came back, as if on call like a doctor responding to a message from the hospital. The lazy day was just too sweet not to enjoy, with good sandwiches made of bologna smashed through a grinder, magic sweet pickle relish on white bread, potato chips, and a bottle of Coke to share. Junior ate his egg sandwich and calmly watched his family.

When the sandwiches were finished, it was time for a little fishing. Junior jumped up and headed down to the lake, motioning to the boys. James and Patrick gathered their fishing poles and tackle boxes. They walked down a well-worn path with a slight incline that led to a dock.

"He's crazy if he thought this makes up . . . " Patrick barely got the words out of his mouth before James hauled off and punched him in the arm.

"Shut up, Patrick." This was not smart, and not like Patrick, James thought.

Patrick dropped his fishing pole and took a stand. James, so much taller than Patrick, smiled and shook his head. "I'm sorry. I...," he knew he was too big to be pounding on Patrick, that was his mother inside, but he knew and feared what he had seen and learned from the master—the quick punch, slap, angry words, all intended to intimidate.

"Well, if you're sorry, stop doing it. Okay?" He was serious. Patrick had had it with his bigger brother. Maybe he would get his tail kicked, but he didn't care. He glared at James until James nodded. Certain that his point was made, Patrick picked up his fishing pole and glanced back at the girls sitting on the blanket with their mother. Elizabeth stared off into the distance. "Elizabeth seems weird but not like her usual weird self," he remarked.

"I don't know . . . I don't understand girls."

"She hasn't been the same since the salvage yard."

The boys continued down the path and quickly saw Junior kneeling on the dock with a cigarette dangling from his mouth. He held the fishing boat close to the dock.

"Hurry up, boys, the fish won't wait," he laughed. It was a beautiful day. "Get in and get those hooks set."

James and Patrick, with fishing rods in tow, slid into the boat. Junior followed, and then pushed off from the dock. James examined his line—his bobber was in place, ready to go. He found a tin can full of dirt and worms, evidence Junior had worked hard to make it a good day. James dug in and pulled a fat worm that wrapped itself around his finger. He pulled the worm straight and stabbed it with a hook and felt strangely like his father.

The boat slowly sailed away with their father manning the oars. Junior, with his constant cigarette companion, maneuvered the boat to the middle of the small lake. He reached over and threw the anchor into the lake. He had been a fisherman his whole life, in a state with man-made lakes and small streams.

"Okay, boys, some good weeds here. Let's catch some fish."

"What are we going to catch, Dad?' James took advantage of anytime his father was in a good mood. This was a grand day.

"Anything, if we're lucky."

Junior laughed resulting in a smile from James who then threw his line into the water. Patrick lowered his hook into the lake and looked at his brother. How easy it was for James to try. Patrick would never try, not really try.

A bucket of fish sat off to the side of the blanket while Junior napped and Susanne read a book. James motioned for the children. Katherine with John in tow, Elizabeth and Patrick followed. They headed up the hill and away from the lake.

Susanne followed the outline of the children as they disappeared over the incline into an open area of tall grass that was closed off by a row of tall trees. Her beloved children were different from each other—each one special because of the moment in time they arrived. Susanne knew those moments, understood those feelings. The children did not.

James took off and waded through the tall grass. He stopped and waved to his tribe, beckoning them onward, like an early scout on an expedition. The children leapt as they ran. John tried to imitate, but fell down. Katherine ran back, grabbed him and pulled him onto her back. Patrick stopped to look at a flower as Katherine ran by, her hair floating near her face with John holding on with force. He was strong, very much like James, big. Elizabeth trailed, her walk purposeful. They finally reached a small stream that led back down the hillside to the lake, crossed over, and settled under the canopy of trees.

"Tomorrow we look for copper. The days are getting shorter." James was commanding.

Plenty of time passed since the music box was broken, and they were living on borrowed time. "Yeah," Patrick agreed. He needed to make a plan that did not include bulls and trains.

It took a few days of wearing a ball cap, combing his hair down on his forehead (his crew cut had been growing) and avoiding people, mostly his father, until the knot on his head was gone. The first night after the train near-mishap, the headache lasted for hours and he vomited in the night. He felt shaky for days and the rib was slow to heal. The "switching" event came at the right time diverting any attention that might have come his way.

Katherine gathered John close to her, enjoying the freshness of the day. "Oh, this is a good day," she mused as she looked around and saw Elizabeth walk toward the groove of trees.

Elizabeth disappeared into a clump of trees and found one, taller than most, and mounted it with ease. She moved up the trunk like a cat, going higher and higher. Her thoughts this day were more about places far away and less about floating nuns. Each move was a step a little closer to that someplace far away. She stopped at the top and could see for miles. Katherine,

James, Patrick and John looked like ants. There was only open sky as the sun set.

On this day the children seemed relieved, at ease. It was true for all but Elizabeth.

A trip to the Dairy Whirl was special. They never had ice cream. It was a good ending for a very unexpected day. The cone idea had come on impulse as Junior steered his way home along the lonesome highway. Out of nowhere, the Dairy Whirl appeared. The kids were sure they would never stop, but it was an unusual day. The O'Sullivan car surprisingly pulled in the lot and orders were placed. The children had never seen their father eat ice cream, off limits. It would be an event, a good event.

The windows of the car were rolled down and the noise of the night seeped in. The headlights brightened the near dark horizon while Junior drove licking a vanilla ice cream cone, a sight to behold in their memories. John sat in the middle seat with Susanne next to the door. His face was a mess, round as a plate, covered with ice cream. Susanne wiped off his face with a small Kleenex tissue from a travel kit she kept in the glove compartment.

Katherine, James, and Patrick held ice cream cones, each with a different flavor which they licked in earnest. Their minds were empty of worry or promised threats. If their mother's voice had been strong enough, she would have started a song and they would have finished it. But there was still no voice. If they had been at home, she would have steered them to the piano and the music would have filled the house.

Elizabeth kept her eyes on the faint landscape. She refused the treat and her mood was more than melancholy. She was fighting to keep anger where it deserved to be, on the surface, not diluted by any creamy, sweet diversion.

Out of nowhere it came, a bolt. The pavement disappeared and the car dropped two feet plunging downward and back up. The children were thrown from side to side, up and down. Susanne bounced off the ceiling of the car resulting in a whip lash. The children held on to their ice cream cones as if it were the last time any of them would ever have a chance encounter with the sweet surprise. Elizabeth held onto the door.

The crash of the car, as it landed, pushed Junior's ice cream cone into his face. There it was. It was real. It had happened and the joy ride was over.

"God dammit!" Junior shouted. He threw the car into park and pounded the steering wheel. Anticipating the next move, Susanne pulled John close. Junior grabbed the Kleenex box off the seat and cleaned his face. He needed to get out of the car and assess the damage. His thoughts ran to the obvious. Why wasn't the road hazard marked? He didn't think to ask if everyone was all right.

Out of the car, he walked around. No damage done to the body. Good. He looked for any sign that the road was under construction. Laying on the ground was the highway marker that should have been staked and in plain view of the highway. He kicked the ground, swung around, hesitated, then slowly crouched down and looked closely at the wheels. He checked out the axle, connected to the wheels. It was broken. That required parts and a good mechanic. He couldn't fix it, even though he had a natural affinity for what made cars and machines run. He sat down on the ground, put his head in his hands. He vowed to give the county commissioners a "what for" when he got his car fixed. He would ask them to pay for the repairs, he thought.

They were alone on the highway, no way to flag down help. They would have to walk several miles into town, probably okay since he had his insulin and ate a good lunch. He would figure out what to do tomorrow, which was Sunday. No mechanic would be working, but Fred Matthews, the man at church who sang in the choir and loved Junior's wife in secret, might help. He was a good mechanic.

Junior knew he picked the prettiest girl in ten counties, and most men would trade places with him any day of the week. Until the "accident," her voice in concert with Fred's, was an accepted and acknowledged gift for the church. Surely he would help, but not until Monday. Sunday he would be in the choir loft and then have a meal with his wife and ten children. Fred hoped every Sunday that Susanne would return, but she didn't. He grieved her loss in silence and sang his heart out with her replacement, a good woman who could carry a tune and loved to sing, but was not Susanne. No one caught on except Junior.

Everyone Junior knew would be at the Flood Room—it was Saturday night. Drinking and playing cards, that's where he should have been. Why did he think an outing was a good idea? He stood next to the car, smoking his last cigarette. "Just my luck," he grumbled. The last cigarette and there was no way to get another one. Out of nowhere a patrol car drove up beside him as Junior finished the cigarette and stepped toward the cruiser.

There he was—Officer Mike, the war hero. Good grief, Junior thought. Why is he always around? Then it hit him. The man was following them, just as he suspected.

"I think the axle is broken. Damn county. No sign, just came up."

Officer Mike got out of the car, eager to help. He surveyed the car from all angles, then looked under the wheel. "Hmm, not good," stating the obvious and confirming what Junior had said. "I'll call it in and give you a ride back to town. It will be dark soon."

It didn't take Junior even one second to respond, "We don't need your help. Just send a tow truck. I'll take care of my family."

Officer Mike looked into the car as Susanne purposely avoided his gaze. She knew better than to show any attention to another man. Realizing her discomfort, he decided to focus elsewhere, "Hi, Elizabeth."

Elizabeth held her breath and looked straight into Katherine's searching eyes. How does he know her name? Katherine wondered before remembering the event with Sister Mary Paul. He also was the one who brought John home on several occasions.

"As I said before, I don't need your help. I didn't need it the last time I saw you either."

Officer Mike stepped around Junior and headed to his vehicle. "Well, nevertheless, I am here to help. I'll call the tow."

Junior got in the car and turned around to stare at Elizabeth. "Elizabeth, how do you know him?"

Elizabeth couldn't remember the last time her father asked her a real question, not a question that was really a statement like, "You don't like beets, do you?" Yes, she remembered that question, followed by a slap to the head and a retreat to her sanctuary. Best to pretend to be deaf, she decided. Besides, she doubted her voice would even work. She was getting more like her mother every day. Instead of answering, she simply stared, the stare that said "no one is home." That should do it.

"You stay away from him," the anger in Junior's voice was intense. It isn't working, she thought. Perhaps maybe a nod, to show him she was taking him seriously. It was something Patrick did when he was acting like he was listening to you, but, of course, wasn't.

Susanne knew to avoid Junior's gaze, but he still grabbed her face roughly toward him. "He might want a family, but he can't have mine." Susanne tried to move her face away, but his grip was too strong.

"That guy has always had a thing for you. He went away and you picked me. He better stay away."

Yes, she had picked him. What a fool! she thought.

Chapter 14

Most of his war injuries healed years ago, but the pain in his back and the nightmares of the men left behind were a constant reminder. He came home to a victory party, a grand occasion for a conquering hero, with a family-chosen fiancée waiting.

The stairs in the old, but very clean Victorian rooming house, seemed like a trip up the Grand Canyon. He needed to lie down. The exhaustion he felt from fighting the pain and coming so close to her could only be relieved with a shot of whiskey.

He opened his door and felt relief in the place that had become his home against the wishes of his parents. His parents thought he should live with them until the "right one" came along. The right one had already come along and he had missed his chance.

It was a good room with a large window that looked out on the tree-lined street. He shared a bathroom with three men who came and went working on the railroad. The men who occupied the rooms down the long hallway might change, but never their occupation. There were also two square meals each day during the week.

The manager, a solid woman in her late sixties, packed lunches for the men to eat on the train while they worked. On the weekends, if there were men staying, there was a Saturday evening meal and a big family-style event on Sunday. Although he never attended the Sunday rooming house meal (his family would not take no for an answer), he was tempted. The men on the railroad who stayed over were a good lot. Most had been to war and gotten a job when they came back. Happy to be alive, they weren't much trouble.

There was no cooking in the room, but he kept a hotplate for coffee. On his days off, when he wanted to stay clear of downtown and chance encounters, he made his coffee in his room after breakfast and read the paper, or the latest edition of any Raymond Chandler book he could find. *The Long Goodbye* resonated with him, a war veteran on the run. He knew that Susanne loved to read, and he watched her come and go to the library with baby John in tow. She never went into the local bookstore which was out of reach for someone on a limited budget.

The bookstore was really more like an antique store with old books and other old stuff, but just the place to find some gem that had been forgotten. Officer Mike loved the place.

He first noticed Susanne one day staring in the store's window. He saw her, but she didn't see him. He recognized her immediately. She had a one year old boy on her hip, dressed in blue. His twin was a girl in a stroller, and there was a toddler at her side. It appeared Susanne also had another on the way. She was as beautiful as the day he left for war, only now older and with a sense of tiredness. Elizabeth was born four months later.

He practiced what he would say when he saw her again, but he knew it would sound rehearsed. How could it not? "I don't know if you remember me, but I'm Mike Wright."

At the actual encounter, he did better than he thought. She remembered him; that was a good start. She was quiet and shy at first, but opened up when he made a joke. "Mike Wright, but usually wrong." He reminded her of days gone by, before the war. He was pleased he didn't stumble, although he was sure he was sweating beyond what could even be expected in November.

He remembered a previous encounter when she listened intently and laughed a gentle laugh as he described schoolmates, pranks pulled, and favorite teachers. She knew he was a war hero; everyone in town knew that. There was no mention of a wife or children even though Susanne had seen a woman at his side the day they honored him. There was not a notice in the paper of a wedding—she had looked.

Mike reached out and touched the toddler's head but James paid no attention. His mother held his hand firmly.

He looked forward to chance encounters with Susanne when he felt well, but a night of terrors usually stayed with him. He stayed inside himself, and away from people. His parents worried as the years went by. He was handsome, kind, smart, and had a good job, but just wasn't that social.

Although he never wanted to try for advancement, people encouraged him to run for sheriff, but he preferred to stay in his cruiser. It would be easy to win in a town that remembered its heroes; there weren't many with a Purple Heart. He could go to college; there was the GI Bill, and he did take a few literature classes at a small Mennonite college one town over, but that was the extent of his educational desires.

The routine call that brought him near Susanne, and by extension into Elizabeth's hectic circle of life, came over the police scanner: small child missing, probably on his tricycle, name of O'Sullivan. He offered to check it out even though his shift was over. He knew where Susanne lived, the number of children she had, and he knew about Junior. He'd followed her life for as long as he could remember. His heart was pounding so hard he thought it would leap from his chest. He hadn't felt that since the war, and the day he saw her at the bookstore. His life was about to change, but not in the way he had hoped or dreamed.

Chapter 15

The children sat perfectly still as Sister Mary Paul walked up and down the aisle. Elizabeth, stone faced, never looked up when Mary Paul stood over her. The school bell rang, relief. Students put their books away. Katherine looked over at Elizabeth, another day done, and no retaliation, no memory.

"Students, be prepared for your math quiz. Elizabeth O'Sullivan, I would like for you to stay after for a few minutes."

Maybe not, Elizabeth telegraphed to Katherine through a glance.

Oh no, Katherine thought, what should I do? What could she do? She wasn't thinking about Sister Mary Paul. She was worried about the change, a real defiance, in her sister. It wasn't like she ever completely understood how Elizabeth's mind worked. It was impossible to enter the land of possibilities where myths became facts and reality was clouded with "what ifs"—a mind so different from her own. She always felt she could affect Elizabeth's behavior with a look, but that was gone with the train that nearly took Elizabeth's life.

The students cleared out, but Katherine hung back. "Katherine, you can wait for your sister out on the playground," Sister Mary Paul said with a look of disdain. The nun was after Elizabeth, but she knew Katherine held the truth. There was no getting anything out of her—she was more loyal to her sister than to the Church so she would not bother with Katherine. No, she would get the truth out of Elizabeth.

Katherine hesitated, looked back at Elizabeth, and then left the room. Sister Mary Paul didn't hesitate. She went directly to Elizabeth and pulled her out of her seat. She had been waiting for the right moment.

"So, it seems the apple does not fall far from the tree. You're a thief and your father insults the servants of Christ. Oh, you thought I forgot?"

Elizabeth prepared for the assault. She was not going down without a struggle. Those days were gone.

Sister Mary Paul's memory had come back like a very bad headache, a bolt of lightning striking its target. It flooded her senses, causing her to sit up in bed as she recuperated. All she could think about was the smug look on Elizabeth's face.

Elizabeth struggled to get out of the nun's clutches. Mary Paul shook her and clenched her hand to strike as Elizabeth struggled more and dodged the nun's hand just in time. That was the first act of defiance—just like telling a little white lie, hard, but she was growing in confidence. She was small like St. Therese of the Little Flowers and not particularly strong, but she knew she could wiggle her way out of the arthritic hands that were less able. They were crooked, stiff, swollen at the joints, something she never noticed before, sort of like the bad leg that made the old nun seem more human.

"You think you are smarter than anyone else. You think you are better. What do you say to that? Cat got your tongue?

Elizabeth stared in disbelief. "*Cat got your tongue.*" What? Elizabeth wondered. That was crazy; she didn't have a cat. Quickly, she realized the nun was trying to confuse her, but she wasn't going to be distracted.

"You won't hit me. I won't let you, and I don't have a cat." She freed herself but didn't run. Instead she struck out, kicking Mary Paul in the shin. That must have hurt, Elizabeth thought.

Mary Paul grabbed her leg, the good one. This nun was not as dangerous without her poker, and the sanctity of the habit. She was just a mean old woman. Elizabeth wanted the strength of Joan of Arc. No, forget that, Elizabeth thought. *Joan of Arc is dead.*

"Elizabeth, come back here now!" Elizabeth almost laughed; the fear was replaced with a strange euphoria. Why would she come back? Because this evil woman told her to? No way. The nun wasn't a dangerous train; she was just a human and not a very smart one at that.

"If you ever try to hurt me again, you will pay."

The adrenaline was working and Elizabeth was spinning. Using words instead of arrows she had sent her message across the room, and it landed exactly where it was aimed, straight into the place any human would have a heart.

Elizabeth flew out of the room. Mary Paul, stunned, slowly sank into her chair and grabbed her chest.

Elizabeth ran past Katherine who was busy playing jacks on the cement landing next to the front door. She looked up just in time to get a glimpse of her younger sister as she sprinted down the stairs and out into the school yard. "Elizabeth!" she yelled. Katherine was determined to talk to her and find out what happened.

It was as if Elizabeth were deaf; she kept on running. Katherine, with her long legs, could take one stride to every three of Elizabeth's and soon caught up with her, grabbed her arm, and whirled her around. There was a struggle, then a stand-off. Elizabeth pulled her arm away. She was getting good at this pulling away stuff.

"Leave me alone."

"What happened?"

"Nothing." Elizabeth was done telling people about her life. By people, she meant her siblings. They couldn't do anything to help her, not really. They couldn't even really help themselves. She was glad Richard had become her friend, but she wasn't sure what he could do to help her, either. Maybe just having someone to talk to, who wouldn't try to tell her what to do, would be good. He didn't talk much, which was a good quality to have in a friend, she decided.

"We have an errand to run for mom." Katherine was sure that would settle Elizabeth down.

"Go by yourself." Elizabeth knew what Katherine was doing. The mere mention of her mother would usually melt Elizabeth, but not now. She took out running again and never looked back. Katherine watched as she got smaller and smaller. There was an aura of electricity surrounding the figure.

Katherine knew this was more than a mood; it was a moment that reflected the change in Elizabeth. It was true; all her fears were coming into focus. The family dynamics were changing and she didn't like it. While the family was crazy, it was also predictable. Katherine worked hard to keep the pieces together and help her mother, but her hands could no longer guide the awkward looking shapes into place.

Elizabeth sauntered down the street, past houses all similar in appearance and size. She watched her feet as she walked, trying to stay off any cracks in the concrete. "Step on a crack, break your mother's back." She hated the image.

Large trees lined the street and blocked the sun's glare. She looked up through the branches and saw patterns. She loved Fall. The trees came with colors that took Elizabeth's breath away. She knew a little about how this happened, but she didn't really care. She liked the results. The bright orange, yellow and red leaves that fell and landed in her path made her feel so many things—sad, warm, happy, all jumbled up. It was symbolic of the coming and going of time.

A car honked and broke the spell. She looked over and saw Officer Mike's police car pass by slowly. He smiled and waved at Elizabeth. She gave a halfhearted wave and returned to watching the walkway. The cruiser kept going and she was glad. She wanted to be alone, to think. She walked slowly, taking her time. She wasn't interested in any errands. She was done with errands. She knew what Katherine was really talking about. It was the music box. She didn't have the stomach for another expedition.

Elizabeth arrived home, walked up to the front porch, and sat down on the last step. She knew Katherine and the boys would be ready to go soon. She could not avoid it; she had to go with them. She was partially responsible.

Elizabeth heard footsteps and looked up into the sun, squinted, and then into Officer Mikes eyes. They were light and bright, but no longer Gary Cooper's eyes.

"How's the car?" A good way to start a conversation with an eleven year old, she thought. What would I know about cars? Nothing!

"A friend is going to help him fix it, save money," she decided to answer anyway. Officer Mike nodded.

"I never told you, Elizabeth, but you were really brave the other day." He wanted her to know he knew about her life, and appreciated what it would be like to have a child just like her, so full of life.

Elizabeth was astounded. One day Richard tells her he was proud of her, implying that she was good, and today she was brave. Good gravy! What was happening? she wondered. She didn't feel good or brave. She knew what was in her heart and it was neither good nor brave—it was ugly.

He underestimated her disposition. It was too much, too much to take in. She didn't believe him, and she wasn't interested in pretending. Why would he say something so stupid? Adults were certainly strange, and she'd had enough. She was ready to challenge him. She had been able to see through Mary Paul. Perhaps the pretend Gary Cooper was just as small.

"Is that all it takes to be brave?" She was thinking logically, philosophically; to be brave, you had to fear something, then act without concern for the consequences. She knew that. She didn't fear Mary Paul when she hit the deck. Elizabeth could see that the nun was fast becoming just an old, mean nun.

"I think it takes more." Elizabeth was on a roll and she felt strong. "My mother is brave . . . but she can't . . . "

"I know Elizabeth . . . I've known your mother for . . . "

"Then why won't you help her?" Elizabeth interrupted. There she said it. *Did he understand what she was saying? Did he know? Everybody else in town knew.* Elizabeth's anger was growing. The game changed the moment he said he knew her mother. He had no right to know her mother. If he wasn't going to help her, he could just go away and disappear, but she wasn't done with him. The depth of her feelings was twice what she felt when she kicked Mary Paul.

Sober, Officer Mike looked down. "It's not so simple."

"Yes, it is. Mom doesn't have anyone but us, and we aren't very good at protecting her. She used to sing, but now she can't. I don't think she ever will."

"I . . . " Officer Mike began before becoming overwhelmed with guilt and a peculiar understanding he was not talking to a child, but an old soul formed by violence.

Elizabeth looked hard into the eyes of Officer Mike, hoping he might feel guilty enough to actually act and protect her mother. She had sent a message, and he sensed her anger, her sadness. He felt the sadness, but avoided the anger.

Elizabeth was tired of the stupid conversation. She got up and started toward the front door, then suddenly turned around to face the startled officer. She didn't feel like letting him off the hook, and she felt something else stirring. She felt like being mean.

"Are you married?"

"No," he said somewhat surprised at the question.

She remembered what her father said, accusing Officer Mike of wanting her family. The ugly part of her father's disposition burst through, "You should be, and you should have a good family, but you don't, do you?"

She didn't give him time to respond. "By the way, how do you know my mother?" She was curious. He didn't have an answer. A few short conversations, many missed moments, he realized he didn't really know her mother, at least, not well.

Realizing there was nothing more to say, Officer Mike turned around and saw Patrick just feet away. He knew it was time to go—the conversation had taken a sad turn and he had not been ready for Elizabeth's outburst. "Goodbye . . . Mr. Cooper," Elizabeth said almost surprising herself, a little too much of her thoughts exposed.

"I'm not Mr. Cooper."

"I know. I just wish you had been."

Patrick walked up and stood next to Elizabeth. He watched Officer Mike as he made his way to the cruiser.

"Where have you been?" his voice a little too strong for Elizabeth. "Nowhere," she answered equally strong.

"We have been waiting. Mom took John and went to the library, and then she is going to the grocery store. Dad told her that he would be home late. He's working on the car trying to get it fixed tonight.

"I know," she said with a hint of exasperation.

"We had to make up two stories: One, you were staying after school to help Sister Mary Paul; and two, Katherine was feeling really sick and couldn't run any errands or take care of John. With the little bandit along, it should make her trip twice as long and give us more time, but we need to get going. Hey, why did you call him Mr. Cooper? That isn't his name . . . "

"It's none of your beeswax, Patrick."

"You're strange," he said automatically. He was not use to being dismissed.

"No, you're strange," she retorted. He was happy to see the feisty Elizabeth. She seemed almost herself, but there was now a new edge. Patrick dashed into the house while Elizabeth took her time. She watched the car move down the street.

Chapter 16

It took longer to go around the stockyards, but Katherine was not having a second encounter with bulls or trains. It was exactly as Patrick said it would be: a large run-down steel building, weeds all around, with old cars and deserted electrical equipment. A tall chain-link fence stood as its defense against any invaders. Patrick pulled open the gate wide enough to slip through, not much of a challenge. He ran directly to a side door, pulled and pulled. It wouldn't budge. He looked around and saw a second door, poorly fitted and loose enough to allow a child to go through. He motioned for the others to follow.

James pulled open the chain-link gate wider and motioned for Katherine and Elizabeth to go through. Elizabeth slid past, but Katherine wouldn't budge.

"This is wrong. The place is closed. People don't want us here," Katherine said, knowing it would make no difference. James gave Katherine an exasperated look.

"Fine, you stay here by yourself, Miss Prissy. Patrick and I will take care of it. But let me ask you this: Did you really think the place would be open for business?" Of course he was right, Katherine thought as she jumped up to join him.

"Okay, Okay, I get it, but you are not the boss of me," she said. He wasn't her boss and no brother or man would ever tell her what to do.

Katherine slid through with James close behind; Elizabeth brought up the rear. James motioned for her, but she hesitated.

"Come on, Elizabeth. I am not letting you out of my sight."

"You don't need to worry about me," she answered, but he was worried about her. She seemed tired, a little angry, and mostly sad, but he really didn't have time to focus on her right now either.

Elizabeth knew what was bothering her—it was Officer Mike. All that talking disturbed her. He was her last best hope, and he was no match for her father. No one was.

Patrick was the first to squeeze through the heavy steel door; then the others followed. He went to an old refrigerator and circled his conquest while James surveyed the place filled with all kinds of old equipment and appliances distributed throughout the shed. The sun pierced the many slits in the roof revealing dirt floors with oil stains and deep truck ruts.

"We should stick with the electrical equipment that we can get to. That's where the copper would be. It's a conductor."

Elizabeth didn't know what to look for, although the copper from the train event was still in her mind—the small thread that she had seen, bright and shiny.

Katherine tiptoed through stacks of boxes and old equipment. She was hesitant to touch anything. The electrical cords were old and frayed. She looked over at Patrick, who had a long piece of metal, which he held like a sword. He poked at the air, then charged across the dirt floor as if he were in a battle. Goofy, that is what Katherine thought as she watched Patrick lunge and dance victoriously as he felled each and every imaginary soldier.

This is fun, Patrick thought. No wonder Elizabeth likes to pretend. He took the sword and used it as a walking cane. "I am going to be a business man."

"Come on Patrick, get busy. We don't have much time." James was in charge, and he had no patience. He was tired of the show; he had work to do. This was just like the paper route, or the job at the bowling alley. It didn't matter the weather, or if there were an event with his father like the night before which left him empty, he was determined to do what needed to be done. Playtime was over.

They went to work pulling the backs off appliances and anything electrical. Patrick and James were methodical. They knew what to look for and they were fast. Elizabeth watched and marveled. How do they know these things? she wondered. Did they sneak off to a special school where they learned about machines and electricity? Patrick was probably born with this stuff in his brain, she thought, but James was different. Maybe he learned it working at the bowling alley.

James was quiet and worked hard. The men at the bowling alley liked him. He wasn't old enough to work so they paid him under the table, but he was always on time. Sometimes he looked tired, but he never complained. He liked to work and he wasn't showy. He had a mind for anything electrical, and he learned it quickly. His real job was to set the pins and stay out of the way of the heavy ball careening down the alley.

Elizabeth and Katherine sat on top of an old car that was missing its doors and wheels. Katherine got down, jumped inside, and pretended to drive as James and Patrick laid out their bounty. The boys did their job stripping the wire out of the old appliances. There wasn't much, but it was enough. The girls tried to help, but they were useless. Their role would be expanded as soon as they could cash in the copper and get the replacement.

"This looks good. With pop bottles, my betting money, this copper, and your bowling alley money, we will have enough, more than enough," Patrick said with pride. James was sick to his stomach. He had been saving his bowling alley earnings for a new model to work on.

Katherine swung around, stepped out of the car, and joined James and Patrick. "Betting money?" she said. Patrick thought she seemed surprised and a little agitated. Why was she surprised? Maybe she wasn't really surprised at all, and just needed to protest so there would be a little distance between herself and the venial act. Either way, it made very little difference to Patrick because gambling was not a mortal sin.

Patrick flashed a smile in Elizabeth's direction. "Yeah, betting money. I know we'll have enough. Elizabeth helped me out with that one."

Katherine didn't want to ask, but she had an idea. *How did Elizabeth teach class and where did she get all the answers?* Then it occurred to her. *Of course, Patrick! I could just bean him!* But right now, she was more concerned about replacing the damaged music box.

Elizabeth wasn't interested in reliving past events. She scaled a car at the other end of the building, perching herself on top. She couldn't hear them and they couldn't bother her. She saw Patrick shake his head.

"Something happened today with Sister Mary Paul and I think it was bad," Katherine volunteered looking over at Elizabeth.

"It's more than that. It's like she's thinking really hard all the time," Patrick offered.

"Elizabeth, get over here!" James said. His look was stern; he was not playing. "We don't have much time. We need to check out the music box replacement, see how much it costs, and if we have enough money, we need to buy another one. We don't have much time, so we need to get it right." The plan, as Elizabeth would learn, was all about timing.

"When we get to the house, we get in and get out. If dad is home, we stop. If mom is home, we stop. We don't want her involved."

Patrick knew what he needed to do. He had to find his friend Edward Whirley who would be downtown. Edward owed him for a homework assignment and he was also the scrap connection. He wasn't actually a friend; there weren't really any friends except his siblings.

Patrick earlier approached Edward with the idea on the day he gave him the math assignment. Patrick thought his idea was nearly perfect, a genius idea. Edward, however, was not a genius, hence the need for homework assistance.

The plan was for Patrick to take the scrap to Edward, whose father owned the only car dealership in town, and Edward would say he had started a new business. Edward had no business acumen, but he was charming and all the girls liked him. The father would recognize the wisdom of his son, his prodigy (not a bad thing for the son), and agree to take the scrap in exchange for cash. Patrick was banking on a simple truth: most fathers wanted to be proud of their children, especially their sons. He had seen pride in his father when he brought home his report card filled with A's. Patrick was a little nervous because he had already delivered the homework assignment, however, Patrick held the trump card—his brother James. Edward would not mess with the biggest kid in the eighth grade.

James walked over to Elizabeth, bent down and motioned for her to jump on his back. She wrapped her arms around his neck, and her legs around his middle section. He held onto her legs. He always knew what to do.

"Boy, you weigh a ton," James teased. Elizabeth wrapped her arms tighter around James' neck. "You are as big as a gorilla. How did we get you? Did we go to the zoo?" The only zoo they had ever been to was in Topeka. That was over a year ago and there wasn't a gorilla to be seen. She knew that he was trying to be funny, and it made her smile.

"No, just got lucky," Elizabeth laughed and startled herself. She remembered what the men from the railroad event said. Yes, she heard them and everything they said. She knew that in many ways she was lucky. She was lucky to have brothers like James and Patrick, and a sister like Katherine. She smiled and thought of John. For some strange reason, she wished he was there because she wanted to squeeze him.

Elizabeth put her head on James' shoulder, which Patrick noticed. She hadn't smiled in days. He wondered when she would start pretending again that she was a race car driver, or maybe a member of the Flying Wallendas. He missed those days.

James ran like a racehorse with Elizabeth holding on like it was her last ride. With each stride, a giggle would erupt. Her laughter was contagious. James joined her revelry and let out a laugh, but he didn't know why. He was just happy that Elizabeth was back from the place that had swallowed her up. He stopped abruptly when he reached the fence and looked behind for Patrick and Katherine.

Patrick gestured for Katherine to jump on his back. She simply smiled and cocked her head sideways. He got it—Katherine was taller, and her legs would drag. She then motioned for Patrick to hop on her back. She really thought she could carry him, but he knew what would happen if she tried. He had wrestled his older brother his whole life. Patrick's weight was all muscle and he was solid, but it might be fun to try anyway.

He did a running leap as Katherine braced herself. His landing shook her very foundation. She staggered like her father without sugar. She took one step and they immediately fell to the ground. Caught off guard, Katherine involuntarily laughed. It came out unexpectedly like a cough. The two giggled uncontrollably; it was a moment of relief.

The sight of the twins, the tall and lean, and short and solid, falling on the ground made Elizabeth smile. It was a good day, indeed.

Downtown was a jumping place as cars cruised by with teenagers hanging out windows. It was the Friday before a big game. The local teens also loaded up buses to travel down the road to cheer for their team. The coaches at the high school hoped James would continue to grow and come out for sports his freshman year. The town was small and they could use all the players they could get.

James didn't really like sports that much; he liked working. He avoided the subject of sports when he was chasing pins at the bowling alley. Big boys were always cherished in a town with Friday night fever.

As for Patrick, he liked sports and saw the connection people had with their heroes who could throw, catch, or hit a ball. He liked people much more than James did, but there wasn't any room for that kind of child's play in Patrick's future. Although he went out for the after school team and could keep up with the other boys, he was not big enough to make a career of it. That was clear. He did well in baseball, but his ambitions took him in other directions. He wasn't old enough for a real job like James at the bowling alley, but he knew how to make money. He still liked doing homework for his fellow students, who were usually older and wanted to appear smart, but now he was moving into the big time. He was in the salvage business, cashing in on scrap copper. This could be a gold mine, he thought.

James, Elizabeth and Katherine sat on the curb outside the Five and Dime. It was busy with people coming and going, and the children heard a bell ring on cue when anyone entered the store. They waited for Patrick who was off looking for his business associate.

There he was—Edward Whirley. He looked nervous, his first negotiation.

"Got the cash?" Patrick knew it was pennies, but he wanted to sound grown up; he'd heard the term on the TV show *Dragnet*.

"I was thinking...,"

Patrick had a bad feeling; the kid was thinking. Good gravy. "I want a cut," Edward continued. He must have watched *Dragnet*, too. So the kid was not as dumb as he acted, just lazy. He wanted a cut of the profits like a middleman. Smart, but not smart enough, Patrick thought. He pulled out the big gun.

"Well, I work for my older, bigger brother, and I doubt he wants to share. In the future we could work something out. You already got what you needed with the homework." The negotiations were over. Edward led Patrick around the corner. He reached down behind a dumpster and pulled out a jar with pennies.

"My dad thought that a guy who was as smart as me would really understand the value of a penny so . . . " There it was—five bucks worth of pennies, five hundred pennies. "That's the most he will pay for whatever you brought, and he didn't care how much you brought, not a penny more." So, Edward told his dad. Patrick figured he would. He also figured the father would be really proud of his son for showing initiative.

Patrick didn't want to appear too eager, so he slowly put his hand out. "Okay, now we count." That was not anything he learned on TV.

Joining his siblings outside the store, Patrick reported, "We got five bucks. Well, five hundred pennies, easy to cash in at the bank, but we have to hurry. They close in a few minutes. Kids do that all the time with their piggy banks." He did not believe in piggy banks. Anyone could steal a piggy bank. He kept his money hidden away in the closet.

James slapped Patrick on the back. "How do you do these things?" he asked with delight. Patrick ignored the question. The fact that he had inferred to Whirley during the critical negotiations that his brother was his enforcer would remain his secret.

"I have my ways. You know that kid who pays me to do his homework?" he said, not missing a beat.

"No." James was not surprised with this revelation. He wished he could be as crafty and as smart as Patrick.

"You do someone's homework?" Katherine rolled her eyes, feigning disgust. She was not surprised with the revelation either, and on some level, she was glad he had the skills he had.

"Oh, Sis, I like homework, and he usually gives me a quarter. What's the big deal? I am just helping the kid out."

"Well, for one thing, it is against the school rules." She felt she had to say something.

"I don't believe I have ever read that rule anywhere." There, he was done with that, so he continued on, "His dad owns the car dealership and will take the copper off our hands. He is the middleman. His dad thought he was smart to find someone to do the dirty work. He wouldn't take a cut from his kid."

"Why don't you take it directly to the salvage guy yourself?" She was no dummy.

"Someone might ask me where I got it. Nobody is going to ask old man Whirley."

Katherine finally understood the value in the transaction Patrick arranged, and the fact that everybody won.

"Okay, Patrick, you and Elizabeth go to the bank, Katherine and I will go in and check out another music box." With that, James led the way into the Five and Dime.

Patrick looked at Elizabeth who sat on the curb. "Come on, you'll go with me. You have a sweet smile, when you smile. Do you think you can smile today? Maybe you can act like a princess or something." He then reached down to Elizabeth who was mesmerized. Her focus was on the marquee of the movie theatre across the street. The marquee was empty; a pimply faced youth on a ladder was preparing a new title. Gary Cooper was gone. Of course he was, she thought. Who needs Gary Cooper?

The bank teller, a short chubby woman with tight curls in her hair, peered awkwardly over the counter. Every old lady has tight curls, Elizabeth thought. Stinky stuff made it look like that. She wanted her mother to do that to her hair, but her mother told her that her hair was lovely just the way it was.

"What can I do for you today, young man?" she said with a pleasant smile. She was nicer than Elizabeth expected. She had not been inside the bank before, and she was a little overwhelmed. The ceilings were high and the windows were large. It reminded her of the time they went to Union Station in Kansas City. The building was so big that when she looked up at the ceiling, she became dizzy. They made a connection on the train to Chicago, a big outing for the family. They did it only once and used their passes. That was the one good thing her father did for them. He worked for the railroad, and they got a pass to ride the train wherever they wanted to go. She just wished they could take a train every week. "Madame," he thought he should be formal. He didn't really talk to women other than his mother, or to nuns who were not really women.

The woman smiled again. Who is this little man? she wondered. She liked him immediately. Everyone liked Patrick.

"I have decided to cash in my pennies for dollars." Patrick pulled out the jar of pennies.

"What are you going to do with all this money?" she asked, not really all that interested, but willing to learn more about him.

"It's a surprise for our mother, a music box."

"What is your name?" He knew that might come up and he had a plan.

"James O'Sullivan." Elizabeth stepped back. What was he doing?

"Oh yes, here it is. You have a saving account." She studied him. "It says here that you were born on…"

"June 26, 1943," Patrick said without a beat.

"My, you look young for your age."

"Yes, I am, but I have to say I work very hard after school and save my money." Elizabeth could hardly contain herself. *Yes, he worked hard, but at fooling people.*

"Well, I was small for my age too." There it was—the connection. Small people have to work extra hard. He did have a way of finding what made people click.

"It looks like you have three dollars in your savings account," she said. Patrick smiled. "Yes, I need to take out two dollars, and with my pennies I think we will have enough for the music box."

❧

Elizabeth shot Patrick a quizzical look. Boy, James was not going to like them looting his savings account. Patrick saw the look, and returned one of his own that said, "Don't ask."

The clerk stopped for a moment and stared. "Are you Susanne O'Sullivan's son? I think I have seen you at Mass with your family, but I would have bet there was an older brother?" Her statement was more of a question.

"Yes, there is; that's Patrick." Elizabeth could hardly contain herself listening to her brother's response. She knew Patrick would love being the oldest.

"Your mother has a beautiful voice. We can't wait for her to return to the choir."

"Yes, ma'am. She can't wait to return either." He knew he was twisting the truth. She couldn't wait to return, but she never would. He knew this as fully as he knew his own name, and Elizabeth was enthralled just watching him work his magic.

"What is your name, sunshine?" the teller asked. "Oh, my name?" a moment, then a smile. "Katherine."

If Patrick could do it, so could she. She loved deception.

"How are you today?"

"Fine, just fine, Madame." Somehow the Madame sounded really silly coming out of her mouth and she wanted it back as soon as she said it, but it was too late. The little lady with tightly-curled hair smiled and turned to Patrick. "So you won't be putting any of your piggy bank money into savings today?"

"No, but next time that's what I'll do. When the piggy bank gets full, I put it into savings unless I have something special I have to buy," he said with complete conviction.

"What a very bright boy you are, James."

Elizabeth could have left it alone, but decided not to hold back. She was feeling strong. "Yes, James is." She shot Patrick a knowing look and a smile.

There it was—the replacement. How much would it cost? James was sure they had enough; it had been a productive few days and Patrick had made it happen. Now James needed to follow through, get the replacement, and make the switch.

After getting the money from his brother, James went back inside the store. He picked up the music box again, confirming the $5.00 sticker on the bottom. He smiled and handed it to Katherine. It felt like Christmas to Katherine; she was so happy. James knew there was more to be done, but he was confident. They proved they could work together. Of course, there were a couple of near misses, but things were looking good.

Katherine didn't know much about retail, or how much anything cost. Her mother made their Sunday church clothes and school uniforms. All other clothes were hand-me-downs from the thrift store. They never went anywhere, really, except church and school functions, and the once a year choir party at the director's house after Christmas caroling. She loved that party. It was the best, with eggnog for the adults and hot chocolate for the kids, and lots and lots of cookies.

Christmas at their house usually meant a great meal with all that their mother could cook in one day, great pies, and one present. The children always hoped to get what they really wanted, but some years it was like the gift-giver (the kids knew that Santa Claus was not real from the beginning) got what was available and affordable, and not what was wanted.

Usually, a good day followed Midnight Mass. The music from the night before would still be in their heads.

Their mother would have sung "Oh, Holy Night" as if she were in a great opera house and the church members were wealthy patrons of the arts. The children would have been proud because they were always proud of their mother when she sang. Their father was usually on his best behavior during the holiday, and sometimes even worked on Christmas Eve; he got both time-and-a-half and holiday pay. He didn't mind. He liked making the extra money. The only event of the evening, if there was one, would not be of the O'Sullivan's doing. Someone else's relative, after an evening of merry-making, might come drunk and late to Mass, sit in the choir loft, and then be asked to leave. Today was not Christmas; it just felt like it.

James circled the house and looked into the first floor windows, taking his time. He didn't see any movement. He stopped at the back door where large bushes close to the house provided ample space for hiding. He whistled, meaning the coast was clear. Elizabeth could not whistle no matter how hard she tried, but the boys were accomplished.

Katherine, hunched down close to the ground under the bushes, was given the box to hold and keep safe. Her fingers were like a vise grip. Her fear played a part in cementing her hands on the gift. She would not let go. Patrick and Elizabeth emerged from the bushes and joined James at the back door.

The plan, as James envisioned it, required Elizabeth to go through the kitchen, tiptoe into the living room, and then go up the stairs to check out the bedrooms and bathroom. Elizabeth knew that all the floating practice made her quite light on her feet. She decided to summon her inner ballerina, and walk on her toes. She needed to move slowly up the stairs, and in case there was a mother sighting, simply dance downstairs, go to the window and wave to her collaborators. If her father was home, an image that normally struck terror in her, she would dance very quickly down the stairs, through the kitchen, out the back door, and around to the back of the shed, all the while repeating to herself "only a man." Her siblings would meet her there; but if all was clear, she would be at the front door.

Elizabeth hoped that her once-monster-now-human father would be gone, still working on the car or out bothering nuns, or whatever it was he did when he wasn't home. She didn't need to use her mantra yet. She knew her mother might be in her room reading, something she did whenever she could while John was napping. He would be tired after an excursion to the library and grocery store where, no doubt, he threw a tantrum because he wanted a Tootsie Roll pop. His fits wore him and their mother out, but usually resulted in a happy, tear stained face, and a hand holding a cherry Tootsie Roll pop. His tantrums were legendary.

The plan was: if there was no signal at the window or the door, or no exit to the shed, it meant Elizabeth was caught. She knew she was the best choice for the job because she had a mantra that helped her remain calm. She also had the most experience being a sleuth, as evidenced by the fact that the father never figured out where all his missing items had gone, or who had taken them. Of course, no one knew she had that talent. She looked at James and smiled when given her task—she was ready.

She opened the back door without a sound and crossed the porch to the kitchen (which was empty), and then went into the living room. Next were the stairs, those crazy creaky instruments of notice. It didn't matter how quiet she was if someone was in the house; it was a small house. She would do her best and maybe she'd get lucky. Not a sound, not a note coming from the stair boards; she felt like air, light and worthy.

Once at the top of the stairs, she sprung into a ballet move, something she had seen on the television once. She didn't know the name of the move, but it felt right. She made up the rest of the dance as she went along. Out of nowhere came beautiful pink ribbons attached to soft-sole shoes, fitted to perfection on her feet, which quickly wrapped around her ankles finishing in a bow. The heels of her feet lifted up and she stood on her toes. There she was, on stage, her hair in a bun, her dress with sparkles, and a tight-fitted bodice with a flowing skirt. Her cheeks and lips were cherry red, and a beautiful tiara was placed sweetly on her head. As a ballerina she danced down the hall peeking into each room. She realized that the magic that had disappeared could be summoned back when she needed it to deceive.

Susanne and John contentedly meandered down the street. The library was a success. John liked the story time, and seemed to like the reader—he sat when he was told, and listened intently without moving around. When it was over and time to leave, he did not even object to his mother reaching for his hand. This was a major change for a child who would dash out into the street, just daring someone, anyone, to try and stop him. On this day, somehow he understood his mother needed to hold his hand. His face, his chubby cheeks, his smile, and his laugh lifted her, and in his small little being, he knew.

The last stop was the grocery store. With John at her side, Susanne was limited in what she could carry home. She understood John's good behavior was probably all used up at the library, and the real John would emerge intrigued by something that shimmered, sort of like a squirrel darting around gathering up every nut in sight. Susanne chuckled thinking how Elizabeth had once described him that way, with nuts bulging from his mouth. However, today he seemed amiable to his mother's suggestions. Maybe she could handle John and two bags of groceries.

James started to get anxious and paced. Where was she? Worry covered his face. Elizabeth should be signaling either from the living room that their mother was home, or she should be out the door running for her life if she had run into their father. If the coast was clear, she should be standing at the kitchen door. He looked over at Patrick who shrugged his shoulders, he knew better than to speak. Patrick finally motioned that he needed to go in and check on her. If it was clear, he would make a safe sign like referees do when a base runner slides into home plate. He would use the out sign if someone was there. He would do that from the kids' room.

Susanne grabbed a grocery cart. John was big for the seat, but he liked being up high and she did not want to ruin a beautiful day with a screaming and angry three-year-old. Although his hair was fair, his eyes her eyes, he was not of her temperament. His disposition, when upset, was closer to Junior's. She imagined that her husband might have been a darker version: black eyes and hair, charming, willing to throw kisses when asked by an adoring mother. Yes, there was no doubt that Junior was very much like John when he was a little boy. She certainly loved John like Vena loved Junior so his behavior was overlooked.

She started down the aisle, first milk (they always needed milk); orange juice (they were almost out); bread; and meat. Next, pork chops for dinner with a side of potatoes, mashed with gravy and green beans or maybe corn. The kids preferred corn with a little butter on top. That would not be too heavy to carry home.

Pork chops were 39 cents per pound. She needed several pounds, and that was within budget. She liked that the children, except for one, would eat almost anything, and that child ate almost nothing. Susanne worried that one day Elizabeth would just blow away. Of course for Elizabeth, it would have to be a tornado the size of Texas to take her away, and she would somehow ride it out and land in Disneyland. Susanne smiled, but she did worry after her daughter's sickness last year. Elizabeth ate so little, her small intestines filled up because she didn't eat enough to help push the food through. She was sick for a week and it meant enemas were needed to provide relief. It was a task that Katherine helped with, but hated. Even Susanne hated it, but Elizabeth never said a word. She kept still and silent when most children would have been screaming. Susanne knew that Elizabeth's ability to be somewhere else helped her in moments of distress when the real world was too overwhelming. She worried, but was thankful for her youngest daughter's disposition, antics, and imagination.

There she was, dancing down the hallway, nothing on her mind but the audience that was showering her with applause. Elizabeth dipped slightly to acknowledge their appreciation as Patrick watched with wonder. In that moment she whirled around, stopped short, and smiled.

"It's okay. No one is here."

"It's just that . . . never mind. I need to let James know." With that, Patrick dashed to the kids' room, looked down at James, and gave the slide sign—safe. James, relieved, went immediately to retrieve Katherine.

A hand came through the bush which Katherine took without a word. James indicated for Katherine to head into the house. She stopped and pulled out the mounted dancing ballerina from a box. There were no smiles; they were in a critical stage and it was go time. He took the empty box that he had to get rid of later, and dropped it behind the bushes close to the window, well-hidden. Katherine needed to get into the house, replace the damaged music box, and get out.

James and Katherine went quickly through the back porch, into the kitchen, and then into the curved opening that led to the living room. Patrick went at his station at the bottom of the steps leading up to the front porch. That was the plan—he needed to be ready to whistle the alert if their father was spotted, then make an attempt to distract Junior, if for only a moment. That was his job. James went to the front door to serve as the last barrier.

Elizabeth very calmly stood at the top of the stairs leading to the second floor—her newly acquired stage. She could see James at the doorway, and he looked uncharacteristically scared. Perhaps she should have taught him her mantra, but she knew that James was far too practical to repeat words that held no real meaning for him.

She watched as Katherine went directly to the side table, slid off the damaged music box, and put the new one in its place. Just as quickly, Katherine needed to get up the stairs and back into bed. She had to play sick; her mother would notice.

Katherine reached the top of the stairs and slid by Elizabeth, and out of sight. A whistle from Patrick sounded the alarm and Elizabeth made her way down the stairs.

"Man, man, man, only a man," she mumbled to herself. She was quite steady, moving quickly but purposefully. She glided toward the music box and reached for the ballerina to covet in her hands. She stared at the dainty, dancing girl as her fingers. touched the skirt. She waited for her father to appear.

James watched Elizabeth from his vantage point and wondered what she could be thinking. She seemed to be talking to herself, not exactly a new phenomenon, but still a little strange, especially given the current situation. He felt anxious, but the fear of his father began to fade. He grew stronger and bigger every day. It would not be so easy for Junior to take him down anymore. He understood that.

Patrick sat down as his father passed by, nonchalant. "What's up Dad?" It was better to act carefree. Junior turned, paused, smiled at Patrick and sat down next to him.

"Nothing, son. Done with the car. It's fixed. Need a little rest, poker night. I should teach you to play poker."

"That would be grand, Dad."

Junior stalled, like he couldn't quite get going. He was caught in a moment from his past, a night when he was a little boy watching his father play cards with the railroad gang. He so wanted to be invited into the room, but the invitation never came.

Junior was tired. He stood up slowly and glanced at James as he passed by. He saw for only a millisecond the features of a man from poker nights long past whose cold stare matched his own.

"What are you up to?" Junior was a little surprised to see Elizabeth. She had been scarce the last few days. Undeterred and well aware that her father was coming, she calmly answered, "I was just admiring the beautiful music box."

"It's fragile . . . be careful. I don't want that broken. It's special. Not another one like it around. I had to order it through a catalog." He took the treasure out of her hands and placed it back on the table.

"Susanne," he called. It was automatic when he came into the house, the need to find her.

"She's not here," Elizabeth blurted out. "She went to the store with John. Katherine wasn't feeling well so she stayed home. That's what Katherine told us." She liked having information he didn't have; it was a small victory. She was talking more to her father than she had in her whole life. It was easier for her when she was pretending and acting.

Elizabeth smiled and thought how much she hated him. She would probably go to Hell for it, but maybe not. He was evil. She should get credit for fighting evil like Joan of Arc. She didn't have any armor like the saint, at least none that could be seen, just her wits. She might have to rethink her feelings about Joan. She tore the holy card in a fit and now regretted it.

In any case, the deed of replacing the music box was finished, and she had done her part. She was pleased.

It was all there, everything Susanne needed for dinner. She lifted John out of the grocery cart, preparing to pay. Now, how will I get all this home? she wondered as John wiggled free and started out the door. Susanne turned to chase him, when out of nowhere, two large arms grabbed him.

Susanne giggled slightly, caught by surprise to see Officer Mike out of uniform.

In her very soft voice, she greeted him with, "Thank you."

"You need help getting home?'

Susanne was astonished. Had he no memory of the broken axle event? If she showed up with groceries, and child in hand with Officer Mike by her side, she would pay a price of accusations, taunts, and slaps. Junior might even start a fight with him, although he would have to be drunk to take on a police officer, in or out of uniform. He had never been to jail.

"I would like to help."

Her face asked the questions she could not allow herself to force into words. Her throat was a metaphor for her life, raw and uncomfortable. Could he help her run away, help her pay her bills and keep her children? Could he keep Junior from finding her? There could be no divorce; Catholic women didn't get divorced. Junior would kill her first. Officer Mike's face replied, with eyes cast down, lifting slowly, and smile widening like a naive child. Yes, he thought he could, but she knew differently.

Today she made it home by herself. John cooperated and Mike followed slowly, out of sight. She saw him as she had seen him for years, just out of reach.

Chapter 17

Days had passed without any events, and fall was fast approaching its zenith. By now, Sister Mary Paul gave Elizabeth a wide berth—she saw the fire in Elizabeth's eyes, and she recognized the feeling attached to such a stare. It frightened her because it was newly born, more fresh and more elastic.

The evil eye had come quite naturally to Elizabeth, even without practice. She would likely use it again, but not today. On soft days like this when all was still, a day when there was no school, no brothers or sister in the house and father gone, music hung like ripe fruit ready to be plucked and enjoyed.

Katherine took John to the park and hoped that Elizabeth might come along, but she refused. The boys were down at the bowling alley—James was working and Patrick watching and learning. Elizabeth knew this was a chance to be alone with her mother. Her father was also gone, something about a part-time job. Elizabeth was relieved and happy when she heard the slam of the front door, and the quick footsteps down and out onto the concrete path. She knew his steps; all the children knew his steps. If he got the part-time job, he would be gone more which was perfect.

There was never a time in Elizabeth's life when she thought about who her father was. The fear that seeped out whenever he was around engulfed her. That he would work extra to bring more money into the home wasn't something she knew about. Or, that he attended night school at the state college in Emporia two towns over with the hope that he would earn a degree one day. A major accomplishment for an O'Sullivan. He would be the first. She only noticed when he was around.

She thought maybe when he was young, he might have been handsome, but that was long before she knew him. Why her mother married him was a mystery, but not a mystery Elizabeth cared to visit very often.

Elizabeth loved to watch her mother at the piano. She would like to learn how to play it, but she was aware her mind was way too active for hours of practicing. She wished her hands could one day just know the keys to play the music that made her want to dance. She loved the movies with Ginger Rogers, and she loved to dance. Why couldn't a saint dance? They probably did, she surmised. Her mother was not interested in passing on to her children this piece of herself. The music that filled her senses and every part of her body was conjured from moments that had passed by; she kept them close. There could be no sharing.

Susanne sat at the old upright piano and ran her fingers across the keys as she slowly began to play and sing. Her voice, still small, softly floated out.

Of all the money that e'er I had,
I spent it in good company
And all the harm I've ever done
alas it was to none but me
And all I've done for want of wit
To mem'ry now I can't recall
So, fill to me the parting glass,
Good night and joy be to you all.

Elizabeth began to move too. It was so pleasant, she danced around the room. She wished this moment could last forever, but she knew it wouldn't. She stopped and looked into the kitchen, the place no one escaped from, the dreaded dinner meal. It was where the food was served that kept the family fixed in place, where orange juice was like gold. Why did it have to be that way? Why couldn't there be music, laughter and softness in this house all the time? Why couldn't she wear dresses with full skirts that lifted and swirled when she danced? A place to dream when you were awake, she thought.

Elizabeth loved the song that had been carried across the water into her mother's soul. She stopped dancing and slid in next to Susanne. She knew the words well, so she joined in the chorus. Her voice sweet but not mature. *So fill to me the parting glass. And drink a health whate'er befalls. And gently rise and softly call. Good night and joy be to you all.*

Music filled the house.

Of all the comrades that e'er I had
they're sorry for my going away
And all the sweethearts that e'er I had
they'd wish me one more day to stay
But since it fell unto my lot
that I should rise and you should not
I gently rise and softly call Good night
and joy be to you all
Fill to me the parting glass . . .

Abruptly the music stopped; Susanne sat still. Simultaneously, her shoulders slowly slumped like air leaking out of a balloon. Her fingers were idle, still placed on the ivory keys. Elizabeth turned to face her mother, and lifted up Susanne's right hand to kiss it. She then slowly reached up and ran her fingers across her mother's throat.

Susanne looked down at Elizabeth, turned her head toward the living room doorway and stared. Elizabeth followed her mother's gaze to the doorway where Junior leaned up against the frame with a cigarette dangling from his lips and a beer in his hand. He pulled a drag from his cigarette and exhaled. The last note played lingered and then drifted away. Elizabeth wished she could do the same, but she kept her eyes on Junior as Susanne looked away.

Junior smiled, walked toward Susanne, and stood at her back. He reached down and kissed her head. "My copper penny," he said with distinction and pride as if to say he owned her. Elizabeth, closer than she wanted to be, slid toward the end of the bench. She could smell the booze.

Elizabeth had only one memory of perceived closeness with her father. He picked her up and put her on his lap during a Christmas Day music concert performed in their living room by their mother at his request. For the few minutes she sat on his lap, her heart pounded; she felt sick and wanted to run. Today her heart did not pound and she wasn't sick, but she knew she might need to run.

Junior had a good voice and Susanne would encourage him. She always wanted him happy. Very slowly Susanne's fingers move across the keys but she kept her voice inside. He boomed out the lyrics.

And drink a health whate'er befalls
And gently rise and softly call
good night and joy be to you all
But since it fell unto my lot
that I should rise and you should not
I gently rise and softly call
good night and joy be to you all

There was a churning, an urge to throw something at his head, perhaps the music box. No, that would not do. She and her siblings worked too hard to replace it, that would be too unfair to them. She wanted to hit him, knock his head off and send him sailing out the door, down the street, along the railroad tracks so he could meet a train. She had one in mind for him.

The music was soft as she moved toward the front door while staring at Junior. Why didn't he just leave her alone? Why didn't he just leave?

Elizabeth couldn't stand the sight of Junior's hands on her mother, or that he kissed her. She knew what might make him move away from her mother. She wasn't ready for action, but the moment was here. Perhaps today was the day; he had been drinking—not good for him. Before she knew it, it happened.

"Kiss her now, but you'll hit her later." It was if someone else said those words. They slipped out with conviction, floating like a balloon and then falling like a dead weight. The instant fire in his eyes, distracted with just a flash of sadness, quickly found her. It was a moment when flight was the only answer to Elizabeth's rash and senseless comment.

She dashed out of the house, her heart pounding, her mind racing. How did that get out? It wasn't time, she silently admonished herself. She didn't have a plan, not really, only bits of ideas that floated in her head at night when others were asleep. But she had really done it now, and there was a gathering of clouds, just the right condition for the tornado to appear straight off the Plains, sweeping down, gathering speed, destroying everything in its path.

Watching Elizabeth's quick departure, Junior was now stunned. Susanne stopped playing and closed her eyes. Elizabeth had gone out the door, down the stairs and was a block away before Junior could fully comprehend what just happened. Elizabeth could feel his grasp, but he wasn't there, and neither was she.

A gazelle, she was a gazelle. No one could catch her. She ran past house after house until she could run no further. She stopped and held her side; she was out of breath. She quickly recovered and ran into the distance. She ran as hard and fast as she could, and never looked back. She would never look back again.

Elizabeth walked along a creek, then stopped and took off her shoes. She gently put her toe into the water, pulled it back out and then plunged her whole foot in and back out. It was cold, just the opposite of her father's eyes the moment the words left her mouth and slapped him in the face. She liked the image; she relished it. It must have stunned him, maybe even sent him to his knees, but probably not. He was, however, not expecting it. She liked that too. What now? she wondered.

She might make it work, this idea she had, but she needed to do something. She couldn't go home now, maybe never. She hated herself for being so quick to act. It saved her the other day with Mary Paul, but doomed her today. Maybe she should pray and ask for forgiveness, but really, she wasn't sorry for what she'd said. It was what everybody knew, but no one admitted. It was the ugliness the world didn't want to see. She wasn't sorry, only afraid.

She suddenly realized she was hungry. How many days could she hang out, and would anyone come to find her? She needed a plan and she wished Patrick were there to help her. She also wondered what happened after she left. Did her father hit her mother? Did he decide to take it out on James? As the moments passed her worry became more intense. What did she do? Elizabeth walked and walked, shoes in her hand.

It didn't take Junior long and he was back, out of breath, minus Elizabeth. Susanne was relieved and grateful. What would he do now? Whatever it was, at least it wouldn't involve Elizabeth for the time being. Thank God! she thought. Why did Elizabeth say what she did? It didn't really matter in the end because the deed was done. Susanne needed to think and act in a way to slow him down so she began to play the piano.

Maybe he couldn't deal with Elizabeth right now and punish her for what she said, but he could show Susanne he could take her. That excited him; he was revved up. He knew it was his right. He was head of the household, and he didn't really have to ask, a husband didn't have to. Besides, there wasn't really much asking that went on before, during or after.

He came up behind Susanne and laid his hands on her neck. She didn't pull away, and in her own way, began her mantra by breathing slowly, encouraging by not withdrawing. He had been drinking, but wasn't drunk. He could do the deed. She hoped he kept drinking and fell asleep. She would make sure he had a beer in his hand the moment he was done.

Elizabeth used the rocks to guide herself across the creek to the other side. She stopped and sat down in a sun-lit space. Starring into the sunlight, she blinked, closed her eyes and let the sun shine on her face. She decided to rest a while and just breathe; it felt good to breathe. She could feel the sun, like a great warming hug. She didn't have a name for it but knew she always wanted it. She also knew, and was not afraid to admit, this was not her first act of defiance toward her father. She accomplished that with the first stolen article that belonged to him—a small gesture, but a beginning, with each step a little easier. This time she used words. She lay down and let the sun take her away—she breathed, floated, smiled, and rested.

A group of squirrels, playing tag in the trees, dislodged a branch which fell and landed squarely on

Elizabeth. Startled, she opened her eyes and spied the playful little animals bouncing from limb to limb in the large tree that now shaded her from the sun. The tree was big, but not too big and the branches reached out so she sauntered over to it. She wanted to join the squirrels having their field day, and see if she could match their exuberance.

She reached up, grabbed a branch, then swung her leg over. She straddled the limb, grabbed another branch a bit higher, and hoisted herself into a standing position. She continued her movements, which for her, were automatic, like a recipe. The perfect way to climb a tree, she went higher and higher. The branches engulfed her into darkness and the plan was coming together somehow.

The trees led her out of the wooded area, slowly mixing with other trees that lined the streets. She went from tree to tree along the friendly-looking path with nice houses and equally nice people, or so she suspected. There was always a limb she could reach, and when there wasn't, she eased down, jumped and raced to the next. She felt a bit of remorse for the trees whose limbs weren't quite long enough to reach the next one in the row. She gave them a hug when she departed.

She saw herself as Jane of the jungle, swinging from limb to limb with Tarzan at her side, and her baby, Boy, holding on for dear life. It occurred to Elizabeth that she would never make it to the convent, let alone be canonized a saint. She lied and lied, and on top of that, she wished for her father's death and then stole his belongings along with a holy card which she would never give back. She had certainly fallen far from grace.

Suddenly, she was there. She had made it to his house.

Chapter 18

Perched outside Richard's house on a very strong branch she waited to be noticed, leaning from the tree, holding on with one hand and stretching, trying to see into his house. He was home, she saw him go inside.

She decided to climb higher and look into the first available window where she hoped to see him again. If she did, she could jump straight from the tree into the room. The limb was that close, but there were problems. First, there was a window screen that let the breeze in and kept out bugs, and people swinging from trees like Elizabeth. Second problem, she hadn't a clue what to say when she landed in his room. She thought the best approach might be to act as if it were just an accident when she showed up. "I planned to turn right at the last stop sign and climb the tree around the corner, blah blah blah, but I took a wrong turn."

Just as she leaned forward, Richard's face came into focus, a regular smorgasbord of emotions. Disbelief, fear and adoration were smeared across his face. It was a tough combination to decipher, and before Elizabeth could utter a word, Richard spoke, "Wha, wha, what are you doing here, Elizabeth?"

"Well, I just happened to be in the neighborhood."

"You, you, you are not telling the truth." Good friends didn't lie to each other. It was an unspoken rule that somehow they both knew. Shamed, Elizabeth lowered her head. She had gotten so good at lying, she forgot that lies hurt people as much as they helped.

"Can I come in?"

Richard unhooked the screen and reached for Elizabeth's arm. There was a small overhang just below his window, a perfect step. He guided her through the opening onto a window seat that held her for just a moment before she gently stepped onto a floor of polished wood. It seemed so sweet, so lovely. One bed neatly made, knickknacks on shelves, a small desk with books stacked just so, and matching curtains and bed spread. Cowboys and Indians, horses and mountains covered the walls—a boy's room.

"Is this your room, your room all alone?" Richard nodded. He was not sure what she was doing in his room. He felt self-conscious; it seemed very intimate. He had never been alone in his room with a girl. Well, just his mother, and she wasn't really a girl, so she didn't count. He was an only child. His parents had sisters and brothers, but he didn't, and his cousins lived far away.

"I've done something really stupid." Tears started to well up in Elizabeth's eyes. She quickly looked away, but Richard saw the tears.

Here it was, the moment of truth. Could he be the man his father told him he could be, and the person his mother wished him to be? He was showered every day with compliments meant to erase the stutter that began with his first words. He knew he needed to concentrate, take deep breaths, wait, and with a rush of air make a sentence to help her with whatever it was.

"Well, what?" and instantly he was interrupted. There was a knock at the door. People knocked in this house, surprising Elizabeth.

"Richard, dinner will be ready in a few minutes. I made your favorite, pork chops." Elizabeth could almost hear Richard's mother breathing outside the door. He was used to having his privacy; his mother would not enter the room without being invited in.

"Okay," he replied and quickly looked back at Elizabeth.

"Wait here. I'll be back. I want to help." The words came easy and he meant them. He would not hurry dinner, although his first inclination was to feign sickness and rush back upstairs, but that might provoke more questions. No, he decided it was best to act normal and take his time, enjoy his pork chops, smile a lot, and listen to his parents talk about whatever they talked about on days like today. But this was no ordinary day in an Indian summer—this was the luckiest day of his life.

With a flash, Richard was out the door. His footsteps could be heard as he sailed down the stairs. Elizabeth looked around his room. She was sleepy and hungry. It had been a long day and it would be a long night. Perhaps she could lie her head down for just a moment, and when she did, the sleep came quickly and deeply. She felt safe in this place of cowboys and Indians, horses and mountains.

The boys arrived home early and knew their father would be home soon. The house looked empty; that was strange, and then they heard the noise from the bedroom. It was a small house. It was the awkward sound of adults doing what was whispered about.

Junior was not spent, and he decided to get something to eat. He rolled over as Susanne moved slowly to pick up her dress and undergarments off the floor. Susanne noticed he was calm, happy and incredibly handsome. She remembered those first moments when they met and he swept her off her feet, but that was a long time ago.

The here and now meant she needed to keep Elizabeth out of sight when she came home. She knew Elizabeth would come home; of course, she would come home. But what if she didn't? And there it was like a thunder clap. All these years she wondered when she might be killed from a night of rage. She worried about the children, but it always seemed his anger was meant more for her. He would never hurt John, never even spank him. Katherine was off limits; Patrick was a target on occasion and James most often. Elizabeth was always just a few steps away from incurring his wrath. What if he killed one of them? It had never seemed possible, but the boys were now growing less afraid and she could see it. Elizabeth, however, could be collateral damage.

For the moment, her fear was not of Junior, but for Elizabeth. What would she do and where would she go? Her heart suddenly ached. Elizabeth was probably somewhere in the woods, alone and frightened. She needed to send James and Patrick to look for her when they got home. They would find her, hide her, and she would make sure Junior was distracted.

Junior stood at the door of the bedroom, and out of nowhere said, "I think I might need to paint the house while it's still nice outside. I love Indian summer." Was he asking her or telling? Probably telling, no need to answer.

"What do we have to eat?" It was his way of saying *fix something*. "I want to go check the siding."

Good, Susanne thought. I will fix something—something that he can choke on! Steak and sex made him more vulnerable. It was the second weapon she had in her tool box.

Elizabeth's eyes opened, and there he was sitting at the window seat looking out into the garden below. She cleared her throat and sat up. "How long have I been asleep?" She waited, certain he knew.

"That depends on when you went to sleep," he said as if distracted by the warm breeze that danced through the screen. It was like he was soaking it all up. He looked calm, Elizabeth thought, or at least that was what she thought calm looked like. No one in her house was calm, even when they were asleep.

"I can't know that," Elizabeth said with conviction. She felt rested, stronger.

"What did you do?" He was now talking with ease. He was indeed calm with a happy feeling inside. He felt it the minute he came back into the room and she was still there. He wasn't sure if she would stay.

"Oh that, well I don't know if I can explain. I guess I said something I should not have said."

"You guess?" He was part of her life now. She came to him for help. She couldn't get away with half-truths, even if he liked her half-truths, even if he liked everything about her. She came to him, and he needed to think through it and help her. He knew she probably acted impulsively again. He had seen it at school; he had seen it when he knew she took the holy card; his eyes were always watching her.

"Is it something about Sister Mary Paul?" Richard volunteered.

That was a good guess, Elizabeth thought. She shook her head. What could be worse than Sister Mary Paul in Elizabeth's life? he wondered. He really knew nothing much about her life otherwise. Yes, she talked about her family, and he knew the size of it—large, but not the largest in the parish, just average. He figured the hole in her stocking he occasionally saw was just part of being one of many. Lots of the kids in his hometown had holes in their stockings. He would never wear a pair of socks with holes because there was no competition for socks, or love, or food in his house. The problem must be big to make Elizabeth near tears.

"Where do you live?"

"1828 Ruby, the other side of town," she answered without hesitation. Then with alarm, she wondered, Why did he want to know that?

Needing a distraction, she blurted, "Richard, I'm hungry." She didn't want to talk about her father. It was a mistake to come here. What could he do, really? She needed to get out the window and away; however, the hunger was real, but food had to wait.

"Okay, I'll get something." There it was again, the fluid language. He had refused dessert, eager to get back upstairs. He decided to ask for a piece of apple pie, also his favorite, to take to his room. It was not the usual routine, but allowed on days the parents sat down to watch Lawrence Welk. As he turned away, he looked back. There she sat on his bed. It seemed right that she was there, and she was his friend. She smiled at him and realized his determination to help. Maybe he could hide her here until he knew what to do.

He returned quickly—the pie plan worked perfectly, but Elizabeth was gone. The room was empty. He knew he must find her.

The black headdress of Sister Mary Rose swirled as she walked toward a small figure in the distance. The schoolyard was empty, evening was coming.

"Elizabeth?"

Elizabeth looked up from the swing as Sister Mary Rose moved toward her. The nun's long stride seemed somewhat awkward, the pace of a tall woman. This time, she wasn't floating.

"Hello."

Sister Mary Rose stopped in front of Elizabeth and the swing.

"You want a push?"

The nun stepped behind Elizabeth and pushed her gently, then faster. She pushed her high over her head, and then dashed underneath. Elizabeth swung high into the air, pumping her legs to go higher. Sister Mary Rose stood silently to the side and watched Elizabeth swing until she stopped pumping her legs and merely glided by. The swing slowed down, but did not stop.

"What are you doing here, Elizabeth? It's not a school day?" the Sister inquired.

"Oh, I don't know. I just happened by here." She did just happen by because she had nowhere to go. She couldn't go home, and for how long, she wasn't sure. The church was locked. She had no money for a movie, and Richard had been plenty kind but he could get in big trouble if she were found eating pie on his perfectly made up bed. She wished she hadn't impulsively bolted—one of her worst habits—because pie sounded really good right now.

"I don't think so, Elizabeth." Sister Mary Rose was kind, but firm.

Elizabeth drug her feet and the swing slowed even more.

"I can't go home."

Sister Mary Rose reached out and stopped the swing. "Elizabeth, where are your shoes? It will be dark soon."

Elizabeth got off the swing and walked toward a nearby tree. Ignoring the question, she repeated, "I can't go home." She then scaled the tree. It was small but it put her above Sister Mary Rose.

"You can't stay here. I'll take you home."

Elizabeth looked down at Sister Mary Rose. "Nope, I don't think that is a very good idea."

"Elizabeth, what happened?"

Needing to be closer, Sister Mary Rose scaled the tree. Her habit followed her, getting snagged on a small branch. She pulled and tugged accidentally ripping the hem. Freed, she advanced and Elizabeth moved over making room for the Sister on the small but sturdy branch.

"Do you think I am smart? My mother is smart; she reads all the time. She used to sing . . . I can't sing."

"What are you talking about?"

"My mother doesn't talk much, can't really. She used to talk. She used to sing. Now she only plays the piano. My father took her voice away, but I've got mine. No cat has my tongue."

Sister Mary Rose reached out and put her arm around Elizabeth. "Whatever are you saying? Tell me what happened."

"When? Which time?"

The nun halted; the words stung as if a belt had been laid upon her own back. A reminder of the pain she had seen before in other children with fathers who drank too much, mothers unable to stop them, and children who paid the price.

"You've met my father. Mary Paul told me. You can't help. No one can . . . my mother tried."

Elizabeth looked into Sister Mary Rose's eyes and saw her own reflection.

In a flashback, she was there in the past. It was as if she were out of her body watching. The memories were real and came crashing down. Moments forever seared into her soul.

She hears the sound of the belt hard upon her, indiscriminately connecting with different parts of her body and the inconsolable silence of the witnesses. The sounds turn into images, a replica of a movie.

Susanne jumps on Junior's back, a dropped belt and James and Patrick struggle to gain control. Junior whirls around, throwing the boys to the floor, and quickly grabs Susanne by the neck. He squeezes hard as she gasps for air. James and Patrick attacked him again, pulling at his arms, worried they would not be strong enough. The inconceivable truth that this might be the time he killed their mother, they strengthened their grips and pulled harder.

Katherine takes John in her arms and retreats. He had seen too much; there had been no time. Their father's rage came on without warning. Katherine knew it was because of something Elizabeth said or did. It had been festering, and she wished she had seen it coming and gotten John away a little quicker.

The boys tugged at Junior's fingers, pulling with all their might. They were determined to break his fingers if necessary. Junior's grip finally loosened and he dropped Susanne to the ground. Then, with what was left of his anger, he elbowed James in the ribs causing him to fall to the floor. Just as quickly, Patrick stepped back but slipped and fell also, bouncing his head off the hard surface. Within seconds, Junior swayed, sweated, and losing touch, landed on Patrick. Patrick pushed him off, which was not an easy task. He turned and saw Elizabeth staring with vacant eyes. It was as if life had left her too.

James tended to Susanne while holding his side as she moaned. Patrick heard her sad muffled voice, and for a moment, he was relieved until the sounds of a convulsing father alerted him back into action. Patrick took control, "Elizabeth, he needs juice now!"

Elizabeth moved slowly off the couch, without gesture or the slightest bit of emotion, although the pain from the belt could not be overstated. She went to the refrigerator and got the orange juice. The ritual had begun again: Patrick opened his mouth, Elizabeth poured the juice. Junior would come back to the present, but he would be spent. By then, Susanne was breathing and had opened her eyes. James hovered over her with tears streaming down his face.

"Mom, we need to take you to the hospital. I can drive. I know how. I've watched Dad." They all knew that was a lie. He had to say it to make them all feel better—to pretend for just a moment there was a way out, but there would be no hospital. Susanne moved her head ever so slightly. They couldn't take her to a hospital, too many questions without real answers. Instead, they needed to use the neighbor's phone, but what would they tell them? That their father was in a fit of rage and tried to kill their mother, or would they say she had fallen? The marks on her throat would prove that story false. No, they needed to protect the family. Junior said nothing, his memory of the event long stored somewhere out of his reach. It was better to hope for the best. They decided to wait for the morning, a new day. James and Katherine were in agreement, but Patrick was less inclined, and since he didn't have a plan, he went along.

Reliving those memories, Elizabeth crossed over to a new reality and there was no going back.

As if waking from a deep sleep, Elizabeth looked closely at Sister Mary Rose, the reflection was gone, only dark brown of the nun's eyes. "You can't help. You don't float," she said as she reconnected with the present, leaving the memory of damaged lives behind. She then jumped down and Sister Mary Rose followed with her habit flowing behind, blocking out the light.

Chapter 19

The room was quiet with thoughts frozen in time. When James hit Junior, the sun rose in the West and the world was turned upside down. The North Pole was the South Pole and the moon became the sun. The world had changed.

Susanne and John now huddled in a chair, just feet from the other children. Junior sat at the kitchen table with a box in his hand that held the damaged goods. He found it by accident when he noticed something just under the bushes.

He got up and went into the living room and took the substitute music box off the table. He smashed it to the floor, then put the original one in its place. "It's a good thing I decided to check out the windows before I started painting or I might have missed this little item left behind." He looked around the room, his eyes searching.

"Where is Elizabeth?"

A knock at the door interrupted, and Junior looked over at James as a slight pain in his head reverberated and grew bigger. Where was Elizabeth? Oh yes, he saw her running. His mind was clouded.

"Get the door. I don't feel so good." Without hesitation, James went to the front door as Junior sat down. He opened the door and immediately sent a distress signal to Elizabeth with his eyes which puzzled Sister Mary Rose. Just as Elizabeth turned to leave, the nun grabbed her hand.

"Hello, James."

"Hello, Sister."

Sister Mary Rose stepped into the foyer with Elizabeth just behind her. The hand so perfectly connected to Elizabeth's began to shake. She could feel it; this was bad, and she quickly began her mantra, mumbling to herself. Her mind whirling, she realized Sister Mary Rose was afraid. Elizabeth knew she better get some strength.

Sister Mary Rose's grip tightened around Elizabeth's hand. She surveyed the room, completely quiet. She stepped back and pulled Elizabeth back behind her.

"Mr. O . . . "

"What do you want?" Junior stepped forward, uneasy in his steps. He smelled of alcohol and demanded again, "What do you want?"

"I had hoped . . . I wanted . . . "

Junior tried to focus; he squinted and saw Elizabeth.

"My daughter? My daughter! You want my lovely daughter," he snarled and continued, "the daughter who likes to ridicule her own father, who doesn't respect her father, who needs a good whipping so she can learn?"

Sister Mary Rose, terrified, stepped back. Like a wild animal, Junior could smell her fear and he moved closer. He began to play, as a cat with a mouse, slightly nudging, back and forth with his paws.

"Maybe my family? Oh, no, that would be the war hero . . . he wants my family. You just want my daughter. Well, you can't have her, Sister whatever-your-name-is. She is mine. They are all mine!"

Sister Mary Rose was totally untethered. He made no sense. Junior shoved an object at the nun, and she dropped Elizabeth's hand to receive the empty music box. Now her hands were full, and he could pounce. They all felt it—a new victim was at the ready. The foundation was shifting, his claws ready to slash, his teeth ready to tear. They had never seen him venture out of his family's cage to satisfy his need to hurt. Surely he could not do to others what he had done to them. A boundary would be breached and the world invited to view his wrath. A covenant was broken.

Sister Mary Rose turned quickly and looked at Elizabeth in desperation. She was locked down with fear and her legs became solid pillars. Elizabeth moved her mouth—there was no sound, but her enunciation was perfect. The muted word, "run," flashed its meaning into Sister Mary Rose's eyes, into her brain, down her spine and into her legs.

The good nun stepped back and now her legs were working. The message had been received. The father was out of control. She didn't take her eyes off Junior while she felt for Elizabeth who was already gone. She needed to be like a cat, quiet and quick. She needed to keep just out of his reach.

Junior slurred and his voice slowed, "You see they broke the music box, but they won't tell me who broke it. They don't care about me, no one . . . " Junior turned toward Susanne and pointed. "She knows but she won't . . ."

Before finishing, he abruptly turned and pointed at the children on the sofa. "They hate me . . . she sang like a bird . . . she was my copper penny . . . "

While he incoherently rambled, Sister Mary Rose saw her chance to bolt. She turned just as Junior stepped toward her. The nun's long legs stretched and she was out the door onto the porch. She reached down and found the heavy wooden rosary with beads the size of marbles that circled her waist. Her fingers searched for the cross she held close to her body; it was an instinctual reach for security.

He followed her and lunged forward pushing her off the porch and onto the steps. She grabbed the railing attached to the wooden steps, splinters entered her hand, reminding her that it was all real. She held on just long enough to regain her balance and move down the steps and out onto the sidewalk."Stay out of my house!" he screamed as he descended the steps.

Was he really trying to hurt her? Was he more than a coward who beat his wife and children? Would he really put his hands on a nun? Why should she be spared his anger?

She knew the answer, it was because nuns were special—they gave up having a family, marriage and love. Others thought they were somewhat magical, and deep down she thought it too. A sick thought caused her body to react. And she was embarrassed; however, she was not waiting to find out what Junior might do. He was still just behind her when the door slammed behind him.

Anguished and broken, Sister Mary Rose had never witnessed such anger. As she ran, she saw images of the children. She must get help. She needed to find a house with a light on and hopefully a phone. Not all houses had one. Junior turned and raced toward the front door, but it was locked. He kicked and kicked, then silence.

James and Patrick simultaneously looked toward the kitchen. The door to the back porch—was it locked? It was not. Junior moved quickly through the small yard to the back door, into the kitchen, then through the living room. Like a tiger, he leapt toward Susanne. She jumped up and tried to escape his reach, knocking over a chair. He crashed into the side table sending the music box reeling and crashing to the floor.

Junior caught Susanne's dress and pulled her close. As he went for her neck, James hit him on the side of the head with a book. His swing matched the course charted by a big league baseball player going for a high-one way out of the strike zone. He was aiming for the fences.

One last punch into Susanne's back and she dropped to the floor, but he wasn't done. Junior whirled around and clutched James by the neck. Patrick jumped on his back while Katherine grabbed John and ran into the hallway.

Elizabeth backed into a corner in the kitchen with a full view of the battle. What could she do? She could do nothing unless she could maneuver her way through.

She was not going to wait her turn for a bashing. She had to have her wits; she needed to be ready because she could feel his eyes upon her.

James fought Junior; it was hand-to-hand combat. He pulled up images from his favorite war movies, prying Junior's fingers off his neck, and then punching him in the gut. When the fist landed, a part of James' former self fell away. He never intended to hurt his father. His dreams were of making airplane models, learning about electricity, buying a boat and sailing away. He knew one day he would be a husband, a parent, and from that he felt some affiliation with his father. But who would teach him how to be a man? He landed another punch as tears sprung up and out onto the young face, now red with struggle and loss.

Patrick was on Junior's back, his arm under his neck holding on tight, almost choking him. Junior moved from side to side—he couldn't fight them both. Patrick held on for dear life while James landed one last fist to the stomach. Junior buckled, his breath taken away and down he went. Patrick rolled off and quickly ran into the kitchen. He grabbed a frying pan; he was ready.

James moved to his mother to protect her from a last assault, if there was one. Her eyes were open, but she looked dazed. He grabbed her up into his tense and angry arms, and she grimaced as he loosened his grip.

Junior rose and tried to speak, but his tongue was thick. He blinked, staggered, then collapsed in a chair. No sputtering. No shakes.

Katherine suddenly appeared with John behind her, his face streaked with tears and terror. Patrick stood ready with the frying pan as Junior slowly slid off the chair onto the floor. Patrick kept the frying pan raised as he crept over to Junior and knelt down, then looked into his father's eyes. "Better get him some juice."

The many years of first-aid had hardened Patrick to distress. His command was half-hearted, but real.

He looked at Elizabeth who could see him through the kitchen door. She stared at her brother with cold eyes and no expression. She didn't move.

"Elizabeth, get the juice." The same words, the same plan, always to save the man who brought such madness into their lives. Elizabeth paused. She saw the chaos: the broken side table and music box, James with rage in his eyes, Katherine with fear painted on her face, and John in tears. Patrick was focused and wanted to finish the business of securing Junior and attending to Susanne. It was a scene she had witnessed too many times.

Elizabeth looked at her mother, and in a moment, an unspoken request was made. Feelings were sent through the air, picked off and swallowed. How does she want me to help?

Without compassion, Elizabeth watched Junior. A realization became a river and broke through, and her face became a valley of tears. She was ashamed and conflicted. Fleeting possibilities raced through her mind of a life that could have been, but never was, and of a father missed.

Elizabeth stood and walked with a deliberate gait around the corner, and out of sight of the other children. She opened the refrigerator door and pulled out a pitcher of orange juice. The pitcher was nearly empty, but there was enough. There was always just enough. She opened the cupboard and found a small glass. She slowly poured the juice into the glass. Yes, there was definitely enough, even with any spills, to stop her father's reaction and restart their tragic lives.

She felt an intense tugging, a wish that her life was different, that there were Gary Coopers who showed up and saved the day, nuns that really floated, and saints that winked and danced off the face of a holy card right into her hand. But that was not her life. Her life was here in this moment. She knew she wasn't strong like James, or as clever as Patrick, certainly not as caring as Katherine, and she didn't have the charm of John, but now she held the fate of the family. They couldn't see her, and they would never know what she did, but she would know for the rest of her life. Her stomach churned, her insides screamed—loud unrelenting fear smashing every cell in her body. She needed to find relief. She must survive.

A voice from the other room interrupted her thoughts, "Elizabeth, now!" Patrick's voice was desperate.

As if on cue she raised the glass to her mouth. The moment the sweet juice touched her lips she knew there was no going back. Her hands were shaking—they had not caught up with her mind that was resting, and suddenly a calmness came over her, the hands were still. She drank the rest of the juice, never spilling a drop. Then, through the stains of salty tears that covered her face she saw a figure standing at the kitchen window. He apparently followed her, and now he knew her life and who she was. Elizabeth mouthed, "Richard, help" and in a moment he was gone.

She quickly decided to do her best impression of a lost and terrified child. Although she was no longer lost or terrified it would not be hard to pretend. She'd felt that way most of her life. She just needed to pause for a moment and collect herself because she had an audience to convince. The watchful eyes were gone.

Elizabeth stepped around the corner from the kitchen with the empty glass causing a collective gasp. Patrick's mind raced, Where had the juice gone? There was plenty this morning when he sneaked into the kitchen and took a swig.

Richard shook and his heart was racing. He needed to get help, but where? How? What would he tell his parents? Why had he gone out the window to follow Elizabeth, nearly falling to his death? He wasn't very good at climbing, or anything athletic, really. He could run, but he was not fast. He was clumsy. As the questions surfaced, he slid out of the bushes.

There she was, Sister Mary Rose. The crazy father threw her out. He should have followed her, left when she did, but he couldn't leave Elizabeth.

He watched as the nun went from house to house. She knocked as hard and as fast as her fist allowed. No one answered. Oh yes, she remembered, bingo night. No one would be home, but then a porch light came on and a woman cautiously opened the door. Richard couldn't see her face, but he was sure she would be confused as to why a nun was at her door. He could hear Sister Mary Rose's voice, "Help, call the police."

"Well, Sister, we don't have a phone. Maybe next door," the woman offered. Sister Mary Rose flew off the porch and straight to the next house. The woman stayed on the front porch, watching and reflecting on other nights at 1828 when the noise came, crashes were heard and the police were never called.

Sister Mary Rose pounded harder at the second door. Richard's heart was racing, his head throbbing. Would she get in? Oh please, let her in! he silently prayed. The fear was overwhelming and he felt a warm rush of water run down his leg. As the door opened and Sister Mary Rose stepped through the threshold, she sensed something. She turned and there was Richard. Terrified, he couldn't move and he looked down at his pants. Relief had come.

Chapter 20

Officer Mike rushed into the house. He found Susanne conscious, groaning and lying on the floor. The house was a mess with overturned furniture and a smashed music box. It was a peek into this family's life.

A slight smile came to Susanne's face then a grimace. Officer Mike stared and retreated to a time long passed: Graduation, enlistment, and a train station full of parents and girlfriends. At that time, he hoped Susanne would somehow magically appear with the other girls, and she did. She threw him a glance, not a smile of longing or regret, just a glance with the hint of a smile. She liked him, but nothing more. He held onto the memory of that smile through the years he spent killing and saving lives, but today the smile was one of appreciation, and he could see it for what it was. A reckoning, with the future that did not have Susanne in it, came over him. She would be a good friend, the sister he never had, and he would care for her, but it would never be more. At his core, he knew the glances she threw his way were never anything more than kindness. Now he must shed the past and deal with the present.

The children huddled together next to their mother, Elizabeth in the middle, surrounded by her siblings with John on Katherine's lap. A small empty glass sat on the kitchen table, a lone piece of evidence, the non-familial witness to the event. Elizabeth kept her eyes on it. The domestic destruction was as real and cruel as any battle.

Junior, was unconscious but breathing; he was in trouble. Why were the children so still? Why were they watching? What happened? All were questions to be answered, but there was no time—they must get him to the hospital. Where was the ambulance? The call came in from a neighbor after an out-of-breath nun showed up at her door. Sister Mary Rose's only words were, "O'Sullivan's, ambulance." The dispatch knew the family and the address. There were plenty of calls for a wandering little boy, but never an ambulance.

Officer Mike picked up Junior like a rag doll (he was lighter than he looked), and scanned the room. The ambulance could also take Susanne to the hospital; it was on its way. She was breathing and conscious, and his training told him to triage.

Elizabeth and Patrick were tied together with anxiety, their arms neatly at their sides, sitting on hard and uncompromising metal chairs at an equally cold table. Katherine sat next to Patrick, off to the side, only inches away with John in her arms. He wiggled, a three year old with an agenda, which included the need to escape the arms that bound him and explore this new place, the police station.

Katherine wished she had brought a book to read to him. A book, her salvation, would have taken her mind off their circumstances and kept John quiet. Her stomach was queasy and she wanted to throw up. There was no way to explain the situation. She needed to leave that up to someone else, probably Patrick. The truth was that she rarely spoke to anyone other than her siblings, and she talked to them a lot. She discussed matters with them which she held back from others. She was still kind to her classmates and occasionally spoke to them when they played Jacks. She also spoke to her mother some, but never her father, and only if required to a nun. Her stomach churned more.

The interrogation room was bland, stuffy, an afterthought. The door had a small window just big enough for the curious people wanting to get a view of the kids. The news spread quickly from the mouth of the neighbor, echoed, and was shared from house to house. There was talk of strange goings-on at the O'Sullivan's—police rounding up kids, mother taken by ambulance. The father was saved by the fast-acting Officer Mike. Oh, how Junior would have hated that!

Officer Mike came into the room and sat next to Elizabeth. "When James comes back we'll be done. He needed to visit the restroom." The children didn't say a word, no acknowledgement. Silence was their friend; it had always been their friend. Words didn't work because no one listened. Silence was always there. Of course James had to go to the restroom, Elizabeth thought, he was probably sick as a dog.

James looked less in stature than normal. Exhaustion occupied his face as he walked into the small chamber with an older officer, a captain on a small team of law enforcement. James looked over at Elizabeth, then took his place next to Katherine. They were all in order.

In a small office were two desks, a small stack of paper, and two chairs. Officer Mike sat down and pulled out some paper while Captain Parker settled into a chair.

"You been on the force for a while now," not really a question. "Doesn't this whole incident seem strange?"

Officer Mike was taken aback; he wasn't expecting any questions. They had both been at the house and the Captain knew there was an altercation. The father attacked his children and his wife. What more was there to say? No, it didn't seem strange. *What was he getting at?*

"I don't know what you mean." Officer Mike was worried about Susanne and wanted to check on her. Her injuries would take a while to heal, but the doctor said she was lucky. A reoccurring thought interrupted;

it wouldn't go away, lodged like a piece of meat stuck in his throat. It hurt and made it hard to breathe. Did Junior permanently damage her throat? He imagined Junior's hands squeezing Susanne's neck with the right amount of pressure to push out a raspy sound. Junior's actions must have taken away her beautiful singing voice, and left the woman almost empty. A quick cup of regret poured into his consciousness. He could have stopped it if only he had listened to Elizabeth. He should have helped.

The captain took him away from his musings. "It's just that they are all telling the same exact story, almost rehearsed, like something out of the Twilight Zone. The father gets all worked up over some music box, the nun shows up with Elizabeth, gets thrown out, then he starts swinging at people, grabs his wife, goes for her throat, the boys jump on him, he falls down, has an insulin reaction . . . and they don't have any juice in the house. They don't have a phone; they panic. They are afraid to leave their mother."

"Yeah."

"Just kinda funny—the exact same words."

Officer Mike finished filling out the forms and handed them to the Captain who looked them over. "So?"

The older man continued, "So, I just think it's funny. I am not saying that's not how it happened. The nun told us the guy had been drinking and was diabetic."

Officer Mike's voice cracked, "I've known Susanne my whole life. Nothing funny about this. I understand your concern, but really, what's the point? If he survives he won't be the same – that's what the doctors say." Then, with anger, he let his emotions flow. "Actually, I guess the point is that if those kids had anything to do with their father's circumstance, they had a right. He is a bully, a monster. No one helped them. Susanne hasn't even recovered from the last assault."

"What assault?"

What could Mike say? That he had seen the small lingering remnants of bruises on her neck one day as she looked through the glass at the bookstore, and that he watched her just out of sight? After that one time, she was gone, vanished. Mike looked for her, but there was no Susanne walking to the grocery store, or playing with John in the park; and no beautiful, timid smile and sweet eyes to greet him. Each day he awoke and took to his cruiser, riding around town and down her street, hoping. He wanted to see her again even though he knew he could never touch her hand or have anything but a chitchat if they happened to meet on Main Street. He felt selfish wanting her to be around because he knew, from the sadness he saw just under her sparkling aura, she needed to go, run away and disappear.

"There's no record of another incident. This is the only time the police were called. We can't do anything about that. She should have called the police before."

Officer Mike repeated again, "They don't have a phone." He knew that even before the event. He had looked through the telephone book, but didn't find anyone named O'Sullivan.

"Most of these cases are caused by the woman. She said something, the guy who had a beer or two whacks her and she forgets about it that night."

Officer Mike was shocked. They were both at the house, and it was plain this wasn't a small domestic dispute.

His face was red, tears welled up, and he choked back any remaining thoughts. He was ready to explode. He knew he needed to calm down, but it was there and he had to say it. "No one needs to smear them." He stopped; he was speaking to the Captain. His army training (never far from his reach) had taught him that talking back to a superior was off-limits. "I'll go by and visit with Sister Mary Rose. She is really the only witness not in the family." *That should satisfy the Captain,* but he had things to do and the first was to check on Susanne. It was not entirely unreasonable for the first officer at the scene to have follow-up questions. He also planned to use the same excuse to visit Sister Mary Rose. If anyone asked, follow-up is what he would tell them.

He also didn't want to think what he was thinking: Here is Susanne's chance. What will she do if Junior survives and is disabled? What if he survives and faces charges? He realized Junior would never go to prison, but maybe he might die. That would be good. Either way, disabled or dead were both good options, one more workable than the other. He was ashamed, but happy for Susanne, and happy won out. No matter what happened, it was still her chance to escape. He needed to take one more look in on the kids. The good nuns offered to house the children until Susanne came home.

Officer Mike walked by the interview room. He looked in at Elizabeth and their eyes met. He paused, then continued down the dimly lit hallway. His walk slowed again before stopping; Elizabeth's voice was in his head. *"That's what we give our dad when he has a reaction. Juice. We always have enough juice at home, always, and we know exactly what to do. It's important to do it fast, no lollygagging around. We always have enough juice at home, always, and we never panic."*

A shock of recognition went through his body. They would have had juice, and they knew what to do. They would never panic because it was routine. They were lying. He felt a chill, acknowledging something not easily explained. They were covering up, but for whom? Susanne? No, she was a victim. Who, which one? They could not have planned this.

He stopped cold and it hit him like a ton of bricks. He knew what happened. He saw her eyes—the gateway to a soul—not quite of this time and place, a contradiction of sweet and detached, welcoming and hard.

He inadvertently made the case for further investigation, providing the motive, and he had made it to his supervisor. How stupid could he be! If he could get Sister Mary Rose to bring assault charges—Junior did put his hands on her when he threw her out of the house—then everything else would fall into place, and the kids would be left alone. No one would question a nun. He didn't really care who was responsible for the coma.

Chapter 21

Elizabeth envisioned the internal workings of the convent and was sure that it was holy, magical, and filled with incense and chanting. It was none of those things, more creepy than not, she realized as she came through the back door close to the kitchen. The place was as bare as her house, not like the sanctuary at church with beautiful murals, stained glass windows, honorable statutes of saints, and the larger-than-life crucifix.

The children were placed at the convent and given cots to sleep on in the basement until their mother could come home. After school, they were encouraged to play at the school grounds adjacent to the convent, that was Sister Mary Rose's idea. "These children have been through a lot and they need to play," she said. Mother of the House had her doubts, but Sister Mary Rose was persuasive. Sister Mary Paul was silent on the issue and the other sisters sided with Sister Mary Rose. The nuns took turns making dinner, did small chores and prayed. It was good for Elizabeth to see what the life of a nun was really like, and she was glad she had given up becoming one.

Once the dinner bell rang, the nuns came quickly to the dinner table. They ate and then retired to their quarters to read and pray. The children played until Sister Mary Rose called them in with a bright and happy smile. She stayed close to them, especially Elizabeth. She knew there were unresolved feelings between Sister Mary Paul and her.

Dinner wasn't much, usually soup and bread, and not nearly as good as Susanne's cooking. Breakfast was not much better, and lunch was just a sandwich. Elizabeth wondered how Mary Paul stayed so plump. After dinner, the children cleaned up and did the dishes. They thought that was fair, and they were used to doing that particular chore at home. After or during the clean-up, there was no horseplay. They took their places at the table and did their homework. It was an easy time, but also a lonely time.

They weren't afraid of the footsteps on the stairs, but Elizabeth knew the Penguin, and knew she would eventually show up and attempt to get revenge. She could also feel the presence of the monster-turned-man who had been the center of their lives, and who at that moment, was in a hospital bed. Elizabeth sensed his struggle, trying to wake up, trying to remember, trying to lift his arm, or move his lips to form words. "It will take time," the social worker said. A nagging feeling lay just below the surface, sadness and shame. She was responsible.

It was arranged, if the children stayed for more than a week, a member of the Kennedy clan would come and get their clothes and wash them. It seemed the nuns, most expressly the Mother of the House, didn't think that the good sisters wanted to look at or touch the boys tighty-whities, although most of the sisters had brothers with "nasty drawers."

The children never were far away from their mother, only during times when she was sent to the tuberculosis hospital, but that had been a long time ago—long before John, and they were all very young. Not being with Susanne was strange and made them feel empty. John was taken to foster care, and they all longed to see his fat face and reckless behavior. They worried about him, knowing that it all made no sense to the little guy. He would miss Katherine as much as he missed his mother, maybe more. Each child was half a person without John.

The basement was dank and dark. In the past, she might have thought of it as a dungeon—a place that Joan, as in Joan of Arc, was confined. She started thinking of people, and even saints, by their first names. She missed Joan, but she was gone now. Joan suffered during her incarceration and was burned at the stake; there was nothing magical about that, she thought. She was rash when she tore the holy card in half and left it on the floor of her hideaway, all alone. Maybe there was a way to go and get it with no one in the house.

Elizabeth knew it was important to have her wits about her, in case that vile and very mean human Mary Paul, decided to show up. The kick on the shin could not have been forgotten; indeed it had not.

Their lives at the convent became routine after just a day or two. For Elizabeth, school was school. Sister Mary Paul was reserved, her eyes always resting for just a moment on Elizabeth.

It was hard for her to make a connection with Richard. Girls didn't normally talk to boys on the playground, and there could not be any passing of notes, too dangerous. She saw Sister Mary Paul's watchful eyes, but she needed to talk to him. That seemed strange—it was like they had some sort of intimacy. They'd shared secrets and he now knew her better than anyone else on earth, including her siblings.

She tried to get his attention for two days, but he wouldn't look at her. Kids had been talking. Elizabeth couldn't care less that her classmates gave her a wide berth. They didn't have the facts, but knew that something bad had happened at the O'Sullivan's. In fact, the whole town was talking, but not Richard. Thank goodness for that, even though she wasn't sure he really understood what happened. He saw the juice, her trembling hands, the fear and the tears, but did he understand what happened? What she had done, and why she had done it? She wasn't a bad person. If only she could make sure he knew that. Her thoughts were moving round and round, like revolving doors on the front of a large department store she had seen in an old movie.

At night, the chatter that had once been the mainstay of the children when they dissected their day, was replaced by silence. None of them wanted to talk about what happened that resulted in their temporary stay at the convent. They all had their suspicions about that night, and Elizabeth was in the middle of each theory. They would each revisit and rewind the night over and over before they found sleep. Elizabeth was the only one who had closed the door.

Katherine, who was most concerned about the souls of her siblings, asked herself: Why wasn't there any juice? She asked that question daily, even hourly. Elizabeth was the last one in the kitchen and the thought caused Katherine to freeze. How did she let this happen? What could she have done differently? But in the end, it was done and everything had changed.

Patrick knew there was juice, and he could see that Elizabeth was play-acting when she came back into the living room holding the empty glass. He knew her that well. Where had the juice gone? Had his mother done something? Although he wished she had, he knew she hadn't. Maybe James or Katherine? Not likely. Wouldn't it be great, he thought, if John had somehow made it into the refrigerator and drunk the juice? He was innocent, just like babies who died before they could be baptized and went to Purgatory. They were all guilty by omission, but only Elizabeth would carry the burden. He felt sick to his stomach.

James knew he wasn't very good at understanding people, but how could it be anyone but Elizabeth? He should have taken his hands and choked his father, or bashed his head with something; his own anger was that big. It was that simple for him. It was his job and he had failed.

Elizabeth had spotted a dust covered Encyclopedia Britannica set sitting in a bookcase next to the stone basement wall. Right before the lights went out Elizabeth would pick at random a volume and commence to read. She didn't much care what she read. It was a way to avoid the sad eyes of her siblings and help her forget where she was and who was steps away in the nun's quarters waiting to pounce.

It was night and the basement was not warm, nor cold, but blankets kept it just right. Elizabeth was hungry. A bowl of soup and a chunk of bread did not keep her fed. She could not imagine how James was holding on. He ate like a horse. The whole setup, although it could be worse, was not much to Elizabeth's liking. She suddenly had an idea—a quick trip down the row of trees that lead to Richard's house might result in food. At least she hoped he was still her friend. She had to find her pedal pushers—laced soft-soled shoes—and short-sleeved shirt in the dark, which was not an impossible task, but certainly not easy. She must not wake anyone.

It was time to go. Everyone was asleep, nothing stirring in the house. She looked at her siblings, each in deep sleep and relaxed. She managed to quietly move several boxes directly under the window so she could step up and push the window screen out. The space was small, but so was she, and she was out of the basement window in a flash.

She sprinted across the lawn, a silhouette from an Olympic dash—knees flying up to greet her stomach with arms at a 90-degree angle. Acting in tandem with her arms, her legs landed hard on the ground stretching her torso. Her heartbeat kept pace with the rhythm of her feet. She was scared, but it was a different kind of fear—her adrenal gland fired sparks that kept the anxiety just at bay. A full moon acted as a floodlight and she hadn't counted on that good fortune. It was good to have a beacon, like patriots in the Revolutionary War—*One if by land, two if by sea.* History came in handy, and she liked thinking of herself as a patriot, especially now when she tried hard to avoid fantasy. That was child's play, but she felt exhilarated, ready to scale the tree just feet from Richard's bedroom.

She wondered how she might get him to open the window. He would be asleep; that was the concern. She wasn't afraid of the darkness that surrounded her as she moved under the canopy of trees lining the street to his house. She was an expert runner and soon found herself again on the tree limb inches from Richard's window. Good, she thought. The window was open, screen in place. Stretching, she used the end of the tree limb, the thin and willowy part, to gently scratch like a cat swiping at a fly. She saw a lump in the bed moving. Now, in a quick soft voice, she called, "Richard." More movement. Maybe just a bit louder, she thought. "Richard!"

Richard sat up, confused. "What, what time is it?" his voice clear, unrehearsed and easy. Who was saying his name? He wondered. After his eyes adjusted, he saw a figure just outside his window, but he couldn't make out the features. The moon's light landed on the back of the silhouette. The person was small, with hair that was long for a boy, but perfect for a girl. Recognition! Who else could it be? His heart jumped a beat as he closed his eyes, shook his head, and slowly opened his eyes again. She was still there; this was no dream.

"Hi Richard," she said in a nonchalant voice like she was passing him on the street. Of course, it was

Elizabeth! Who else would show up outside his window in the middle of the night and act like it was the most ordinary thing to do?

"Hi to you, too," he replied acting as if it were just another day in the life of Elizabeth. He knew her life in recent days had been anything but ordinary, even for her.

"I was wondering, well . . . I'm really hungry. They don't feed us much at the convent." That was not totally untrue, but she needed to talk to him and find out everything he saw the other night

Sparse servings of food seemed reasonable and appropriate for a convent. Richard wondered if she wanted to come in or sit out on the tree limb and eat whatever it was he could find. A tidal wave of astonishment came over him. Good gravy! What was he thinking?! He never, ever, entertained the idea of sneaking into the kitchen to retrieve leftovers for a visitor sitting in a tree outside his window. Come to think of it, he never sneaked into the kitchen late at night for a snack, even for himself. His family had rules. You ate your dinner, had dessert, and no late-night snacks. "Not good for your digestion," his mother said.

Then, because he was getting used to strange occurrences when it came to Elizabeth, it only slightly dawned on him this was the second time she had come looking for food. Would she stay or disappear and force him to follow her like before? Life, with a friend like Elizabeth O'Sullivan was not easy.

As Richard tiptoed down the hall, he realized that the stakes were higher this time. If his father got up to go the bathroom and ran into him, what would he say? The last time he went on a mission hunting for food for Elizabeth, he could legitimately say he wanted the dessert he had passed on during dinner. Maybe he could do a fake sleepwalking routine. He heard stories about people who walked out of their houses during the night and found themselves on a park bench in their pajamas. He finally decided not to worry about that now, or why Elizabeth was outside his window. He had a job to do and he felt important.

Creeping along, he heard a loud snoring sound coming from his parent's bedroom as he passed by, which was a good sign. There were advantages to being an only child and this was one of those times. There was no one else to worry about. They didn't even have a dog although he often hoped one day he would come home from school, and there would be a dog waiting for him. A dog would be a spectacular addition. They didn't look down on boys who stuttered, but a pet would never happen in this very clean house. Perhaps that was what drew him to Elizabeth. Her life was messy, and he had seen the worst of it.

The stairs, shiny hardwood, were sturdy but not so old that they bellowed when he stepped on them. Clear. Now he was heading into the dining room, a space filled with the ever accommodating table and chairs, a buffet used for special occasions when his parents entertained people from the bank, and a china closet. He rounded the table heading straight to the kitchen, stubbing his toe and wanting to scream out, but he held back. Holy heck that hurt! he thought.

At last, there it was—the refrigerator, fairly new with a light that appeared as the door opened. He never experienced the light in this manner, kind of spooky, but he had to move fast. *Aha! Leftovers!* Although his mother was very frugal, she cooked like she had ten kids.

Macaroni and cheese, one of his favorites was good hot or cold. He could make her a sandwich too—peanut butter and jelly, or bologna, but which one? Okay, both, he decided, but how could he do that in the dark? Well, maybe no sandwich. *Oh, here it is...chicken!* He found what he was looking for; *perfect!* The next day, his mother would be sure there were three pieces of chicken left over, and not two. If asked, he would need to lie about taking a piece—a second time lying for Elizabeth. He was fairly confident it would not be the last if he intended to keep her as his friend. That was a small price to pay. He had changed, and it started the moment he threw caution to the wind. His father always told him to go for the gold, and to be all he could be. Well, apart from a lie or two, he was being the "all" he could be, he thought.

He was better at working in the dark than he could ever imagine. He found a plate, a fork, and even a napkin. Now, up the stairs without a sound. I can do it, he kept telling himself. The moon that led the way for Elizabeth earlier was just as helpful for Richard. He felt a calm come over him. He was doing a good deed and nothing could strike him down.

There she was, with perfect posture, sitting on the branch that was now her throne. That's how he saw her, more like a princess. He put the plate of food down on his desk and took a long hard look at the figure behind the screen. She was definitely out of place, sitting on a limb outside his window, especially late at night. That wasn't normal, but in the world he had entered, it was becoming more real and more expected.

She stepped on the overhang like the last time while his hand unlocked the screen as he gently lifted it out toward Elizabeth. She pulled it over her head, ducking just underneath. She felt for Richard's hand and found it waiting as his second hand attached to her forearm. He wasn't intending to let her drop. She stepped through the opening as he guided her up into his room, step by step, like moving up a ladder. "Oh, boy. What a day!"

She was actually going to act like this was a casual visit, but he knew better.

Richard gave her the shush sign to be quiet and Elizabeth nodded. She forgot for a moment where she was, and what she was doing. It was because of the excitement of the journey, the disregard for all things scary.

"I got you chicken, and macaroni and cheese. Leftovers. Hope you like them."

"My favorite, thanks." She smiled as the moon shined on her face. He looked away, embarrassed. He told himself it was just Elizabeth, nothing to be embarrassed about. But he felt special and happy. He knew he meant more to her than just macaroni and cheese.

She dove in, relishing each bite and it didn't take long before the plate was clean. Richard marveled at that, but it made him a little sad. He wished she weren't so hungry. He wondered what she would do each of the next many nights she spent at the convent.

"How long will you be at the convent?" he whispered. He doubted she knew, but someone had to talk. He couldn't just sit and stare at her because she might leave. What a thought—he was going to carry the conversation! But it was easy to talk with Elizabeth.

"Well, that depends on what happens to my dad. You met him, sort of, didn't you?"

How should he answer that? He witnessed the ongoing scene from his vantage point outside the house in front of two windows, right at the intersection of the living room and kitchen. He saw Elizabeth move from the living room into the kitchen, and the father lunge at and eject Sister Mary Rose. He remembered quickly retreating under the hedges as the father sprinted to the back of the house. He also saw the faces of the children when the father entered through the back door. He saw him pass by Elizabeth and go for the mother. He saw the terror and would never forget what he witnessed. He saw Elizabeth drink some juice. He finally decided to confess, "Elizabeth, I didn't meet your dad. I saw your dad through the window."

"You know what I mean." It was getting really hard to dance around the truth, and especially to him, her one true friend.

"Yes, Elizabeth I do."

Okay, an opening, she thought. "You could see what he was doing?"

"Yes, it was hard not to see what he was doing."

"By the way, why were you there?" She was truly interested.

"I came back to my room and you were gone, and . . . " Now it was his turn to dance around the truth a little bit. What could he tell her? No, he couldn't tell her why. "You show up, tired, hungry, and talking about stuff that doesn't make any sense, then you ran away. It just seemed I should find out what I could do to help. I am going to be an Eagle Scout one day, you know." Elizabeth was impressed and liked the way Eagle Scout sounded, but what was an Eagle Scout? She didn't have an idea. There was a lot to this kid.

What she wanted to know was if he saw her drink the juice. "I was a little flustered," Elizabeth explained. She was stalling.

Richard thought back to that moment and she didn't seem flustered. She may have been a little scared, but she was definitely not flustered.

"When did you get to the house?"

Why did she care? He admitted he saw her crazy father. She went in the kitchen, drank some juice, and that was strange, but Elizabeth could be really strange. He saw her and she saw him. He ran to get help, saw Sister Mary Rose and heard her pleading with a woman, "Please help. Call the police to the O'Sullivan's." He remembered that clearly. He also thought Sister Mary Rose saw him, but he didn't say anything and neither did she. At that point, he got scared and ran home. He hoped the nun missed the accident when he wet his pants, but it was the most frightened he had ever been in his life. What would Elizabeth think of him if she knew? The shame he wanted to ignore was slowly growing and changing into anger. He suddenly wanted to lash out at her for putting him in that position. She could be exasperating.

The long pause was a fertile field for her anxiety. Elizabeth was trying to figure it out, but it was a struggle. Maybe she should just ask him if he saw her drink the juice? No, that wouldn't work. She was getting scared again, and her heart was racing. She thought she was done with being afraid and she needed to get away.

"I have to go before they figure out I'm gone. They get up in the night a lot. I can hear them walking around." They are probably searching for food too, she thought. Yeah, that's how the Penguin stays so square. She eats at night.

"What about your dad? What is going to happen?" It popped out of his mouth like a kernel of corn that flowers when heated.

A gallon of cold water seem to land on Elizabeth, poured from the most unsuspecting of characters. She shivered. "I don't know. I can only hope." The truth at last—they both knew what she meant.

He realized the conversation was finally over. So, that's why she came; it was all about her father.

Richard didn't react; he was tired. The lack of sleep, mixed with moments of high anxiety, caught up with him. He opened the screen and watched as Elizabeth scaled the tree like an African monkey he had seen at the Topeka zoo, and she was every bit as quick. Eventually he needed to tell her the truth, but not now. He ran away after what he witnessed.

Each nun was awake, rooms apart and sitting up looking out the window. The bright moon caught their attention and drew them to the view. Forces with equal strength were plotting. Scalp caps were off exposing hair as different as the women, one straight and thin with too many years forced in place, the other curly and trying to reach out.

Sister Mary Rose wanted to help the sweet children in the basement, especially Elizabeth. But how? There was a convent in St. Paul. Maybe they could help too? Officer Mike suddenly popped into her head, the handsome Officer Mike. Where had that come from? She shook her head to try to erase the image that invaded her thoughts. Why was she thinking about him? Okay, maybe he could help. She could almost shake his hand; he seemed so real.

She was lucky when she got tossed out of the house by Elizabeth's father, only her pride took a hit. She'd admonished herself many times since that night. She thought that facing her fears was enough, and she could somehow talk her way through the mess that occurred that night. Elizabeth warned her, and it was a good lesson in humility. Maybe she should be thankful for what she learned, but it should be just that—a lesson. Charm, righteousness, and pride should be replaced with strategy. Officer Mike is charming in a quiet kind of way, she thought. And there he was again.

Sister Mary Paul, at the other end of the hallway, felt only anger. The devil child in the basement would get what she deserved; she would not get away with hitting a nun. She couldn't care less about Elizabeth's suffering family—they were all deserving of what they got. The father was a drunk, the mother a fool, and the children's lives predestined. They were all failures, even the smart one. There was rank when serving the lord, and she was never so ill-treated except . . . there it was, a ping, hard to the heart. A slight gasp, she forced back tears for the gentle bird down the hall who was under the spell of the evil one, and who had broken her heart. She prayed for forgiveness and vowed not to allow herself to think of Sister Mary Rose again. She must keep focused on the one who came between them—the one who'd captured the bird's love.

They both saw the flash. It was a person. A very small person. The nuns' minds were working in tandem. It wasn't an adult; it was a child. Who would be so fast? Who would be out this late, running across the school grounds? Who would break the unwritten rules of a small community that all small children should be home in bed at this hour? Maybe a child without a home? There was no question. They both knew.

The window cracked open, but without response from her siblings. Elizabeth slid in the small opening and dropped to the cement floor. The illumination from the moon, that led her through the neighborhood, was still her friend. The siblings, asleep, had found comfort in hard cots, and she was not missed. She found her spot and slipped into the bed without changing her clothes. Within seconds, a creaking sound announced a visitor descending the basement stairs. Look away and keep eyes closed, she told herself. She didn't need to open her eyes to confirm the identity because there was a special odor that came with evil.

Chapter 22

The kitchen was a busy place in the morning, made more chaotic with the O'Sullivan children. Sister Mary Rose oversaw the congestion of people. Nuns ate their oatmeal as children waited with their bowls. When a nun left, a child sat down.

There were six nuns, not a large convent, but the school wasn't large either. It would have been larger if the Mexican church didn't have its own school with dark-skinned, Spanish-speaking nuns from the old country. Certainly, the Mexican church and school were small too, and they could have joined the white church, but that was the way it was. They did not mix. The nuns said it was because there were enough old Mexicans who did not speak English so it warranted a priest from Mexico and their own church. Why they had a separate school wasn't clear to Elizabeth. The public school could accommodate all the children in town, but it was important to the Catholics they have their own schools, something about heathens and pagans, and the one true church.

They needed to get out the door. Father would not wait for a nun to start Mass. It looked very bad if the nuns came in late, and they would be summoned and reprimanded. A letter would be sent to the Motherhouse in Atchison.

"Sister Mary Rose will take the children with her when they finish their breakfast." It was the same every day. The Mother of the House made the declaration which was a sign that the nuns needed to get out the door, and the children would follow soon.

Sister Mary Rose knew she needed to keep her eyes on Elizabeth and Sister Mary Paul, to be a buffer between them. It was one thing to have them in a classroom together, but in the same house was a different matter. She sensed something had happened, but she wasn't sure what. She was certain the small comet that flew across the convent lawn the other night was Elizabeth. She didn't go look as she wasn't sure how to handle it. She thought it a good thing Sister Mary Paul was asleep, or at least that is what she believed. Sister Mary Rose would not rest well until Elizabeth was safely away. She knew the child was up to something; that something had caused her to leave the nest and take risks.

The church bell rang. "Come on children, choke it down," Sister Mary Rose said, laughing. The children laughed too—they liked her.

Chapter 23

Junior lay in a bed with an IV drip. An elderly man and woman, William and Vena O'Sullivan sat at his side near a window. The couple was well dressed: William as handsome as the day Vena met him; and Vena, sturdy and aching. Her heart was breaking because her favorite child was the sad conclusion of unconditional love. Also standing next to the bed near the door was a young woman, Marilyn. She briefly turned when she heard the throat clearing cough of Officer Mike as he came into the room. She was a beauty with long black hair that framed her flawless face, and eyes large and bold, but sweet. Otherwise, their looks were so similar there could be no doubt that she and Junior were brother and sister. She never took her hand off Junior's arm as she offered Officer Mike a slight smile, and then quickly returned to her brother. Like the others in the room, she waited and wished for acknowledgement from Junior, but none came.

Standing near the door, Officer Mike could see Junior's eyes. He was awake, but not all there. The fire that flared at the slightest provocation was extinguished. He was recovering, but his brain was damaged. The doctors said the recovery would take a long time.

Vena got up and approached the visitor. William was left to consider the past—the part where he was right and Junior went wrong, and where regret started and never stopped.

Officer Mike made the first move by offering his hand, "Mrs. O'Sullivan?"

"Yes" she said in a quiet hospital voice. She looked toward the young woman. "My youngest daughter Marilyn and my husband William." The sadness that engulfed the room was undeniable.

"They say your son is going to recover, but . . . "

"A long road back and the doctors want to move him to Topeka for more care," Vena interrupted. "Then we will see what happens, but how is Susanne? She doesn't want to see us." A pained look covered her face and her lip quivered. If only she could talk to her, she would tell her they would take care of them all. They could come live with her and Junior's father in the big house in Topeka.

"I'm sorry, but he's still in trouble," Officer Mike reminded them.

"Yes, I understand, but he was a good boy." The excuses began, the excuses of an old mother trying to make sense of their lives. She wasn't all that different from many of the other mothers she knew. Her son was her making; he was loved. If anyone were to blame for his abusive behavior, it was her husband who never accepted him. "Everyone in the neighborhood loved Junior . . . then he got sick and the troubles started."

"Yes, but it's not smart to beat up your wife, and throw a nun out of your house." Junior might want to forget he had a family, and the nun might forget what happened, he thought to himself.

Vena turned, "Maybe he could . . . just . . . disappear . . . could you help with that?" It was as if she'd read his mind.

"Or maybe his whole family could disappear." Officer Mike walked toward the door. *Why did I say that?* But he knew why. He never allowed himself to consider the thought until he looked in Susanne's eyes the night of the event. She looked at him with appreciation, but not love. She was never his, and never would be. She had a different story and life, and it never really included him. She could leave, and probably should.

"That's not what the other police officer said. He said there would be an investigation," Vena offered, almost pleading that he would disagree. Officer Mike turned around quickly.

"What officer?" he asked trying to seem only slightly interested.

"Parker was his name. He came by a while ago. He said they needed to get all the facts before they decide whether to press charges."

Their rooms were on separate floors of the two-story building, a small city hospital. Susanne wished they were in different cities, the further apart the better. It was a big decision for the hospital staff to decide where she belonged. Perhaps they could put her on the surgical wing, but she didn't need any surgery. Her broken ribs would heal slowly without any intervention. Not OB GYN—too many new mothers taking a peek at a possible future. Not internal medicine, although it would have been appropriate, but that put her too close to the perpetrator; they saw the evidence. They finally determined the first floor, with the aging and infirm, was the perfect place. Most of the patients had been in their family home, fallen, and needed care. Some injuries resembled Susanne's, but not inflicted by a loved one, at least not any wounds that could be accounted for.

Her broken ribs were wrapped, and her throat was sore, but no bones in her neck were broken. A lucky swing by a son had made the difference. The knot on her head was slowly shrinking, but the bruises were more deliberate and harder to heal. Especially the internal one, caused by a kidney punch. Her mind, working overtime, took the pain and put it on a shelf. She avoided the pain pills; they made her drowsy. She knew she must be strong and alert so she slipped them under the mattress. Elizabeth wasn't the only one with a plan. Yes, Susanne knew who drank the juice. There had been enough, and Elizabeth was the only one in the kitchen.

There was a knock at the door and a face she had seen but really didn't know appeared, his hat in his hand. Who was this guy dressed in a suit? Who would be selling insurance here? Well, maybe not such a bad idea, just a little after-the-fact, she almost laughed.

"Mrs. O'Sullivan, is this a good time to visit?" he said as he stepped in the room.

Is that really a question? she thought. What would he do if she had said no? The big question of her life: What if she had said no to other things? A small pang of sadness and regret surfaced, but this was not the time.

"I am Captain Parker with the local police," he said with a hint of pride.

Well, good for you! she thought.

"I am here..." he hesitated for just a second.

"I know why you are here," she said in a monotone voice. She sounded like the walking dead, something out of the Twilight Zone. Most people he interviewed (and the truth was there weren't that many in a town this size) were nervous, even if they had never done anything wrong. She didn't seem afraid, just kind of apathetic. Her act was convincing so he would go slowly.

She wasn't going to help him. She didn't feel like being kind or accommodating. She decided to tell him nothing because she would not put her life in the hands of someone else, especially a nervous detective with fake insurance salesman confidence. Pain had a way of clarifying and proving you were alive. She was alive, but pretended she wasn't. A great irony, she thought.

"Can you remember the events of a week ago, when you were injured?"

There was no hesitation. "No," she replied.

There was that damn "something" again she was not telling. *What was she up to?* He was here to help her. If he got the goods on Junior, he would pursue charges. He needed her in order to do that. The nun didn't really see anything, and the kids weren't very reliable. *Who would believe these kids, besides Officer Mike? Was she lying or was she just doped up?* He decided to try again," Are you sure you don't remember anything?"

"Not much really. I must have fallen down, hit my head."

"Mrs. O'Sullivan, someone beat you up, and I doubt it was one of your kids. I think it was your husband." He was getting mad, which was not good. He had met his match, and there was nothing he could say or threaten to make her talk.

She had her own idea of the future, and it did not include this place or this man. She watched his mouth move, but she wasn't listening anymore. Her mind was in a different place and planning. Where was the box of family photos she had saved? She needed to find them and remember who was who in that family. She never really knew, but first she needed to get rid of this guy, close eyes and feign sleep.

The small parking lot was only half full with plenty of room for visitors driving Fords and Chevrolets. "Hey," Captain Parker turned around seeing Officer Mike standing next to his cruiser. "What's up, Captain?" Officer Mike was nonchalant, too, but not as convincing as Susanne.

"Trying to find out what happened at the O'Sullivan's," Parker said. What was Officer Mike doing here anyway? he wondered. He was a hero, yes, but still a patrolman. Of course, he could have been a captain, probably a member of Congress if he wanted to. President Eisenhower had come calling, but he didn't answer. "What are you doing here?"

"Just cruising around and thought I would see how Susanne was doing. Just following up." He was not going away.

"That's not exactly your job." Captain Parker was a little peeved. This was his territory, but he knew how much Officer Mike cared about the kids and wanted to make a case. The officer needed to back off. "I just talked to her. She is kind of out of it to tell you the truth, not talking a lot. I'm no doctor, but she doesn't look very well."

Officer Mike's mind wandered. He didn't know if he wanted Junior to go to jail or just leave. He wanted to get to Susanne, talk to her and figure out what she wanted. Surely she wanted Junior to go to jail. But what if there was a trial? Would she get a divorce? Certainly she could get a divorce after this. But how would she support her family? She had to get a divorce, to hell with the church! Suddenly, he felt very protective, like a big brother—a new feeling.

"Like I said, she wasn't talking much. The nurses said it will take another week before they let her out. They want to make sure her internal injuries are healing properly."

The mere mention of injuries gripped him. Her injuries were so public, there was no going back.

Captain Parker hollered as he walked away, "See you at the station." He sauntered off and then stopped to throw out a crumb. "Hey, do you know a kid named Richard Robinson in Elizabeth's class at school? His dad is president of the bank."

Officer Mike was blank. "No," he didn't know anything about Richard and didn't know his dad. Wait, he did know Richard's dad. Robinson...Robinson, he thought. *Yeah, Thomas Robinson.* He had forgotten all about him because they had no need for interaction. Officer Mike didn't get a loan for anything. He either had the money or he didn't. He only went to the bank to deposit his check once a month. He only saw the name on an office door, but nothing further. It was a small town, but enough of a town that there were different crowds. He didn't hang out with the folks who hung out with bankers.

He vaguely remembered Robinson from high school, a pleasant guy who stuttered. He didn't go to war, somehow stuttering and war didn't go together. He still remembered the guy's face as they went through the physical. Robinson smiled, did a thumbs up at Officer Mike, and disappeared behind a screen. Mike figured he would see him at the train station waiting with all the other guys who had signed up right after graduation, but he didn't.

"Sister Mary Rose mentioned him."

Sister Mary Rose. A smile came across his face and he tried to hide it. *Why did he do that when he thought of her?*

Captain Parker noted the smile, and thought, That's odd—he smiled at the mention of a nun's name. This hero was batting around zero, definitely strange.

It was that simple. Sister Mary Rose had nothing to hide or really offer when she met with Captain Parker. He dropped by her classroom right after school as she cleaned the black boards. She was eager to get to the convent, to keep track of the kids.

She told him about the crazy look in Junior's eyes, about the smell of the alcohol on his breath, and about how he threw her out of the house. She didn't really see him hit anyone. She was scared and might have missed something.

She pondered, then offered, "Yes, there was something strange. Richard. I think he was at the house and might have seen something."

The detective was trained to watch for a hesitation, like summoning up an untruth.

"Perhaps I should have called his parents. His father is a banker, very respectable. They live in a beautiful house across town . . . well, I just got caught up in what was happening. I forgot all about it. He stutters, but he's shy and smart. Sister Mary Paul thinks he will make a great priest, apart from the stuttering of course. Perhaps a monk." She stopped; she was rambling and suddenly very aware she was nervous. Her palms were sweating, and that was new.

Captain Parker looked up from his notes and locked eyes with Sister Mary Rose. *What was she hiding?* He would talk to Richard Robinson, but first he needed to talk to the parents.

A sweet breeze, neither hot nor cold, snuck into the classroom, very common for this small Kansas town. It was part of why Sister Mary Rose liked her assignment.

The day had been good but the children seemed antsy. She understood; she was antsy herself. The black tunic and apron that made up the nun's uniform felt unusually heavy today and weighed her down. The click-click of the rosary that hung from her woolen belt under the apron irritated her as she walked around the room. The starched white fabric surrounding her face and covering her head and neck was itchy. She wanted to rip it off. *What a thought!* Tear off the black veil pinned to the coif that signified her obedience to the church; yes, right at this moment if she could. Her meeting with the detective was unnerving.

Maybe it was the thought of the children, the ones she had adopted as her own, who now lived in the basement—not the ones who showed up each day to learn the mechanics of life, reading, writing, and arithmetic, and in the case of her best students like Patrick, pre-algebra. For a moment, she longed to be a mother, but immediately shoved the thought back. It was replaced by the unending itching and desire to run.

Suddenly, her arms were on fire. She didn't really want to connect the feelings of motherhood with the O'Sullivan children. They weren't her children; she was simply a guardian, just as she was the academic and spiritual guardian to the other children in her classroom.

She rolled up the first set of sleeves that formed the habit, then the second set of sleeves that covered her arms. She scratched and scratched, but her nails were cut short and barely brought relief. She wished she had a comb, that might work; but she gave up combs when she came to the convent. Why would anyone with little or no hair need a comb?

Obsessed with finding a solution to the itching, she rummaged through her desk drawer. Maybe there was a lost comb or a comb collected from an inspired Elvis fan. She had seen a photo of The King which one of her students left behind on a church pew.

Elvis' hair was a work of art; something she had never seen before. She noticed that some of the boys in her class began putting some sort of gunk in their hair during recess to keep it upright like their idol. They needed a comb to make it work. She always asked for a comb when it was sighted, but gave it back at the end of the day. It was required to return confiscated items.

The gunk, well, that was another story. There was no getting gunk out of the boys' hair during school. She doubted there was any shampoo that would work, although she knew next to nothing about gunk or shampoo. She wondered if Officer Mike put gunk in his hair. She hadn't seen his hair because his head was always covered by his hat, just like her.

She didn't hear him come into the room, but she had a flash of recognition, kindness, a scent vaguely familiar and pleasant. He waited. He had never seen a nun's arms, but hers looked red and streaked. That was strange. It also seemed oddly intimate, this moment, watching her.

She looked up and smiled a curious smile. How long had he been there?

He took off his hat. His thick hair did need some gunk, she decided, and perhaps a comb. She could take care of that. I COULD TAKE CARE OF THAT—Oh my dear God! she thought. She quickly rolled her sleeves down and placed her hands under the apron, out of sight. She was fighting an urge, but the urge to do what?

"Sister, sorry, am I interrupting? I had a couple of questions for you about the event at the O'Sullivan's."

Sister Mary Rose was not listening. Greek was flowing from his mouth. It was as if he had seen her unclothed, and she did not mind. The feeling she had was strange, but not scary, and there were no feelings of sin, only an urge to touch him.

"Sister. Sister," she heard him say, as if he were calling her back from some distant place.

He watched her, waiting for a response. Then a smile coupled with embarrassment crossed her face. She was sweet in a soft-strong way, he thought. He wondered what her hair looked like under the headdress. Was her hair like his mom's, a dull brown? Probably not. Her beautiful eyes were dark. There was an uneasiness coming over him. He felt less than honorable, as if he were betraying someone. He wanted to know her, really know her. He couldn't control the feeling.

"Yes, Officer Mike, how can I help you?"

Shame was in conflict with the thoughts he couldn't control. *What was this?* He turned around and walked to the window. He never felt this way about Susanne. He yearned for her, but this was lust, and for a nun no less! Susanne was perfect like the porcelain doll, always admired and loved, but never touched.

He closed his eyes and thought of baseball. Yes, baseball, and the Cardinals to be specific—the only team whose games were carried throughout the Great Plains states on the radio. Stan Musial, "The Man." Yes, he was still the man. An All Star every year, and not the least bit attractive to Officer Mike. There, the distraction was successful and he was okay.

He turned around and saw a flush glow on Sister Mary Rose's cheeks. She looked down at her feet.

"About the events of September 2, I wanted to follow up. Do you remember anything you might have left out of your first interview?"

Sister Mary Rose looked up, hoping her inner thoughts were not on her face, but her face felt hot. "I told the captain that there was one detail I forgot about and it was not included in my initial interview . . . Richard Robinson. He is in Elizabeth's class, and he was there. You know that, don't you?"

He avoided her question, but his curiosity was doing the job by keeping his mind off things he should never let himself envision, like a naked nun, this nun.

"Well . . . he was just standing next to the house, close to the bushes. He must have seen what happened. It frightened him."

"Did you talk to him? Did you ask him?"

"I didn't have to. The light from the street told the story."

"His face? Was he crying?"

"No, he wet his pants."

Officer Mike understood immediately.

Sister Mary Rose had taught school for ten years and had several brothers. Children didn't have accidents unless they were scared out of their wits. No eleven, almost twelve, year old boy could withstand that humiliation.

She had only seen one boy wet his pants. The parish priest chastised him in front of his classmates after Mass for dropping the communion wafers. The Father came into Sister Mary Rose's class and made sure everyone was aware of the mistake, but there was no need. Everyone witnessed the error for themselves, and now the extra humiliation by the priest—a double gut-punch for the child. Sister Mary Rose hated that priest. Yes, she knew the significance of the thought, but she knew, too, the child would carry that shame with him for his lifetime. It was those kinds of moments, and there were plenty of them, all special for their reckless indifference to the children and inflicted by a nun or a priest who felt trapped, that made her question again her decision to enter the convent.

No one saw the accident. Sister Mary Rose stepped in front of the boy and whisked him out of the room, but the child knew. The family left town soon afterward, and now she was worried about Richard. He was a gentle spirit, and there was no leaving town for him.

"I didn't want to tell the detective, but he was relentless and said that if he were to make a case, he had to come up with some new evidence. Mrs. O'Sullivan doesn't remember anything." Mrs. O'Sullivan—that sounded so foreign to him, but yes, she was Mrs. O'Sullivan.

Officer Mike knew a good defense attorney could plant the seeds for willful children, lying and eager to bring down a strict parent. What he didn't understand was why Susanne didn't remember anything. She wasn't unconscious when he got there.

"I think it was a mistake to mention it," Sister Mary Rose considered.

"You think lying might be better?"

"Not saying something is not lying."

"Who told you that, Mary Rose?" the officer wondered.

Where had the "Sister" in Sister Mary Rose gone? His language was casual, like people who knew each other for a very long time. His tone was not that of a professional talking about his job, or was she just wishing?

She knew he was right about telling the truth and holding back, but how could she put a boy on display for ridicule. It wasn't right, and why would they believe him anyway? He was just another child with a story. She was, however, confident he'd seen more than any child should see.

"I just don't want that mentioned, about how afraid he was."

She was a nun willing to lie, to leave out pertinent information to protect a young boy. Officer Mike liked her sensibility. He liked her, and it wasn't just the great smile or the generous heart she had, or his overwhelming desire to kiss her. There were no easy answers today.

"So you told Parker that Richard was outside Elizabeth's house but nothing more?"

"Yes"

"Okay, let's just keep it that way." They both knew it was a crime not to report what he might have seen.

They stared at one another. They were on a dangerous path, and they could feel it. The intimacy of the moment was palpable. He reached for her arm, found her hand, and squeezed it. She held on, not wanting to let go. They both knew they were embarking on a journey that had changed—from one of personal responsibility to protect the vulnerable, to conspiracy and a state of confusion. A map was lost and a new course charted.

A strong sense of dread came over Sister Mary Rose and she pulled her hand away. She looked to the door, but no one was there, but she could smell the remnants of a tortured soul, the very essence of Sister Mary Paul. Officer Mike noticed Sister's Mary Rose's defenses rise. He followed her eyes to the door. "What's wrong?"

"Sister Mary Paul. I am afraid she was there, outside the door. She hates Elizabeth."

"We weren't talking about Elizabeth."

"No, but we were talking about Richard. Sister Mary Paul must have heard us talking about him."

"I am not following." He was truly confused. He needed to talk with Richard. It was strange he was at the O'Sullivan's, but he would find out why.

The two nuns talked very little since the night in the convent when Sister Mary Paul had made her mad with incoherent statements. Sister Mary Rose avoided her, never agreeing to share chores. She didn't even allow herself to ever be alone with the other nun; and she didn't know what to do about her. The memory of that moment was ingrained. She tried to push it away, but it surfaced.

This time there were more people involved and it was not good. How much did Sister Mary Paul hear and did she see them holding hands? Nausea swept over her; she felt like throwing up. If Sister Mary Paul knew about Richard, what would she do with the information?

Richard was Sister Mary Paul's pet. Sister Mary Rose wanted to make sure he was kept out of the chaos, but she knew in the other nun's eyes, Elizabeth would undoubtedly carry the responsibility for Richard's involvement. It would not matter why Richard decided to stand outside the window. It was still Elizabeth's fault as far as Sister Mary Paul was concerned. All things derelict, insolent and arrogant came from that evil child. If she thought Elizabeth had somehow soiled Richard, brought shame upon him and his family, and lured him into her foul world, Sister Mary Paul would do all in her power to hurt Elizabeth.

Sister Mary Rose turned away. She was embarrassed and there was too much to consider.

"Mary Rose. Mary Rose," he repeated.

Oh no, not Mary Rose. He has to stop saying that, she thought. Besides it was not the name she wanted him to call her. Bridgett was her name before she took her vows. "Call me Sister Mary Rose, please," she said stiffly.

"What's wrong?" Officer Mike said. He knew what he was feeling.

"It's just that there is so much going on right now. I worry about Richard and Elizabeth, and what Sister Mary Paul will do to them." She almost choked saying Sister. She had come to realize Mary Paul did not deserve the title. She was no Sister. "Mostly . . . what she will do to Elizabeth," Mary Rose continued. "She was the one who switched Elizabeth, for no reason, and that was not the first time. I have never stopped her, not really. I tried the day she fell and hit her head."

It was the first time he remembered seeing Mary Rose. He rushed into the room, with Sister Mary Paul lying on the floor and coming to, but unable to speak. Katherine was off to the side, the older sister of Elizabeth. He knew that much. Mary Rose was kneeling beside the lump on the floor. He never before paid attention to any nun; they were some kind of other being. They were untouchable, but even in that moment, he felt an ease. They were like partners. She started to cry, buried her face in her hands and leaned on Officer Mike. It was natural. He touched her back gently, bringing her close. There was no struggle because it felt right. She had not cried since she left home; on that day, she cried both tears of joy and sadness. She felt good about her decision to become a nun, but she knew she would miss her family. Still, she was confident that doing the work of Jesus was what she was called to do. Today she knew the work of Jesus was more than teaching. She was protecting.

It was becoming clear. Elizabeth had gone to Richard's the other night. What did she need from Richard? Did Richard see something that others did not see?

The room was cold, but Sister Mary Paul felt hot with anger. She paced her small room, thinking: *so the little witch has been at work on Richard*. He was at Elizabeth's house. Oh how she wished she had heard all of the conversation. She came in late and only heard Richard's name. Her anger rose. Richard was a sweet boy, very naive. He would grow into a great man, a leader in the church, and she was the one who found him. Sister Mary Paul knew it the first time she saw him. He was a respectful boy with a desire to serve. He did have a small problem with speech, but that would eventually go away with a little effort. She prayed for him, gave him special attention, made sure he made A's.

What did Richard see the night he stood outside the window of the O'Sullivan house? What could she get him to say that would send Elizabeth packing? It was not about Sister Mary Rose anymore, only about Richard. She was done with the young nun; she was a witch too. She had seen the hand-holding. Where else had her hands been, she wondered. Sister Mary Rose was now her enemy.

The two "felons" weren't far ahead of her. That's what she thought when she thought of Officer Mike and

Sister Mary Rose. Imaging the two of them in jailhouse uniforms, she almost giggled. This was helpful and she felt lighter. Mary Rose with her skull cap dressed in stripes, and the hero, tall and slender with his officer's hat firmly on his head. The stripes laid on them for all the offenses they committed against the church, and more specifically, her.

The lightness left like a switch the moment she thought of Elizabeth. What a conniver that girl was! She used Richard, and she had to be stopped. It boggled Mary Paul's mind how daring Elizabeth was, and for a moment, it gave her a fleeting sense of admiration for the crafty, evil child. It now made sense that Elizabeth left the convent late at night because she had some place to go—Richard's house. The felons didn't know about that. I've got one on them! Mary Paul thought smugly Elizabeth wasn't out for a stroll; she moved too fast and was on a mission. Mary Paul knew she was wise to go to the basement and check on her. No matter how clever she was, her breathing was not that of someone in a deep sleep. She knew what that looked like; she had a history of checking other sleepers.

Elizabeth went to Richard that night to get help. What had he seen? What had she done that would require his help? But it was certain—he definitely saw something in that house. Two minds were thinking in tandem.

Chapter 24

Richard sauntered along, kicked a rock, and kicked it again. He wondered if he could kick it all the way to school. Autumn was the best time in Kansas, right before the trees that lined the streets started to change and color the landscape. There were no tornados to run from like in May; and no swimming lessons, thank goodness. No Boy Scout camp that came with mosquitoes to swarm you at breakfast, lunch and dinner. No blizzards that could come up like a spring storm and take a life just as quickly if unprepared.

This year everything changed. The school year was barely started, but he felt so different. There was Elizabeth, and everything that came with her. He was older than she, but in the same grade because he was held back. Scarlet fever had made him vulnerable and his parents worried. He knew his life was much different from Elizabeth's. He had seen it. He was protected and she was forced to grow up, but she was still every bit his age.

Life had been quiet, but not reassuring since the event at Elizabeth's house which was followed by a late night visit and an empty conversation with his now best friend.

He tried to forget how scared he was and what a coward he had been, but the memories of the liquid trickling down his leg and the embarrassment he felt, would not go away. Many nights the terror and memories came rushing back. He felt like he was drowning in sweat. The proof of the night's struggle would wake him; he changed his bed linen twice a week and he wondered when his mother would notice.

To complicate things, Elizabeth was being very erratic, more erratic than usual. She looked at him like she had something to say, but then looked around the room, searching for something. He was sure it was the nun she was watching. He wished she would just say something like, "Meet me at the whatever," and he would show up and they could talk. Elizabeth definitely had something on her mind, and he missed their talks and walks.

Out of nowhere, right before he rounded the corner of the school on the sunless side of the building, a cloth-covered nun's arm reached out and pulled him into a small doorway. It was dark, and his heart was pounding. He struggled slightly, but her grip was serious.

He couldn't make out the face, but she was a lot taller. Thank goodness, he thought, it must be Sister Mary Rose. The Penguin was much shorter; there he went thinking strange thoughts. He needed to thank Elizabeth for that, too.

She looked so out of place. Nuns didn't ever just pop up alone, but there she was. What he could see of her face seemed to telegraph worry, very much like the night of the event. He stopped his failed attempt at struggling.

"Hello Richard."

Oh no, not that, he thought, acting like this was totally normal. The nun reminded him of Elizabeth for just a moment, but of course she was much, much taller. This was not normal, and they both knew it. He defaulted to his Boy Scout training: be polite and honest, and get to it. "What do you need, Sister?" There was no hint of the stutter although he certainly knew it could come out, especially because he was straining to be calm. He had to play along.

She was taken aback. He didn't stutter this time, not one little bit. He knew she noticed. "Okay, we will dispense with pleasantries. I need to talk with you, and you must promise never to speak to anyone, ever, about our conversation. I know you will keep this promise because I know you are friends with Elizabeth."

He liked the way that sounded and felt surprisingly "cool" as the older boys would say. A realization occurred to him. Of course she knew he was Elizabeth's friend! He was at her house looking in the window, the nun had seen him. Either she was his friend or he was a pervert looking in other people's windows.

"Why were you at Elizabeth's house?"

"I had a hunch that she was in deep trouble. I followed her. She had come to my house and said she had done something stupid, but just when she was going to tell me what she had done, we were interrupted."

"What time of day?" she demanded. Richard was getting worried, and Sister Mary Rose's voice was getting loud. If she didn't want everyone to come running, she needed to lower her voice.

Before he could answer, she continued the interrogation, "She walked up to the door and asked to speak to you? Did your parents see her?"

One by one he answered her questions very calmly: "Dinner time. Late afternoon." No, she didn't go to the front door, and no, his parents did not see her. She came to his window, up the tree next to the house. She was a very good climber.

A smile enveloped Sister Mary Roses's face. Of course Elizabeth was a good climber. She saw it herself on that very same day when she showed up on the school grounds.

The tension was slowly draining away; Richard could feel it. He was relaxed, although aware that he stood in a dark doorway with a nun; one more experience he could attribute to Elizabeth. It was time to tell her everything he saw. He was sure that was what she wanted to know; and of the visits from Elizabeth.

"I followed her and watched through the windows. You saw me there."

"Yes, I did." A small sense of embarrassment came over her. She knew what she was admitting.

Richard didn't stutter or stop. He knew what the nun saw and it bothered him, but what was he to do? It felt good to talk about that night. Maybe his own memories could fade once he shared them, and he could forget.

"I saw you come in with Elizabeth. I saw her father lunge and grab you. I saw him come around the house and go in the back door. I am really glad he missed seeing me in the bushes."

He let out a deep breath. He was on a streak and could not slow down or he would stumble and sputter like an old car. "Mr. O'Sullivan was locked out, but the boys forgot about the back door. I looked again and he was back in the house. It happened so quickly. I saw him come after Mrs. O'Sullivan, try to choke her, the boys jumping on his back, and then Elizabeth left the room. That is the strangest part. She went to the fridge and got juice and drank it all. I could hear them calling her name, but she didn't move. She is really smart. I would not have moved either. Then she saw me." His voice began to tremble, "And she asked for my help. I saw you and I . . . ran away."

Richard dropped his head, tears flowed; Niagara Falls had nothing on him. His body shook as Sister Mary Rose grabbed him and held him tight. He didn't feel like he was twelve. He felt like a baby, but he could not hold back. He wouldn't be a real Eagle Scout anytime soon, or maybe ever. "I am a coward," he said through the tears.

"Oh, Richard, you didn't hide. You let me see your fear, which made me knock harder." She let him cry and cry. She had seen only one other person cry like that, and it was her mother the day her sister died. Now she was a mother, and he was her child. She held him until the shaking stopped and the tears dried up. He stood before her and wiped his face.

"I wondered if I should tell someone, like the police."

"No, not yet. Let me think first. Whatever happens, don't tell anyone what you saw Elizabeth do. No one, even if the good Sister Mary Paul asks." She needn't worry about Sister Mary Paul; he knew what she was, and it wasn't good.

"Elizabeth came to see me the other night and said she was hungry, but she wouldn't tell me the real reason she came. She left in a hurry; it was very late at night."

"Yes." Now it was Sister Mary Rose's turn to be truthful. "I know." She hesitated, then decided to bring Richard into the scheme.

"There may be a detective coming to ask you questions. I accidentally mentioned your name. No . . . truthfully, I was afraid, and I made a mistake, or maybe not . . . it depends." Now she was stumbling and felt ashamed. "Regardless, I mentioned you, but not how scared I knew you were." He knew what she meant. Thank goodness, he thought.

Talking to Sister Mary Rose was somehow like being debriefed by a comrade in the Army. Well, what the hell? he was becoming a recruit and it was for Elizabeth. How, he wasn't sure, but his commanding officer told him so. He was never much of a daydreamer nor did he think he was very creative, but pretending was becoming very acceptable.

For Sister Mary Rose, the pretending was over. It was as if the more she learned about Elizabeth, the more she learned about herself, and the more free she felt. If she could keep Elizabeth, and by extension Richard, out of Sister Mary Paul's way, the more complete she would be. Perhaps that is why she had come to this place, why she took the path she took. She was becoming someone else, or rather, she thought, she was becoming herself, ready to live a different life. If these children could be so brave, so could she.

Chapter 25

Susanne sat in a chair next to the window. She held a letter to her chest and tears streamed down her face. The tears were of hope and happiness and she felt strong. Her ribs were healing as well as her kidneys, and her voice was better, not perfect and maybe never pitch perfect, but it was the first sign. She'd talked very little since her arrival.

The room was a safe haven. The children came to visit, but John was not allowed in the unit. She missed her constant companion and was afraid after ten days he might forget her. She had not seen him since the event.

She'd found a place for her family without Junior—that was huge. Now she needed to get her family together and get on the road, but she knew she needed all her strength to make it happen. The children had done their part. James found the box in the closet with letters and cards that family members sent, and he was instructed to bring the box to the hospital.

There was a Christmas card with a return address from a cousin whom she fondly remembered. She decided to write to her and ask for temporary lodging until she could get on her feet. If her cousin was still at the same address, maybe she would help. Susanne was determined—if her letter came back unopened, she would find someone else. She would look until she found a way, but there was no worry, and no delay in the response, nor any judging. There was a new home waiting for her and the children. She was remembered and she was no longer lost. Cousin Susanne and children could "come and stay as long as they needed." They had plenty with a big house on Summit in St. Paul. Her cousin and husband wanted children, and hoped one day a miracle would bring laughter into their home. Perhaps this was the miracle, only packaged just a little differently.

There was a grace period between Susanne's return home and when Junior would be released from the hospital. He was sent to Topeka, a short train trip away for rehabilitation. It was a one-of-a-kind place for people who worked on the railroad, and patients came from around the country.

The doctors thought he'd had a stroke, not a reaction. His veins were in bad shape "like an old man's," they said. She kept her stoic exterior intact as the doctor left her room, but it was hard. She was screaming on the inside. *Thank God, a stroke!*

Junior could walk, but only with help, and his right arm would never work again. He could speak, but it was still slurred. His parents came and took him away and Susanne saw them as they wheeled him by her door and down the hall. There was a slight halt at her door, but they knew not to come in. The "No Visitors" sign on the door was meant for them. It was her first act of autonomy. She spoke only to those who she wanted to speak to, and the nurses understood.

She looked out the window to see Officer Mike was back again. What a kind man with such good intentions, she mused. Today she would tell him to let it go; she knew he cared. She was going away and taking the children. There would be no divorce and no charges brought, she could not corroborate the children's story, and she remembered nothing. That is what she would tell him. But, she did remember. She remembered everything. She had plenty of time to think, to ruminate back to the hours that passed before Elizabeth decided to let her father die. What might she have done differently had she not left it up to Elizabeth?

She knew what Elizabeth did; they all knew. She saw it in the children's faces when they came to visit.

There were no words, but a sadness followed them, especially James. Only Elizabeth thought no one knew. Her youngest daughter tried to do what Susanne herself did not have the courage to do. She was driven by the guilt that she had somehow collaborated with her captor. It was overwhelming. She felt guilty not by action, but omission.

The "stroke" diagnosis brought relief, and replaced the constant rumination—damnation averted. Her sweet children were spared the cloak of guilt that could cover them for a lifetime. She knew what it would mean to Elizabeth specifically, and to the other children collectively. It was true she often felt far away and didn't know them, but she did know them, each and every one of them. She knew their character.

How would she parent this brood she had come to compartmentalize? She wondered. They were not an ordinary family. They had memories and secrets no one wanted to talk about, but they did have their strengths. They would learn as they went along. This was their chance to start over and there would be no more secrets. There would be no need. She had to be strong and strike a new path which would not be easy. She had one more step that needed to be taken, and after she did it, they would never look back. She was deep in thought and did not hear the knock.

"Susanne," she heard that. She looked up and there he was. She liked him but she never felt more than that.

Officer Mike felt anxious, but not because his feelings had changed, more because he wasn't sure how to help her. In any case, he must talk to her, help her figure it out, make plans.

"How are you feeling?"

She smiled and she meant it, her eyes a little red but her heart at ease. "Good," she said.

"Great. Listen, there have been some new developments in your case," he said with earnest and concern.

"Stop!" she said, not mean or angry, but calm.

Officer Mike was confused; she needed his help and needed to listen to him. There may be more interviews, divorce is difficult under any circumstances, and how will she take care of herself and the children? he wondered. There were so many questions running through his mind. That, of course, was when he wasn't thinking about Mary Rose, and he thought of her often. In fact, he thought about her even when he was looking at Susanne. He felt very cheap just recalling a vision of the nun in his head at this time, but there she was, smiling, looking like she wanted to be kissed. He was such a shmuck, he thought. It was back to Susanne.

"There will not be an investigation," Susanne said, noting that he seemed distracted.

Where was I? He wondered. Oh yes, Richard Robinson. He ignored her comment and continued. "Richard Robinson, Thomas Robinson's son, was at the house. He was looking in the window. He knows something."

Now Susanne was confused. Thomas Robinson sounded familiar, but she had never heard of Richard Robinson. Officer Mike could see that he needed to explain a few things.

"Richard is a friend of Elizabeth's, and he was outside the house, watching. We don't know why."

"Who is we?" she asked, wondering how many people were in on the investigation.

A shot of red went up his face. "Sister Mary Rose and me."

Susanne noticed immediately. He was fair skinned and showed his feelings on his face; he was blushing. Maybe she would not need to let him down as she had thought. It looked like someone else had his attention. *Good, that's taken care of.* She didn't care what he was doing—or not doing with Sister Mary Rose, but she was a little surprised. Sister Mary Rose had been at their house and had gotten help, that made sense; but she was most interested in this Richard boy. "Oh, what do you think he saw?"

There it was. He was sure Susanne knew what he was talking about. The silence took over the room. *What could he say? What could he admit?*

"I am sure there is nothing he can add to the story that the children have not already told the police, and they are not exactly reliable . . . children you know. I don't remember anything, and I doubt I ever will. Besides, the doctors believe he had a stroke."

Stroke! He was overwhelmed. It was disarming. He and Mary Rose were so worried about what would happen if there was further investigation. The relief he felt sent waves throughout his body. He was stunned and searched for something to say. "Susanne, is there anything I can do?

She said very calmly with a new voice, "I need your help tomorrow, if you are willing." It wasn't like asking, more like telling. He could either help or get out of the way. "Pick John up at the social service office as soon as they open. They'll know you are coming, and then my children at the convent. I am getting out today, and we will leave around nine am tomorrow. We are catching the train to Chicago."

Officer Mike was dumbfounded. He figured he would have to lead her out of the darkness, but she didn't need him. She just told him what to do.

Captain Parker came into the meeting late. Mr. And Mrs. Robinson and Richard sat at the steel table in the small interrogation room where the O'Sullivan children sat almost two weeks before. The chairs were uncomfortable on purpose, and Officer Mike had already begun.

"It seems that Richard really didn't see much at the O'Sullivan's the other night. We got him out of class for nothing. Sister Mary Paul was none too happy and she wanted to come along. He got there, heard loud voices, and just hid in the bushes. He came out about the time Sister Mary Rose started knocking on doors." Officer Mike hesitated a moment before adding the show-stopper: "Probably around the time Junior had his stroke."

"Stroke? That's what they think?" Good, Captain Parker thought, we can get this over with.

"So, Sister Mary Rose saw him. He ran away. It seems Elizabeth climbed a tree next to his room a few days later; she was hungry. He got her macaroni and cheese and chicken. Oh, yeah, apparently she is a very good climber." A slight bit of humor, a moment of relief. Captain Parker grinned. The Robinsons did not.

Richard didn't know what a stroke was, but he did what he hoped to do. He made the point of telling them about Elizabeth's scaling skills so he sounded detailed and truthful. He did think she was a great climber. The first time he lied for Elizabeth was by omission when he just sat there and didn't say anything, but he didn't think that would work this time. The captain had a gun which he could see bulging under his jacket. Better to keep it a simple lie. He did not want to get confused about what happened when and where, and Sister Mary Rose was very clear. "Nothing about Elizabeth," she said. It seemed strange because it wasn't like Elizabeth committed a crime; she just had some juice.

Mrs. Robinson's mind raced. She couldn't care less about a stroke. Her son saw something. He had been jumpy for days and begun wetting his bed. She noticed it the first time she changed the linens. She knew of young children wetting the bed, but not an older one. She was as nervous as Officer Mike, but for different reasons. Her sweet boy did not need any more terror in his life. He suffered from stuttering, although lately it seemed better. He was a caring and kind boy who happened to have a girlfriend (she meant that in the broadest of terms) who came for a visit. Oh my goodness, she thought. He has a girlfriend!

Mr. Robinson remembered Officer Mike, but had not talked to him in years. Until his own stuttering was worked out of his system, he barely talked to anyone. His voice improved when he met Mrs. Robinson; it seemed to be the same for his son. Love could do that, he mused, and he was happy for his son and a little proud. Richard started liking girls much younger than he had—no priesthood for either one of them.

Chapter 26

Elizabeth needed to get the cigar box out of her hiding spot. She couldn't leave it behind; it held her life. She decided to wait until they were all asleep and slip out. Their house was just a few blocks away and no one was there. A key to the front door was under the mat and she could dash up and get it, and dash out. Easy peasy.

Upstairs, all but two of the nuns were asleep. Sister Mary Rose told the Sisters the children were leaving in the morning.

"It is a good thing," Mother Agnes said, because "the family needs some time alone so they can prepare to help their father when he comes back from Topeka." It was not the truth, but Sister Mary Rose didn't care. Her job was to get the children and Susanne safely out of town.

They needed to be up early, have their breakfast and pack sandwiches. Sister Mary Rose would take care of the sandwiches and Officer Mike made sure they had money for the trip. He included it when he dropped by to tell the Mother of the House of the children's departure. The young nun watched Sister Mary Paul's face. She was turning red and excused herself from the table. She wasn't feeling well and retired for prayers.

Just like her daughter, Susanne had her own rendezvous to make, but it required that she take the late train to Topeka. The train came twice a day in each direction—early in the morning and late at night. She could hop on the Eastbound, get off in Topeka, do her business and jump on the Westbound very early the next day. She was to be released from the hospital late in the afternoon, plenty of time to grab a meal at the diner.

The clerk stared at her. "Kind of a quick trip, going and coming." She smiled in response, "I'm going to see my husband and have to get back for the children." Not exactly a lie.

She knew what she had to face, and what she had to do. Her appetite was really good so she ordered an open-faced sandwich with lots of beef covered with gravy over a large mound of mashed potatoes.

It was like a miniature parade of the Penguins heading to Antarctica—first Elizabeth out the window and across the lawn, then Sister Mary Paul staying just far enough behind to keep out of Elizabeth's sight, and lastly Sister Mary Rose behind her. The streetlights kept all of them in view.

Sister Mary Paul didn't have a clue where Elizabeth was heading, but Sister Mary Rose knew. She was headed home. She must need something from the house; they had left in a hurry.

Sister Mary Rose vowed not to let Sister Mary Paul get her hands on Elizabeth, and she knew exactly what to do when they all arrived at the house. She had nothing to lose; she was already making other arrangements. She wrote a letter, put a stamp on it and had it postmarked. The evidence would be in the envelope. She didn't even have to mail it; it was already dated.

The train was right on time. It was a short ride, and the walk from the train station up to the hospital was only a few blocks. She needed to be careful when she got to the hospital as visiting hours were over. She asked the nurses about the hospital in Topeka, and most had been there at least once in their lives. Everyone in town either worked on the railroad or had a family member who worked on the railroad, and went to the company hospital for care. Susanne, for some strange reason, had never been there, not even with Junior. He always went alone for any appointments, or his mother went with him.

When the train stopped, Susanne felt a little flutter in her stomach. She told herself it was merely a reminder she was alive and going to stay alive. Pain had been the reminder before, but that was then.

The walk took a few minutes. Her shoes, the only decent pair she owned, weren't meant for walking, but she wanted to look dressed up. She was wearing her Sunday best, a shirt waist with a short jacket. It was still pleasant outside, no need for a heavy coat.

She must have resembled all the other women who came in from the country looking for jobs during the war years. She felt self-conscious, aware of her situation. She wondered what she looked like walking alone in the evening. She couldn't remember the last time she was out after dark alone when she saw the front door to the hospital. It was enormous with the feel of a corporation that employed thousands. She suddenly felt small. She could see a clerk at the front desk and she didn't want anyone to know she was there. She decided to wait until the front desk clerk got up, even though it might take a while, but she had the time.

There it was, the house. She intended to be in and out. It seemed a little spooky, but Elizabeth didn't need any motivation. She just pretended it was a dark theater ready for the curtain to go up.

She found the key, opened the door, raced in and up the stairs. Turning on lights was not a good idea; it might draw attention. She knew the room, found the door leading to her sanctuary, went through it, and sat down on her favorite spot as a small drawer sprung open. She searched and found the flashlight, turned it on, looked for the box, and there it was—all the lovely gifts her father "gave" her when he wasn't aware. She especially loved the lighter. Among the other small little trinkets was the holy card, torn in half. She felt sad and a little disappointed in herself. After all, what had Joan of Arc ever done to hurt her? In fact, the saint had smiled and danced when Elizabeth needed a friend; that was, of course, before Richard. She wanted to fix her saintly friend now, so she pulled out a small roll of tape—also taken from someone but she couldn't remember who—probably Katherine. She taped the two pieces together and stared at the card. It made her smile. She waited for the little saint to make a move, but nothing . . . only the strained face of a young girl soon to meet her maker.

Susanne waited for what seemed a long time. When she saw the clerk get up and head to the hallway, she slipped in and through a door that led up a flight of stairs. At the top of the stairs, she could see a directory through a glass door. Good, she could find her way.

It didn't take long to find the rehab unit, and before she knew it, she was standing outside Junior's door. A sign with his name was displayed, a private room. His parents must have paid.

There he was, small and thin. She gasped just a little. She didn't think she cared what he looked like, but she did. She reached for the light switch, but decided to let the moon provide the illumination. The last time she looked into Junior's eyes, she only saw her reflection—weak, scared, accepting of her fate. Tonight, his eyes, although wide open, were empty.

Susanne moved directly in front of the window with the moon at her back. She was faceless, her head an outline. He knew her form so she didn't need to say her name.

He tried to say, "Susanne." There was a resemblance to the sounds that made her name, but barely, with a tiny lilt at the end—something sweet, upbeat and pathetic. A flood of tears, which she couldn't stop, came falling down and there was no holding back. She sobbed, choking back the sounds. Who was this pathetic man? There was so little of him left, and her heart was breaking. He was once the handsomest man she had ever known. His laugh, his smile, and his fearless nature were all a part of him. Yes, she loved him once, a long time ago.

All the things she wanted to say were fading. The planned whisper in his ear, telling him if he came looking for her, she would kill him, was gone. She saw through the shadows of the room that there was no longer anything to fear—he couldn't make a fist, let alone throw one. She needed to see him, and in her own way, forgive him so she could forgive herself.

After a few minutes of silence all Susanne could voice was, "Good-bye." There was no need for anything more. She left the room the way she came, in the dark. As she walked the silent hospital halls, occasionally a ward clerk looked up and smiled. She seemed to fit in; she was the woman staying late, anxious for the morning to come. She took the elevator down to the basement where a cafeteria worker was serving coffee and donuts for relatives and friends holding vigil. The worker served her coffee and made small talk. She smiled; she was at peace. She sat and waited until it was time to catch the train home.

Elizabeth came down the hallway. The moon that showed Junior's face to Susanne in the hospital room miles away, revealed a presence, not quite formed.

"Well, well, Elizabeth. It is just you and I." An odor emanated from the being, covering the space. Elizabeth recognized the scent before the face. It was especially strong, like the manifestation of evil had been working really hard, sweating. Along with the odor, Elizabeth sensed an undertone of fear. Her perceptive skills were blossoming.

"Not exactly, Sister." Sister Mary Rose stepped out of the shadows, a third presence in the room. She was nervous but knew she needed to act.

"Go, Elizabeth. The good Sister won't be bothering you tonight," Mary Rose said with a small lilt in her voice.

Out the bedroom window, onto the tree limb, down the trunk, Elizabeth thinks. But she could not leave Sister Mary Rose alone with this crazy creature.

"Go!" Sister Mary Rose repeated. She was used to telling children what to do.

In her best authoritarian voice, Sister Mary Paul asked, "What are you going to do now? I saw you with the officer. I know your proclivities and I will tell." She attempted to make her point with a superior sense of satisfaction and distress, all mixed up together.

"I don't care. I won't be here much longer," Sister Mary Rose answered. She had an Education Degree from St. Mary's that would allow her to teach somewhere, just not while wearing the scratchy and heavy mantle of the church.

"Sister Mary Rose," interrupted Elizabeth, surprising both the sisters, but mostly Sister Mary Rose by stepping right in front of her.

"We can go. She can't hurt me anymore. I know her smell." Elizabeth was very calm.

The balloon had been burst. Mary Paul leaned against the wall. She was spent and had no will to understand what just happened.

The route home for the teacher and student was spiked with moments of silent declarations. Sister Mary Rose did not need to tell Elizabeth she filled an emptiness in her heart from the loss of a sister. And Elizabeth never mentioned that her idea of a hero changed from an armored young warrior to the flesh and blood woman who stepped in to protect her.

Chapter 27

They didn't have much to pack, only what they brought with them to the convent. Officer Mike picked up the four O'Sullivan children at the convent early since he had the day off. He already had John with him. It was all arranged, the family taking a little trip to help Susanne recuperate. That's how Officer Mike explained it to the Family Service and Guidance staff. They thought it was a grand idea, and pleased that law enforcement was so helpful arranging the departure.

Susanne and her children had a pass from the railroad so there was no cost to travel. And the agency provided a little spending money for meals. Their father was still recuperating in Topeka, and there would be a reunion soon. Officer Mike knew otherwise.

When Officer Mike arrived at the convent, Mary Rose answered the door. She smiled a smile that told him she was ready too. Only Elizabeth, who was first to the door, witnessed the small touch, the brief hand holding. Sisters didn't gently touch men's hands. She had never seen it, not one time in her whole Catholic life. No. Officer Mike and Sister Mary Rose definitely liked each other. The Penguin actually told the truth, a thought that made Elizabeth smile. She needed to look up the word Sister Mary Paul said to the other nun—*proclivities*.

Chapter 28

Baggage carts were lined up, stacked high with suitcases next to the brick building, and a line of people extended out from the ticket office. A clerk, in uniform, drug bags labeled "mail" and piled them on an empty cart.

An old Ford rolled up. Officer Mike stepped out, went around and opened the door. Katherine, dressed in her school uniform, exited first with John in her arms. He had put on weight and wore new clothes. The foster family fed him well, and they wanted to keep him—Elizabeth found that hard to believe. Then came Elizabeth, James, and Patrick. They were all dressed in their school uniforms, and they would be happy to relinquish them once they arrived in Minnesota.

The train platform and station had always held good memories for the children. They loved the trains, the majesty and the wonder of traveling. You start in one place, and in just a few hours, you could be very far away. Along the journey, you played, made trips up and down the aisle for cold water, ate homemade sandwiches, and watched the world whiz by.

It seemed like a million years since they last rode on the train, but it was only a few months. Their lives had changed. They would never forget the train that nearly took Elizabeth away, or the words of the men who thought they recognized them, but only knew about them. Trains meant something different now.

As their feet hit the pavement that formed the landing for passengers, they each hoped that once on the train, they could find their familiar seats, turn two seats around to make a four-spot, hear John giggle, and listen to their mother's sweet voice humming.

John quickly spotted Susanne who looked happy, but was a little tired. She arrived just minutes before from Topeka on the Westbound train that left just as the car pulled up to the station. He bolted out of Katherine's arms and headed straight to his mother. He had not forgotten her. She bent down to greet him, covered him with kisses, and was careful not to strain her healing parts.

Officer Mike disappeared into the station. James and Patrick looked down the long tracks then at Susanne who took a seat on a bench with John in her arms and Katherine at her side. James, Patrick, and Katherine were anxious to leave. Their father was incapable of hurting them, they knew that, but he was alive and would always be a threat if only in their dreams. Elizabeth slid in next to Susanne holding a cigar box as Susanne bounced John on her lap.

Officer Mike peeked his head out of the station door. "The train is late by an hour, it will probably be longer, fires out west."

Elizabeth looked over at Susanne. "I need to do something. I really do. I need to take something to school."

Officer Mike heard and quickly responded, "I can take you. We have plenty of time."

Susanne nodded as Officer Mike grinned and walked over to Elizabeth. He was so happy to be part of any planning, to be helpful. He never thought he would be happy to see her go, but everything had changed. He was making his own plans.

Elizabeth jumped up with her cigar box in her hand and ran to Officer Mike's car. There was a spring in her legs, a youthful exuberance, a happiness. Susanne noticed and smiled. In a few hours, she would be in new home with her children making memories to replace the ones she was leaving behind.

The car passed by houses and through the tree-lined streets while Elizabeth looked out the window. "How many miles away is our new home?" She wanted to make sure it was far way.

"Well, first you go to Chicago, change trains, then go north."

"I love traveling by train. It's the most fun. Will you ever come to visit?"

"I will always remember you, Elizabeth," Officer Mike said. "Your dad will never hurt your mother . . . or you . . . or your brothers or sister again."

"I know," she said rather flatly. She had seen to that, she thought, but she wasn't proud of how she did it. "I know a lot of stuff."

"I know you do, Elizabeth." This was the closest he could come to the subject of the big event, the big night that changed everything. It was not his place. He had not earned it.

"I am going to change my name when I go to public school. There are lots of Petersons in St. Paul, Minnesota; that's what Mom said. I think that's what our new last name will be when we live with our cousins. The church doesn't allow divorce. Did you know that? My mother was never much of a Catholic; she just liked to sing. Maybe she will sing again. I think she will. I hope she will. I think we will be Lutherans."

"Lutherans?"

How strange it was to give up the saints just when she was moving to a city with a big cathedral and a town named after St. Paul, she thought. She read about the place in the Encyclopedia Britannica, her new best friend. She wondered if anyone ever read every book in the set. She thought that might be a good goal to have once they moved to Minnesota. They had long winters, at least that's what the Britannica said.

She watched Officer Mike as he drove with a hand on the wheel and the other on the door. He seemed very relaxed and natural. She had witnessed the momentary hand touching between him and Sister Mary Rose, which of course was a mortal sin no matter how short the moment. That was because Sister Mary Rose was married to Jesus. Although, if the nun left the convent, she would no longer be a Catholic and certainly no longer married. Elizabeth never saw Officer Mike at church, so he was off the hook. He was just a plain old sinner. Maybe they could become Lutherans, too, although there wasn't a Lutheran church in town. She remembered what the nuns said about Lutherans; they really didn't like them. They had very different rules, accepted anyone, and didn't care too much about sin. They didn't have statues or incense either. Maybe Officer Mike and Sister Mary Rose should leave, too.

Elizabeth turned back to the window, hung her head out, and let the breeze blow her hair away from her face. She closed her eyes.

Elizabeth walked down the hall and stopped outside the classroom of Sister Mary Paul. She looked in to see the nun standing at the front. She looked tired. Elizabeth opened the door and walked into the room. Surprised, Sister Mary Paul stepped back, folded her arms and stared at Elizabeth.

"I have something for you, Sisterrrrrrrr."

The nun continued to glare at Elizabeth.

Elizabeth walked up to Sister Mary Paul and opened the cigar box. She pulled out the Joan of Arc holy card which was taped together, and sat the cigar case on the desk.

"Just as I thought!" said the nun.

Elizabeth handed the holy card to Sister Mary Paul. "I don't need it anymore, Sister Mary . . . Gallbladder!"

Sister Mary Paul's mouth fell open. The students gasped and snickered as Elizabeth smiled and looked for Richard, but his seat was empty. She turned and ran out of the room with Sister Mary Paul after her. The nun's limp was apparent; but she was quicker than she looked, tired or not. Revenge is an elixir.

As Elizabeth ran past the open door of Sister Mary Rose's class, she paused, smiled and curtsied. She looked over her shoulder to see Mary Paul hot on her trail. Elizabeth started to sprint as Sister Mary Rose stepped out into the hall, nearly colliding with Sister Mary Paul. Steam came out of Sister Mary Paul's puffing nostrils similar to a bull. She shot an intimidating glare intended only for the interfering nun, but it didn't find a home. Sister Mary Rose had already packed emotionally and found a new life. It would be just a matter of a few months until she made the move. She hoped Mike would come with her. She had stopped calling him "Officer."

Elizabeth burst through the doors and leapt into the air, soaring over the stairs, much like a long-jumper. She landed and looked behind to see Mary Paul at the top of the steps grimacing and out of breath. A few feet away, school windows sprung open, and she saw her classmates cheering. She searched again, but there was still no Richard. She would miss him the most.

She thought about her other classmates. Boy, they will pay a price for snickering! Well, maybe not, she thought. How could that old Penguin switch every child? Sister Mary Paul's arms were strong, but they would eventually wear out. Elizabeth had to remember in the future that there was security in numbers.

Sister Mary Rose stood behind Sister Mary Paul as she smiled and waved at Elizabeth and Officer Mike. He caught her smile, and smiled back. It was a broad smile.

Officer Mike put the car into gear. Elizabeth, out of breath, struggled to speak, and slowly began to laugh. "Oh, boy, you should have seen her face."

"Who?"

"No one. Step on it, Officer Mike!"

The car roared off.

There he was standing steadily next to Susanne. Elizabeth jumped out of the car and ran to Richard. She stopped abruptly, pulling her hair out of her face. What a mess I am! she thought. She was anxious—a new feeling, a grown-up feeling. She really liked him.

"Richard what are you doing here? You will be in big trouble." She laughed, a nervous laugh. She didn't know what to expect, but she was glad he was there. She was excited to be leaving, and sad she was leaving him behind. It has to be, of course, she thought. She tried to be strong, stand up straight and look solid. It was too bad that to make a new life she had to leave the good parts behind.

"I know. I wanted to say goodbye. Sister Mary Rose told me you were going." His voice was smooth, no stuttering with Elizabeth.

"Oh, Richard, this is not goodbye. I will come back one day and find you." Her voice began to tremble, and then her voice cracked. What was that about? She had only cried when the monsters came out or when she was really scared. She didn't understand this emotion, but knew she had to tell him the truth. "Richard, what I did in the kitchen that you saw was wrong."

Richard was stunned. He couldn't really comprehend. "You did nothing. You just drank some juice."

"No, it wasn't just juice. It was what my father needed. He needed sugar, fast." The tears began to roll down her check. "I just wanted him to stop."

"Well, I was so scared, I peed my pants that night and ran away. I wanted to survive too."

She knew it wasn't the same, and so did he, but he told her what he would never tell anyone else. She knew that was special.

"Elizabeth, I saw what your father did. You needed to stop him, I am very sure of that. Cross my heart," he said making the gesture. "Besides, I heard Officer Mike say your father had a stroke."

"A stroke?" Elizabeth didn't understand. She had never heard that word.

"Yeah, that's what Officer Mike said. My mom said that you can't walk or talk after you have a stroke. I don't think it had anything to do with juice."

Elizabeth was confused. The tears rolling out of her eyes were for both relief and sadness. She was glad she hadn't caused her father to suffer. It was a strange feeling. She hated the man, but also felt sorry for him.

Thankful, she wiped the tears away. "Well, I'm sure I have had an accident or two in my life. I just can't remember when." She wanted to move on, change the subject, forget about that night, but make sure he knew she would never think less of him.

"Hey, I am going to change my name. What do you think about that? I want to be called Beth." He needed a way to find her.

He wasn't worried about her name or even his accident. He had something he had to say or he would burst.

"I love you Elizabeth." There it was, and it felt good. He would never regret saying it, and was relieved that he could.

"I know," she said.

He reached out to shake her hand. Instead, she took his hand and then landed a peck on his cheek and whispered, "I love you, too."

She was sad because she was leaving the one person whose eyes had captured her at her worst, and maybe her best moment. No one would ever know her so well, or have the right to say they loved her more than Richard.

Overwhelmed, he knew he never wanted to wash his cheek again. He smiled, turned and placed his hands in his pants pockets. He gave up thoughts of the priesthood the day he knew he loved her. Besides, he never really wanted to be a priest; it was always someone else's idea. He had grown up the last few months in every possible way. Some changes were subtle like his pants were too short, his growing bones ached, and his knees hurt. He expected it—the puberty book alerted him to the hair that would appear, and he was sure he had one or two curly fellows welcoming the arrival of many more down in his private parts. His parents wouldn't recognize him if they looked closely; he hardly recognized himself, but he felt good, almost chipper. He knew he should be sad she was leaving, but he wasn't. He just wanted her to be happy. He knew she meant what she said—she did love him.

He wasn't sure he would ever see her again. She would not be held in one place. She would travel the world and maybe he would too, and perhaps they would find each other again. Or maybe not. He was very practical. He knew he would never forget her no matter what she called herself or how many miles they lived apart or the number of years that would pass without a sighting. She was forever in his heart.

Chapter 29

The train roared down the tracks, and the whistle blew. In a four-seat area, John sat opposite Susanne and Katherine. He jumped up and down, laughed, and plopped down on his bottom. Susanne had her arm around Katherine, as Katherine held a book. John moved to the window. He studied the landscape for the first time—he had grown up too. Katherine joined him at the window, pointing out cows, making *moo* sounds for John to imitate. She would never be far away from him.

Across the aisle in another four-seat area, James and Patrick wrestled. They threw each other from one seat to the other, laughed, and struggled. Out of nowhere, Elizabeth appeared with a small cup of water in her hand. She gently poured the water over the boys. Susanne saw it all. She motioned for Elizabeth to sit next to her. Elizabeth complied while flashing a pretend hard look at her brothers. She had definitely learned how to give the evil eye. They knew she would be back, and they were glad.

As the sweetness of Elizabeth's laughter filled the space, Susanne stared into her daughter's eyes, hoping she might see into her soul and wondering how she would say what she needed to say—that she knew the truth of that night, what happened and what didn't happen. Her part in it all. And how it could have turned out differently and how happy she was that it didn't. Tears start to well up.

"I know mom, I know," Beth offered. There was nothing more to be said.

Although the train, the motion, the noises and smells all seemed the same, they knew they were different and traveling by train this time meant something new.

THE END

ACKNOWLEDGEMENTS

Support comes in many forms and places. To my dears, far and near, made during childhood, in high school and college and all the years since—the ones that have left the earth and the ones still here. Best high school ever, with the best possible classmates, Argentine High, and ladies of the lake. Serina Heikes, who was the first to believe, my editor Vickie Julian, who helped make it better, and Emily Kate Johnson, whose photos made me look better. Crazy Ray Menendez who got me started writing, I owe you everything and I wish you were here. St. Paul screenwriters, who helped me become a better writer. For my women friends, who have made a difference in my life, you know who you are, and how much you have given me. My Kee Nee Moo Sha family, always willing to listen to my stories.

To Maureen Carroll who came into my life at the right time and made me an author. My Beta Readers, whose feedback provided helpful insights and encouragement.

ABOUT THE AUTHOR

Tess Banion became a storyteller at the age of two. It took her many more years to test her writing skills for real. She grew up in a nice size Catholic family with three brothers and a sister. Her first novel is based on truths, half-truths, and flat-out lies.

She raised two children and helped sustain a marriage of 37 years. She's gone to school (got a couple of Masters), worked in politics, changed careers and found her calling. This is her first novel, but not her last. She lives in Lawrence, Kansas.

Contact the author at: www.tessbanion.com.

DISCUSSION QUESTIONS FOR *A PARTING GLASS*

1. Did it take a while to get into the story, or did you get sucked in right away?
2. Was this a plot focused or character focused story?
3. Were there notable plot twists, or character changes?
4. What characters most interested you? Why?
5. Was anything too cliche or predictable?
6. What surprised you most in the story?
7. What were the central ideas the author was trying to explore?
8. What kind of changing/growing occurred?
9. What scene/quote sticks with you the most?
10. Which characters could you relate to most?
11. Did you get an "aha" moment or change of heart from reading the story?
12. Did your impression of the book or characters change as you read?
13. What was resolved, and how did that make you feel?
14. Was the ending gratifying, or did it leave you wanting?
15. Would you recommend the book?

OTHER BOOKS YOU MIGHT ENJOY FROM ANAMCARA PRESS

ISBN: 978-1-941237-08-3
$24.95

ISBN: 978-1-941237-14-4
$12.95

ISBN: 978-1-941237-16-8
$18.95

ISBN: 978-1-941237-18-2
$14.95

ISBN: 978-1-941237-05-2
$8.99

ISBN: 978-1-941237-17-5
$8.95

Available wherever books are sold or at:
anamcara-press.com

Thank you for being a reader! Anamcara Press publishes select works and brings writers & artists together in collaborations in order to serve community and the planet.
Sign up for our email list at:
www.anamcara-press.com

Anamcara Press
anamcara-press.com